They hit the line of zombies [ ]
and he barreled into those co[ ]
Teeth and claw slashed into the dead flesh, skin and bones busting with ease. But there were so many of them. A set of teeth sunk into his hip and he spun, shaking the zombie off, but not before it took a piece of him with it.

Growling and snarling, he fought, his wolf loving the rawness of the battle, the sheer love of being by his mate's side and keeping her safe. Of fighting for her and protecting her.

The zombies didn't break, they kept coming, but from one breath to the next, they were through the line.

"Erik, run!" Rylee shouted, blood dripping from a deep scratch down her neck, and what looked like teeth marks scraping her arm. The older man didn't question her, just bolted for the house. His eyes, so reminiscent of Rylee's, were wide with a fear hardwired into every human. Finding out the dead could truly walk and were a hazard to your health when controlled by a less-than-friendly necromancer were something of a blow to the human psyche. Even one who rode a dragon.

Liam loped behind them, keeping himself between Rylee and the zombies, who were only now figuring out they'd lost their prey. Alex, seeing where he was, dropped back beside him.

That was when the ground rumbled and a hand shot out of it. A hand big enough to grab them both and squeeze the life out of them without even trying.

PRAISE FOR SHANNON MAYER AND THE RYLEE ADAMSON SERIES

"If you love the early Anita Blake novels by Laurel K. Hamilton, you will fall head over heels for The Rylee Adamson Series. Rylee is a complex character with a tough, kick-ass exterior, a sassy temperament, and morals which she never deviates from. She's the ultimate heroine. Mayer's books rank right up there with Kim Harrison's, Patricia Brigg's, and Ilona Andrew's. Get ready for a whole new take on Urban Fantasy and Paranormal Romance and be ready to be glued to the pages!"

—*Just My Opinion Book Blog*

"Rylee is the perfect combination of loyal, intelligent, compassionate, and kick-ass. Many times, the heroines in urban fantasy novels tend to be so tough or snarky that they come off as unlikable. Rylee is a smart-ass for sure, but she isn't insulting. Well, I guess she gets a little sassy with the bad guys, but then it's just hilarious."

—*Diary of a Bibliophile*

"I could not put it down. Not only that, but I immediately started the next book in the series, *Immune*."

—*Just Talking Books*

"*Priceless* was one of those reads that just starts off running and doesn't give too much time to breathe. . . . I'll just go ahead and add the rest of the books to my TBR list now."

—*Vampire Book Club*

"This book is so great and it blindsided me. I'm always looking for something to tide me over until the next Ilona Andrews or Patricia Briggs book comes out, but no matter how many recommendations I get nothing ever measures up. This was as close as I've gotten and I'm so freakin happy!"

—*Dynamite Review*

"Highly recommended for all fans of urban fantasy and paranormal."

—*Chimera Reviews*

"I absolutely love these books; they are one of the few Paranormal/urban fantasy series that I still follow religiously. . . . Shannon's writing is wonderful and her characters worm their way into your heart. I cannot recommend these books enough."

—*Maryse Book Review*

"It has the perfect blend of humor, mystery, and a slow-burning forbidden-type romance. Recommended x 1000."

—Sarah Morse Adams

"These books are, ultimately, fun, exciting, romantic, and satisfying. . . . Trust me on this. You are going to love this series."

—*Read Love Share Blog*

"This was a wonderful debut in the Rylee Adamson series, and a creative twist on a genre that's packed full of hard-as-nails heroines. . . . I will definitely stay-tuned to see what Rylee and her new partner get up to."

—Red Welly Boots

"*Priceless* did not disappoint with its colourful secondary characters, unique slant on the typical PI spiel, and a heroine with boatloads of untapped gifts."

—*Rabid Reads*

VEILED
THREAT

Books by Shannon Mayer

VEILED THREAT

A RYLEE ADAMSON NOVEL
BOOK 7

SHANNON MAYER

TALOS

New York

Visit our website at www.talospress.com.

10 9 8 7 6 5 4 3 2 1

Library of Congress Cataloging-in-Publication Data

Names: Mayer, Shannon, 1979- author.
Title: Veiled threat / Shannon Mayer.
Description: First Talos Press edition. | New York : Talos Press, 2017. |
   Series: A Rylee Adamson novel ; book 7
Identifiers: LCCN 2016039144 | ISBN 9781945863011 (softcover)
Subjects: LCSH: Missing children--Investigation--Fiction. | Paranormal
   romance stories. | BISAC: FICTION / Fantasy / Urban Life. |
FICTION /
   Fantasy / Paranormal. | GSAFD: Fantasy fiction.
Classification: LCC PR9199.4.M3773 V45 2017 | DDC 813/.6--dc23
LC record available at https://lccn.loc.gov/2016039144

Original illustrations by Damon Za www.damonza.com

Printed in Canada

ACKNOWLEDGMENTS

Whenever a book is released, there are so many more people than just the author involved in making it happen. My fantastic editors, Tina Winograd and Melissa Breau are instrumental in making sure Rylee has all her weapons—both of the verbal and more literal sense. I wouldn't want to try and put Rylee out to the world without them.

My amazing cover artist, Damon with www. damonza.com: you always bring flare to my covers and have helped cement Rylee's (and my) brand. I cannot thank you enough for continuing to up the game with each successive cover.

To Benjamin, there is nothing to say except . . . You are the man when it comes to formatting!

A HUGE shout out to Jen Bobish, a reader who helped me develop two new characters for this book (Erik and Ophelia). It was so fun to build the characters from scratch and I think all the readers will love the new additions!

When it comes to my support system, I would not be able to keep up this pace without my amazing hubby. He makes sure that everything not related to writing continues to run smoothly even when I am lost in my words and other worlds.

And in no particular order, thank you to Lysa Lessieur, Creig Lessieur, Poul Bendsen, and Jean Faganello. You have each helped me in your own way to make my books and writing better each time I put pen to paper. Thank you for all you do!

CAST OF CHARACTERS

Rylee Adamson: Tracker and Immune who has dedicated her life to finding lost children. Based near Bismarck, North Dakota.

Liam O'Shea: Previously an FBI agent. Now he is a werewolf/Guardian as well as lover to Rylee.

Giselle: Mentored Rylee and Milly; Giselle is a Reader but cannot use her abilities on Rylee due to Rylee's Immunity. She died in *Raising Innocence*.

Millicent: AKA Milly; witch who was best friend to Rylee. Now is actively working against Rylee for reasons not yet clear.

India: A spirit seeker whom Rylee Tracked in *Priceless*.

Kyle Jacobs: Rylee's personal teenage hacker—human.

Doran: Daywalker and Shaman who helps Rylee from time to time. Located near Roswell, New Mexico.

Alex: A werewolf trapped in between human and wolf. He is Rylee's unofficial sidekick and loyal companion. Submissive.

Berget: Rylee's little sister who went missing ten years prior to *Priceless*. In *Raising Innocence*, Rylee found out that Berget is still alive. In *Shadowed Threads*,

Rylee discovered Berget is the "Child Empress" and a vampire.

Dox: Large, pale blue-skinned ogre. Friend of Rylee. Owns "The Landing Pad" near Roswell, New Mexico.

William Gossard: AKA Will; Panther shape shifter and officer with SOCA in London. Friend to Rylee.

Deanna Gossard: Druid, sister to William. Friend and help to Rylee.

Louisa: Tribal Shaman located near Roswell, New Mexico.

Eve: Harpy that is now under Rylee's tutelage, as per the Harpy rule of conduct.

Faris: Vampire and general pain in the ass to Rylee. He is in contention for the vampire "throne" against Rylee's little sister, Berget.

Jack Feen: Only other Tracker in existence. He lives in London and is dying.

Agent Valley: Senior in command in the Arcane Division of the FBI.

Blaz: Dragon who bonded (reluctantly) with Rylee in *Shadowed Threads*.

Pamela: Young, powerful witch whom Rylee saved in *Raising Innocence*. She is now one of Rylee's wards.

Charlie: Brownie who acts as Rylee's go-between when working with parents on all of her salvages. Based in Bismarck, North Dakota.

Dr. Daniels: AKA "Daniels"; a child services worker and a druid Rylee met up with in *Raising Innocence*. Rylee and Daniels do not like one another.

"Love is a better teacher than duty."
~ *Albert Einstein* ~

1

Rough, broken splinters of wood gaped like an open mouth where a doorway stood not too long ago. Shards lay scattered on the floor at my feet, giant toothpicks. I pushed one with my boot across the thick stone floor.

Liam bent and picked up a piece of the broken doorway; he rolled it between his hands before looking up at me. "This is the fifth one busted to hell." The light from the torches hanging on the wall caught the color of his eyes, making them more silver than usual.

"Five out of five. Someone's going for the gold." I squinted, using my measly skill with my second sight to look around. Nothing was out of the ordinary in the castle. Yet this was a jumping point for those wanting to cross the Veil, and someone was destroying our ability to use it. My guts rolled with acid; our time of respite was up.

I loosened my swords, only the second time in the last month that wasn't for practice. A month of peace, of relative calm, if you didn't count the constant explosions from Milly teaching Pamela how to hone her magic.

Not to mention Alex "singing" the Christmas carols Pamela taught him—at three in the morning—in his sleep, and at the foot of the bed.

Liam and I spent a week in northern Europe with the old wolf, Peter, and his pack. That was the only other time I had to draw a weapon for more than practice. And then, it hadn't even been my own. My hand went to the teardrop pendant hanging around my neck. A gift from Liam from our time in Europe and one that I treasured above anything else I owned; as much for what it stood for as for what it was.

I shook my head, clearing those memories, focusing on what we faced in the castle.

The hallway echoed our footsteps. We were heading to Portland to see Sas and the ogre gangs, and find out if they stood with us or not. After losing Dox, Sla, and the triplets, I wasn't so sure the ogres would see us as friends any longer. The communication with Sas since then had been, at best, lacking.

Not a good sign when looking for allies.

With each doorway we came to, more evidence piled up. Broken, destroyed. No way we'd be using the castle as a means to jump the Veil anymore. I let out a slow breath. While this would make life difficult if we had to move fast, it wouldn't kill us.

I hoped.

"Why wasn't the doorway to the mine broken up?" Liam asked. The answer was already on the tip of my tongue.

"Trap."

He let out a low snarl and energy swirled around him.

"Don't shift." I held up a hand, though didn't look back at him. "Let's see what other doors are busted."

A snort escaped him. "You think any of them aren't?"

We'd traveled back from Europe the week before, and I'd checked in with Doran. The doors had been intact at that point. So this destruction, and whoever had done it, was recent. They might still be here.

"If we are being driven toward something, yes. At least one other doorway will be unbroken."

If I thought his energy had swirled before, it was nothing to what I felt as he moved tight to my side. Power and the scent of wolf wrapped my senses into a nice, tight package that egged me on, urging me to let loose. I drew in several breaths, slowing the adrenaline not yet needed, but drawn to the surface of my skin. Begging to be unleashed.

The wolf in Liam called to my own wildness, the part that wanted nothing more than to turn my back on the world and run free with him to where no one would find us. For the last month the pull had grown stronger, the desire to be away from everything I knew was coming for me. For us.

Especially after our time in Europe.

It had been the two of us, and our connection deepened in that time, if that was possible. Letting him lead, allowing him to truly be an alpha, had strengthened our relationship in ways I couldn't have imagined.

My hand unconsciously went to the gold chain hanging around my neck, touching the pendant through my shirt, reassuring myself it was still there.

In a very short time, it had become a touchstone for me.

But I knew running away was a dream. There was no way we could walk out on everything and everyone and ignore our responsibilities, or those who depended on us.

"I wish you were wrong." He breathed out, his lips close to my ear, though nothing sexual about it.

Okay, maybe a little sexy with the feel of his jawline against the back of my neck. My body knew his too well not to be affected by his proximity, even when my brain screamed danger to me.

"I wish I was wrong too."

While the castle always felt deserted, something was different. A definite chill . . . like a graveyard vandalized and the graves dug open. I had no illusions about this being a place of peace; we'd shed enough blood on these stones to dispel any of those kinds of thoughts. Still, it seemed wrong to break it down and turn it into nothing more than an ordinary castle.

It took an hour before we found an unbroken doorway besides the one leading to the North Dakota badlands we'd come through on the first level. On the third level, near one of the few windows looking onto the courtyard, was the only door untouched.

A part of me expected something black and charred, a literal entrance to Hell or the deeper parts of the Veil I kept hearing about.

This door though was steel, thick and polished to a shine catching light from the window. A heavy, old-school padlock clamped down on a bar that rode across the middle of the doorway. I knew this door;

I'd been here with Alex. Fuck, I did not want this to be happening.

I put a hand on the cool steel. "Does it surprise you this doorway is left standing?"

"No, not really," Liam said, bringing his hand next to mine on the door. He barely touched it and was thrown back, an arc of lightening slamming him into the far wall.

With a groan he sat up, rubbing his head. "Let me guess, the door is spelled?"

I chuckled, knowing it would take a hell of a lot more than a simple bolt of lightning to take him out, and ran my hand over the door, my Immunity to magic protecting me. "I suppose; I didn't touch it last time."

Stepping back I shook my head. "Let's go, there's nothing we can do about this now."

Liam brushed himself off as he stood. "What about Sas and the ogres?"

I slid my swords into their sheaths. "Blaz, or maybe Eve can take us. That'll be faster than driving. We still need them, but not so badly we'd take the long route."

The clank of steel against steel, soft and quickly silenced, rose through the window. Moving to the side of it, pressing my body against the cool stones, I peered out. Liam did the same on the other side.

In the courtyard below, row upon row of red caps covered the ground. Big hulking bastards covered in muscle and armor. They had their pikes in one hand shield in the other. They looked like the Hulk pumped up on steroids. Yeah, they were that big and ugly. Shit, we'd faced them before in the castle and I'd nearly died, and Pamela was with us, blasting her way through them. Where the hell had they come from? Maybe another doorway was still open.

They stood tall and proud, blood trickling down their faces from the gruesome organic hats on the top of their heads. The thing with red caps was they loved their "hats," but only if they were made of the guts of enemies they'd slain. One stood in front of others, a half-head taller and what looked like viscera on his shoulders that dripped with blood. He paced in front of the other red caps, finally coming to a stop. "There are intruders here, ones who have destroyed the doorways."

A deep rumble rolled through the red caps and even at this distance I saw their large hands tighten on their weapons and lips lift into snarls. Shit, this was not good. Particularly since I was pretty sure we were the only intruders in the castle, and I doubted red caps would wait for us to explain we hadn't blasted the doorways apart.

"We should go, now, while they're busy." Liam stepped away from the window and motioned for me to follow him.

"Wait, just wait." A part of me wondered whose side they were on, because if we could get them on our side, they would be an amazing fighting force against Orion. Lots of them and blood thirsty as they came.

Below us, the leader let out a loud snarl. "We will hunt them down and use their bellies to brighten our caps and their skin to shit in." His troops roared their agreement.

Never mind, time to go.

On the second floor, nearing the stairway down to the main level, the first red cap loped around the corner behind us.

He let out a roar, his head thrown back as he lifted a six-foot long pike over his head. That was the opening we needed, but Liam beat me to him.

Liam lunged, his blade snapping forward and driving through the red cap's neck. His head rolled, held by the spinal column.

"Not even a clean cut? I'm disappointed." I headed down the stairs as the body thumped to the ground behind us.

"The blade is too short, which makes it somewhat useless. Besides, don't I even get a 'thank you'?"

No doubt he still wished he had guns. For the safety of the supernatural world, we destroyed the spelled munitions while in Europe. So Liam was back to blades or teeth and claws. I was happier with them gone. The guns made me so damn nervous I could barely sleep at night, dreaming of Orion finding them. In the wrong hands that technology would have literally been the death of our world.

Liam trotted down behind me as the sound of footsteps on stone echoed around us, probably called in by their buddy's last roar of defiance. I jogged faster, skipping steps where I could. We were nearing the first floor, but our doorway was on the other side of the castle.

Not that I was dawdling, but I was doing my best to keep quiet. Red caps en masse were not something I wanted to deal with if I could help it.

And the stairwell was dark and shadowed. Of all the things in my arsenal, night vision was not one of them. Last thing we needed was me falling and breaking a leg or an arm and alerting the red caps to where we were. Liam wouldn't break if he fell; I on the other hand was all too capable of snapping a bone.

"I'll thank you later. Besides, you keep telling me your job is to protect me. See how I let you do your job?" A smile twisted across my lips and Liam laughed under his breath. Being hunted by red caps doesn't seem much like a laughing matter. Yet, in my life, it was a fairly minor deal on the scale of scary shit I'd seen and gone through. At best, a five out of ten.

Water dripped down the walls of the castle, hitting the pitch-covered torches, flames hissing and flickering with each droplet of moisture. But we were almost to the doorway, so who the hell cared if the lights went out? Or so I thought, until Liam grabbed my arm, his voice low. "We aren't alone."

Every muscle in me tensed as my eyes searched the hall ahead of us. With the light dancing, every shadow seemed alive, every dark spot could hold someone waiting to take us out when we least expected it. I'd been ambushed more than once in dark places like this. Being supernatural you'd think I'd learn to avoid them, but honestly it seemed my life was nothing but dark places and battles.

There will be no rest for you, Rylee. You know that. Yeah, I did. The echo of Giselle's voice in my head was not needed to remind me of that particular fact.

Behind us, at the far end of the hallway, came a loud sniff, as if a creature were scenting the air. Red caps didn't scent the air; they were more human like than animal, even if they did bathe in the blood of their enemies and wear intestine scarves.

Liam let out a low growl. "Some sort of hound, we have to move."

So be it.

I strode toward our exit point, the only door besides the steel one unbroken. The shadows beside the door shifted and a man stepped between us and our exit.

Unfortunately for him, I had very little patience for this kind of shit. "Move or I'll move you in pieces."

He let out a soft laugh that tickled along the back of my senses. The hounds behind us let out a unified howl that filled the air, doing far more than tickling my senses.

The man didn't move. His face was shrouded by shadows, his arms loose at his sides. Almost like he wasn't sure what to do with himself or what he was doing next. I didn't like it. His eyes darted from us, to the doorway, and then back to us. Uncertainty was a good way to get killed in our world.

"Rylee. I never thought to see you again, child." His voice was thick with an accent I thought might be Russian.

"Good for you, you know my name. Now move your ass out of our way."

Hesitating slightly, he opted for a sweeping bow, then stepped away from the door. "After you."

Heavy feet and armor, along with the scrabble of claws behind us, propelled me forward. I didn't trust this shadow man, but I didn't have a choice. We couldn't face all those red caps, not without serious casualties. At least once on the other side of the doorway we'd be safe. One of the few perks with using doorways—very little would come through after you.

I yanked the door open and paused to stare at the man. "I suppose you're wanting to come with us?"

He nodded and I pointed to the dark on the other side. "You first."

He obliged and Liam let out a growl. "Go, I'm right behind you."

I didn't argue, took a torch from the wall, and stepped through the doorway. Liam followed, shutting the barrier hard behind him. We crossed the Veil, a tingle of awareness crawling over my skin, and then we were through to the other side, back home in North Dakota.

The air in the cave was cool and still.

"Where'd he go?" I swept the torch high, but saw no one beyond the cusp.

Liam pointed and I followed the scuffled footsteps to see the man leaning against one of the walls.

"Who are you?"

He lifted his eyes to mine. His face was familiar, but I couldn't place him, couldn't remember where I'd seen him. There were flecks of green and gold in his eyes, and he watched me carefully. He ignored my question, staring intently at my face. "You have the coloring of your mother mostly, but those eyes . . . they might as well be my brother's staring back at me. At least in color, if not design." He smiled and I just looked at him, unable to move, his words tumbling inside my head. The implication stunned me to the core. No, he wasn't saying what I thought he was. He couldn't be.

Before I said anything the doorway behind us flew open and the leader of the red caps stepped through.

Funny enough, he didn't look all that happy.

Fan-fucking-tastic.

2

Liam reacted first, shoving me away and putting himself between me and the red cap. What shocked me though was the man—the one who was implying he was my uncle—pulled a sword from his back, one that looked suspiciously like my own. He put his other hand on my shoulder, tugging me with him, away from the doorway. His hand shook a little, a tremor running through him and into me.

"We don't want you too close to that."

I had to agree; in theory, being close to a red cap was not good for one's health. Still, taking a backseat wasn't my style. I pulled my own sword then shrugged off his hand, stepping up and stopping only when Liam put his arm out to block me.

The red cap's lips curled up, showing his pointed teeth, blood dripping down into his mouth. "While I'd love to take your challenge, I am forbidden from drawing blood outside the castle walls."

I pushed my way past Liam's arm, forcing him to let me by. "Then what do you want?"

The red cap folded his arms over his barrel chest, armor creaking with the flex of muscles. "You saw the doorways, broken beyond repair?"

"I figured a little duct tape and wood filler would put them back together." I mimicked him, folding my arms over my chest, though I doubted I looked as intimidating.

His lips twitched downward. "We will slaughter any who come into the castle. There are only three doorways left, and they will be protected. This is the only warning you will get, Tracker. Do not cross this threshold if you value your life."

Three doorways. We'd only found two; I made a note in the back of my mind.

"We wiped your little red caps out once." Okay, Pamela and Liam did, but that wasn't the point. Liam made a choking sound. Maybe it wasn't so smart to remind the red cap we'd killed a bunch of his boys.

He leaned forward, blood dripping in a steady stream down his forehead and off the tip of his nose. "Those red caps were children sent to test themselves. Those who guard the doorways have been trained and battle-hardened. And they like little humans who scream as their bodies are pillaged for intestines and blood."

I clenched my jaw tightly and leaned toward him, my eyes barely above his folded arms. "Go back to your castle and hide, red cap."

He snarled and the blood flowed faster between us. I reached up and ran a finger through the stream of red, rubbed it between my two fingers.

The red cap stood straight and stepped back, his eyes narrowing. "You are warned. That is more than most get. A warning will not happen a second time." He strode through the doorway, his shoulders brushing each side, and the frame rattling as he slammed the door behind him.

Liam stared at the closed door. "Does it ever occur to you *not* to piss off the big ones?"

The shadowed man behind us let out a laugh, even went so far as to slap his thighs several times—almost like he was trying too hard. "Gods, I feel like I've stepped back in time. Rylee, where'd you find this one?"

I frowned at him. "You talk to me like you know me. Who the hell are you? And why would it matter where I found Liam?"

His laughter faded and he let out a slow breath. "My name is Erik. I'm your father's brother."

I didn't give the words time to really sink in, I couldn't. Three steps and I was next to him, close enough that in the flickering light I clearly saw his face. The angles of his jaw, the color of his eyes, the shape of his face. All hints of myself buried in his skin, but that could be said of thousands of people. I'd never tried Tracking someone *related* to me, using that as a marker. But that would be a way to be sure. If it was possible.

Tentatively, I sent out a Tracking thread, focusing on the qualities and traits I had, and got—nothing back. Stupid, of course, it wasn't like my family would be their own species. I stepped back. "There's no way to prove you are any relation to me, nor any reason to think you aren't here just to mess with me."

The creak of Liam loosening his holsters turned Erik toward him. "Is Blaz still with you?"

My eyebrows climbed into my hairline and I would have answered except the door behind us opened again. Damn that red cap.

"What the fuck do you want now?" I snarled as I turned, confusion making me less than charitable.

The doorway had been flung open but what spilled through was not a red cap. Or at least not a whole red cap. An arm, a thigh, a piece of a head sliced down the middle. Yup, our time of respite was most definitely done.

Both my swords were free from their sheaths before I took my next breath, my legs braced for what crawled through the doorway.

Hoarfrost demons. Three of them, their bodies arching upward, part ant, part scorpion, all badass destroyers of worlds. The black snowflake in the middle of my chest sang with a sudden, sharp cold that reminded me how very bad these particular demons were. An apocalyptic winter was not something I was keen on dealing with.

"Motherfuckers!" I jumped forward, hoping to hell we could kill them. The last time I'd faced a hoarfrost demon I'd been inside a pentagram; taking out the pentagram with the scorpion tail had banished the demon.

This time around they were in the physical world, no pentagram to hold them.

"Don't let them sting you," Erik said, calmly, as if telling me what the weather report was for the next twenty-four hours, "that would not be good."

I ignored him, knowing the scar on my chest, the black snowflake, gave me Immunity from the demon's venom. The first demon gave me a big grin, its mandible cracking wide and then chittering together, before engaging me. There was nothing I could do but work to get around it.

Working fast, I drove my swords through the air, through the demon's waving pincers. Black, thick blood poured out of the stumps as the demon reared back in pain, its tail arching high, a thick drop of poison hanging from the tip.

"Come on, bitch. Let's see what you've got." I snarled, sliding around the side and driving both swords through the thickly muscled tail. The demon fell forward, unbalanced without the weight. I grabbed the stinger at the base and jumped onto the demon's back, pushing the stinger deep into its neck. It shuddered once, twice, then went still. Booyah for me.

Liam was on the ground, a demon over him, and— Erik was engaged with the last demon, though he didn't seem to be faring well. He was doing a lot of dodging and almost looked like he was trying to talk the demon down. His lips moved but I couldn't hear the words. Not that it mattered.

There was no question for me. Liam came first. With him pinned to the ground, the demon had its back to me. Stupid, very, very stupid. I swung my two swords in tandem, crossing them in front of me. With one swipe I took the demon's tail and head.

The body shuffled and I scooped up the tail, ramming the stinger into the demon's back over its heart, just to be sure. Flopping like a decapitated chicken, nerve endings still firing, the hoarfrost demon bounced on the ground but it was death throes. Its jaw clicked a few more times even unattached from the rest of the body, eyes dulled and finally it went still.

Liam rolled to the side and we approached the final demon, who'd put Erik into a corner. He was blowing hard, barely able to keep the hoarfrost demon at bay.

"You are in trouble, little man. Orion wants to talk to you," the demon said to Erik, its tail arching high overhead. Even with a clear shot, it never tried to stab Erik with the tip. Neither of them seemed aware we were coming up behind them. Good for us.

Lightning fast, Liam struck, taking out the demon's legs and pitching them sideways. A scream of rage erupted from the demon, but I was on it before it could take a second breath, using its friend's stinger and cramming it into the demon's mouth.

"Suck it, you piece of shit." I pushed hard, felt the stinger drive deep into the back of its throat. It thrashed for a moment, then slowly stilled. I climbed off it, breathing hard.

There was a shuffle of feet and the three of us spun to see the captain of the red caps standing in the doorway.

"Remind me again about how tough you assholes are?" I wiped off my swords with a rag from the red cap arm that had come through first.

"They appeared in the middle of us, through a cut in the Veil, and headed straight for this door; demons are supposed to be bound to the deep levels of the Veil." He seemed truly confused. I didn't care.

"Demons have not been truly bound for nearly thirty years, and some don't need a proper doorway to step through," Erik said, helping Liam to his feet. "Were any of your red caps stung?"

The captain nodded. "Three."

Erik's eyes were grim. "Kill them. There is no cure."

The captain didn't argue, but he did give a slow nod. "I did not see you, Slayer. I thought all your kind were done in during the last rout."

Slayer?

"No, not all. But most, you are correct. Kill your men, captain, and burn the bodies. Dragon's fire is best." Erik cleaned off his sword and slid it back into its sheath at his side.

The red caps' captain stared at him. "It will be done. Your red bitch is on the other side of the third doorway, yes? We will take them to her."

Erik laughed; damn he seemed jovial for someone with the tag of 'Slayer.' "Still cranky, is she?"

"Cranky? Is that what you'd call it?" The red cap turned to leave, paused. "If the demons are truly coming through, I do not know if we can stop them. But we will lay our lives out to try. We will block the doorways from our side." His eyes rested on me for a brief second.

The door shut behind him and I swallowed hard, finally taking in the moment. Demons were being sent through the Veils and coming after me. No, it wasn't ego, it was truth. One of the downsides of all the quiet time for the last month meant I was reading through the big black book of demon prophecies. Besides the nightmares, I'd learned enough to know that the demons saw only one outcome for the future: them ruling the world. A minor fly in their ointment though . . . I was the one who was going to stop their 'messiah.' Which meant, to them, I was the biggest threat and worth taking on at every chance. Nothing was going to change that. I was just surprised they hadn't tried before now.

A thought occurred to me. "Is that why Orion wants to speak to you? Because you are a Slayer?"

Erik paused, his eyes downcast for a moment and I watched him closely. "Most likely." And though I waited, he said nothing else. I couldn't put my finger on it, but I didn't trust him. Or maybe I just didn't trust anyone except my inner circle anymore.

After that, the three of us left the mineshaft in relative silence.

At the top of the shaft, Blaz waited, curled around the opening like a giant, blue and black scarf.

Making friends again?

Liam laughed, though there was no true mirth in it. "You could say that, Blaz."

The dragon lifted his head and stretched his wings and jaws wide. But as Erik stepped from the shaft Blaz recoiled, scrambling back with a speed that shocked me. How could one tiny human scare a dragon so badly? Was it because he was a Slayer?

Please, pray to the sky gods, tell me you did not bring Ophelia with you.

Erik smiled and shook his head and I finally got a good look at the man who claimed to be my uncle. His hair was dark with hints of red here and there between a few sparkling strands of grey. Heavily muscled, even though he had at least ten years on Liam, they were of a similar build. Hell, they could have been brothers except for their coloring. Tattoos wrapped around his wrists and crawled up both forearms, disappearing underneath a loose sand-colored shirt.

Dark green pants and army boots and a heavy cloak edged with fur partially hid the sword at his side and no doubt more weapons than I could see. But it was the tattoos I focused on.

Reading the black-skinned demon book, I recognized them for what they were.

My blade sang as I pulled it out. "Demon marked, I don't think we're going to be friends after all."

Liam let out a low growl, but Erik didn't seem concerned, though his eyes gave a flicker of unease. "No more demon marked than you are; it is the way of a Slayer, to carry the marks of the demons. It keeps us safe from them."

He opened the throat of his shirt and there, lower down than mine, and closer to his stomach was a perfect black snowflake, identical to the one on my own chest. He turned away from me and finally answered Blaz's terrified query.

"Blaz, you can avoid her for only so long, she is your mate." Erik lifted his hands. "But I did not tell her where I was going, only that I needed to go ahead of her to suss things out."

Blaz swallowed hard, his throat visibly bobbing and I couldn't help the laugh that escaped me. "Seriously, are you afraid of your own . . . wife?"

We were paired as children; I have no say in it. And she is not my wife. He snaked his head toward me his eyes glittering with anger, and more than a little fear. I patted him on the snout, felt the heat of his belly fires rumbling up through his skin and promptly went to ignoring him. We had bigger issues than a dragon's love life. Though I wasn't wholly convinced that Erik was harmless, or even here to actually help, I had Blaz and Liam with me and there was no doubt who would

win in a throw down if he proved himself untrust-
worthy.

"Come on, let's get out of here."

Why are you not in Portland with the ogres?

Liam boosted me up on Blaz's back first, and then
he followed. "Change of plans. We'll discuss it when
we get back to the farmhouse."

Erik stood waiting, the late January wind curling
around his cloak. "Well, Blaz, are you going to let
me fly with you or should I call Ophelia now to carry
me?"

You can fly with me, Slayer. For now. With ease, Erik
climbed on board, using the rigging we'd made for
Blaz as if it were the most natural thing in the world,
like he'd done it hundreds of times. And maybe he
had, if he had a dragon who carried him.

Made with thick leather, the rigging went around
Blaz's broad chest, over his shoulders, and tucked in
behind his wings. Three spots were wound in to sit
and strap your legs. It wasn't much different from the
rigging we used for Eve, only scaled for the dragon.

Hell of a lot easier than trying to hang on every time
he rolled mid air, just for the sake of the winter wind
snapping along his scales.

Erik settled in behind Liam, and Blaz leapt into the
air, the dusting of snow on the ground puffing up
around us, then lazily dropping as we soared high
above the mineshaft in a matter of seconds.

Liam and Erik were silent as we flew, but Blaz was
a constant presence inside my head. I'd learned to tell
when it was just him and me conversing and when he
was projecting to all within range. His voice softened

when it was him and me, as if all his confidence fell away. Then again, we could look inside one another's head. Hard to be full of bravado when your rider knows you're terrified shitless. Like your mate.

She is not my mate. Not yet. I'd hoped Erik would keep her busy longer. You may laugh now, but when you meet her, if you meet her, you will understand. They don't call her the red bitch for nothing.

It should not have been a surprise that even Blaz had a fear that kept him awake at night. The dragon let out a long low snort, whether in agreement with me or not, it didn't matter. I didn't speak my thoughts and questions out loud; no need to air his dirty laundry. But I did wonder if Blaz had known Erik was my uncle.

Of course I did. All the Slayers ride dragons. Or they used to. I forget you know none of this, that your childhood was not filled with training and learning the history of your family. Each Slayer rides with a dragon. That is how I knew you, when you showed up on my doorstep. It is imprinted in your skin that you would be my rider, the way you walk and talk. As much or more than being a Tracker, the ability to slay demons runs in your veins, hot like the blood that keeps you alive. He quieted for a moment. *You don't trust him?*

I wasn't sure about Erik, and I didn't like the niggling of doubt that bit at me.

I cannot think of a way he could be anyone but who he says he is, not and keep Ophelia in the dark. I cannot read his mind though, so you are right, we don't know for sure. We will keep an eye on him, but I think you are being over cautious. Blaz was taking my concern seriously, which I appreciated. I snorted at the over cautious comment. That was not a trait attributed to me.

With my chin tucked to my chest and my arms wrapped tightly around my upper body to keep in what warmth I had, a question formed in my mind—two questions actually.

First of all, you didn't ask, which is why I never mentioned him. And you melt down like a fucking volcano when I pry inside your head to see what you're thinking.

I gave a slow nod. That was true. He tried it last month and I very nearly sent him to his home in France. Liam calmed me, gotten me to see that I was over reacting, yet it still burned in my gut. I didn't like people in my head, didn't like the feel of someone knowing my thoughts more completely than I did.

As to your second question, yes, I'd planned on asking your help in dealing with Ophelia. I hoped to find her a mate and continue on as I have been. Alone.

Brows dipping low over my eyes, I clamped my mouth together to keep from asking why out loud.

Another deep rumbling sigh slid through Blaz as he banked his large body. The highway was to our left and though we were only a hundred or so feet above it, no one saw us. The beauty of belief in the human world was our side never existed. And what a human does not believe, they refuse to see. Or they deny. Either works in our favor.

You have only been reading the prophecies within the Black book, so you know what the demons believe. But what they believe isn't necessarily what is coming for you. You and I are bound together, for good or ill, and

. . . he shook his head, scales catching the falling lights as the sun sank to the horizon's edge of the badlands.

He didn't finish his thought, didn't have to. I saw his image as clearly as if it were in front of my eyes. A slate rock covered in blood and dragon scales, a burst of light, demons lapping at the blood. I closed my eyes but the image stayed.

I do not understand the whole of it, Rylee. When it comes, the battle will rage and there will be far more death than life. How can I bind myself to another when I know I will not survive?

"Noble." I whispered, the wind taking the word from me. I was not sure I would be so noble. I would not give up Liam, not even if I knew I would die and break his heart in my last breath. No, I was not so noble.

Blaz's voice stilled inside my head and that was for the best. We had larger problems than whether or not I was noble, or what Blaz would do if Ophelia showed up to claim him. I glanced over my shoulder to Erik. He stared off, his lips moving softly and I had no doubt he spoke with his dragon. His eyes flickered and then met mine. He gave me a slow nod and then a sheepish half grin. Like secrets he held, ones he couldn't wait to see me react to. A chill swept through me. I didn't trust him.

Shit, what if the old bastard was my uncle after all?

Yeah, I wasn't expecting this to be pleasant.

3

The farmhouse stood in the last ray of sunlight as we touched down, which highlighted the fact the entire place needed repairs and maintenance in a rather desperate way.

Milly and Pamela stood in the yard, mud splattered up their boots to their knees as they practiced across from one another. Milly was nearing on six months pregnant—according to the doctor she'd been further along than she'd realized—and her movements were awkward and unbalanced. She often clutched at her belly and waddled like a diva, even though she wasn't that big. Drama queen; even now she loved the drama and attention. But I didn't care. She came back to us, turned away from Orion, even though he held a death threat over her.

Frank, our pack's newbie, sat raising the dead. The only dead I'd let him raise.

"Stop with the fucking bugs, Frank." I yelled as I slid off Blaz. "We have enough inside. We don't need any freak show zombie cockroaches impossible to kill."

His glasses lay halfway down his nose, and he looked up sharply, surprised. I shared a glance with Liam. "He didn't notice a dragon landing in the yard;

he'll get his ass handed to him if anyone shows up for more than tea and cookies."

Liam nodded. "I'll talk to him. See what I can do."

The sound of Erik's boots hitting ground stilled both Pamela and Milly, who turned in unison to face him. Pamela put hands on her hips a split second before Milly made the same stance.

I bit my lower lip to keep from laughing. Pamela tended to take on the traits of whomever she worked with, something I only saw now that she was training with more than just me.

"Who's that?"

I half turned to him, and then waved him forward with my right hand. "This is Erik. He says he's my uncle."

Pamela nodded and accepted that fact like it was nothing. Milly, on the other hand, not so much.

"Your what?" Her green eyes were wide with disbelief and I saw her subtly prep a spell.

"Milly, knock it off. Blaz will vouch for him." I stepped between her and Erik, even though secretly I was glad she had prepped a spell. Just in case.

That I will, witch. He hasn't changed much over the last few years. His voice was loud and echoed clearly through our heads. Frank's face paled and he clenched his bent knees until his knuckles were white. The kid was so green to the supernatural that it hurt my brain. Where Pamela had taken to it like a duck to water, Frank seemed to be in a perpetual state of shock and awe.

Milly strode forward through the mud, slipping and sliding, clutching her belly, wobbling with each step. When she drew close, Liam put out a hand to steady her. His wolf still didn't like her much, but she was a part of this rag tag bunch, despite her past. Maybe that's why she had become more fierce in her defense of those she deemed 'us' against those she saw as 'other.' Then again, maybe the pregnancy was making her a tad psycho.

"You don't really mean to let him stay here, do you?"

Erik stepped around me and gave her a low mocking bow, speaking to her slowly and deliberately. "Rylee needs help, help no one else can give but myself. Unless you know how to fight multitudes of demons she'll soon be facing and win?"

She drew herself up, her eyes flashing with ire. "I do know how to fight demons. I'm a witch."

He grinned at her, all white teeth and mirth. "Then tell me, where does a hoarfrost demon stand on the scale of danger to you?"

She arched an eyebrow at him. "Middling to high."

Erik slowly shook his head. "They are forerunners. Nothing more than pawns in the demon world. If you believe they are middling to high, either you are stupid—which I do not think Rylee would tolerate—or you have been deceived."

Milly glared at him, her anger two high pink spots on her cheeks. "We don't know if we can trust you." She turned toward us. "Liam, you haven't said anything; do you trust him?"

Liam frowned and I realized she was waiting for his word on the subject. Like she trusted him, even over me. Then again, they'd been through a lot together, most of it shitty.

"For now, he can stay. I'll kill him myself if he proves a liar," Liam said, not looking at Erik, but Milly.

Her mouth twitched and she lowered her hands, but the spell she'd prepped did not dissipate. "For now then, as you say."

The wind suddenly howled, and the sun dropped behind the Earth, the dark curling close.

I pointed to the farmhouse, feeling the weight of the day heavy on my shoulders. "Everyone, inside. There's a lot of talking to do and I'm not doing it while we slowly freeze our asses off."

Everyone trooped inside except Blaz, of course. I glanced at the barn and Pamela gave me a small smile. "Eve is out flying, practicing the things Eagle taught her."

That was good; we all needed to be at our best. And that was as far as I would let my mind wander in that direction. "And Alex?"

We stepped into the kitchen and she pointed to the living room area. Splayed out in front of the wood-stove was the werewolf. He might have been a rug he was so thin, sprawled on his belly with only a slow breath now and then to show he was a living creature and not a taxidermist's prize.

"He was doing laps around the whole property until just before you came back," Pamela said. "I think he was marking the territory."

Liam gave a low grunt. "He's not the submissive he once was."

No, he wasn't. But he was still stuck between shapes, half man, half wolf. Maybe it was too late for him to shift. Not that it mattered at this point. Alex was who he was, no matter what shape he was in, and an integral part of our group. According to Giselle, he'd be the lynchpin when it came to the final battle.

Milly, Pamela, and Frank took a seat at the kitchen table. Liam stood near the doorway, and Erik leaned against the sink. Blaz listened in, his presence a steady thrum just under my skin. I went over what we found at the castle, the broken doorways, the one doorway left untouched, and then the red caps and the demons.

Pamela shot to her feet, her blue eyes bright with excitement. "With Milly, I could go in and clean out the nest of them; those red caps aren't so tough."

I shook my head. "What would be the point? There are no doors now. And we don't need to bring another battle to our front step. Not until we have to."

"Are you driving to Portland, then?" Milly asked, but I saw she already knew the answer.

"No, Blaz will take me and Liam."

Erik cleared his throat, his eyes darting to mine. "I'd like to go with you."

Uncle or not, I didn't know him. My eyes slid to Milly; if Orion could turn her, who was to say the bastard couldn't turn an uncle I'd never met? The worst betrayers of my trust had always been the people I considered family. Perhaps he read the answer on my face, because before I said anything Erik shrugged. "Then again, I could always have Ophelia come, that way Blaz would not have to carry me and you would not be able to tell me I cannot fly with you."

We will take you, Slayer. Just do not call your bitch on me, not yet.

Erik laughed and I noticed a missing tooth on the right side. Like it had been knocked out and he hadn't bothered to replace it.

"Good. Are we off then?" He clapped his hands, rubbing them briskly.

Frank cleared his throat and pushed his glasses further up his nose, though there was no further for them to go. "I think before you go, you should see what is on the news." I nodded and he jogging up the rickety stairs and was back in a matter of thirty seconds. His hands held an old computer screen. Using bits and pieces of the spelled weapons and metal we scavenged from the warehouse, he rigged a computer that would run with us all in one room. Not that I'd thought anything of it when I'd first seen it—who cared if we could play solitaire or join Twitter? My only concern was at some point it would have to go. This technology was the last evidence of those fucking guns. Still, the kid was isolated enough; for now I'd let him keep this one connection to the outside world.

Frank flicked on the screen and pulled up videos. He clicked the first one, a shot of a heavily cobbled road, small cars jam packed on both sides. The videographer panned the street; people running one way, staring over their shoulders, mouths wide.

"Where's the sound?" Pamela asked as Erik said, "That's in Spain, I've seen the area."

Frank tapped the mouse. "No sound on this one, and yes, it's Spain."

We didn't need the sound, the terrified people were enough to get the picture. And then came a flood of water. What the humans saw, I had no doubt, was just water, a lot of it, but nothing else. Within the flow were silvery flashes of movement. Maybe they'd put it off as fish, but I saw the truth.

Liam leaned forward, a crease in his brow, as on the screen a hand shot out of the water and pulled a human into the death wave. "Mermaids?"

Frank nodded. "Yes. There's more."

The next clip was a tornado, banshees controlling the winds as they tore across the open plains. Then a clip of a field of eviscerated animals, blood and gore strewn across the dull grasses of winter, hooves and horns broken in half. In all the clips devastation reigned and the causes were creatures of the supernatural. Mermaids, banshees, trolls, and others I'd never before faced, only read about.

Erik leaned forward and pushed the power button. "This shouldn't be a surprise to any of you. You are aware a battle is coming? This is the start; someone has opened the Veil and pulling demons through. Most likely simple tears. They will possess the supernatural creatures first, the easy ones, and use their powers to cause terror."

Digging my fingers into my belt, I held my breath for a moment, thinking. "What is the point?"

Milly leaned back in her chair, her eyes fluttering as if in pain. She ran a hand over her bulging belly. "Orion needs the terror, the chaos, if he is to come as a 'savior' to the humans. He will stop all this and then be seen as their chosen one. And they will give him the world on a silver platter." I lifted an eyebrow. That seemed like a pretty detailed 'guess.'

"How much of that is guess and how much do you know?" I didn't take my eyes off her. She continued to rub her belly in slow circles.

"He talked about it in front of me, one time. I was very young and to be honest, I'd forgotten this particular plan of his; he had a lot of them, you know. Always a contingency plan for this or that." Her eyes held no guile as she spoke, but with Milly I would never truly be sure again. "Orion had plans on plans on plans. Some of them I think he had to confuse those around him; he doesn't trust his minions, nor the demons sworn to serve him. In this particular scheme he thought to use the human's beliefs against them, twist their faiths, and make it seem he was the answer to their prayers."

She fell silent and I tipped my head back to stare at the ceiling, as if my own answers would be written for me to discover there.

Erik rapped his knuckles on the table, snapping my eyes to his.

"I think your witch friend is right, and it fits with the prophecies. This will be his first step; the next will be to crack the Veil open wide so he can physically come through, along with his stronger demons," he scrubbed a hand over his chin, "unless the Veil and the Guardians of it have already weakened. It is possible we are seeing a merging of the two problems."

Milly nodded. "Yes, that would seem a likely ploy of Orion's, to work two possible paths at the same time. Like I said, a contingency plan."

I fought not to rub my arms because it wasn't truly that cold in the house, despite the goose bumps running along my skin. "And the hoarfrost demons, will we see more of them?" Shit that was the last thing we needed, adding a new ice age to our list of problems.

"No." Erik shook his head. "There were only five. I killed one in my youth," he touched his chest. "You killed one, and today the last three have been killed. No, they are all done. Now it will be time for demons that haven't walked this world in many years to show up."

Liam grunted. "Besides those possessing the supernaturals causing all the havoc?"

"Those aren't demons in the sense you are thinking, Liam," Milly said. "They are spirits, controlled directly by Orion. Evil spirits. They don't need a pentagram or a coven to bring them through. A slice in the Veil to the deep levels would be enough to unleash them. But that means someone is opening the Veil for Orion."

I realized as I stood, everyone was looking at me, waiting for me to make a decision. I gave a sharp nod. "Can Shamans cast out evil spirits?"

Erik's eyebrows shot up. "Perhaps, that would help as a way to slow them down."

Pamela scuffed her toes on the wooden floor. "What about Will and Deanna? Maybe the druids could help?"

A second sharp nod. "Tomorrow, Liam, Erik, and I will go to the ogres in Portland, but we'll stop in New Mexico first and talk to Louisa and Doran. Pamela, you phone Will and get him to talk to Deanna and the druids. Milly, you contact Kyle and see what you can find out in regards to the FBI and the Arcane Arts division. If it truly has fallen apart, then bring Kyle here. He and Frank can track whatever is going on in the world, where the spirits are causing the shit to hit the fan." With Kyle's background as an expert hacker, and his understanding of the supernatural world (even though he was as human as they came) he would be a big help.

Milly gave me a tight nod, and Frank's eyes damn well lit up. "Like a command center?"

"This isn't a fucking video game, Frank." I snapped at him, irritation flowing through me.

His eyes dimmed. "I didn't mean it like that. I'm trying to put this in terms I understand is all."

Liam and Milly both gave me a look, one that said I'd gone too far. Again. Damn it all to hell and back.

I damped down my irritation, forcing my voice to soften. "Sorry, Frank. You and Kyle put together something of a command center, it's a good idea."

And with that, we were off in different directions again.

I didn't like it.

Never mind that nothing I planned went the way I hoped.

Not one freaking thing.

4

Rylee was passed out, sound asleep beside him. The last month she'd slept like the dead, heavy and dreamless. Liam ran a hand over her bare shoulder and then slowly pulled the covers over her. She didn't even twitch, her face buried in her pillow. For a woman who'd always been a light sleeper, he didn't know what to make of this change. On one level, he knew it was good, knew she needed to rest and likely that's all this was. A break before the coming storm when she could build up her reserves.

But damned if she didn't constantly smell like Milly now, her heavy rose perfume seemed to permeate everything. He blew a breath through his nostrils as if to clear the scent. Nothing he could do about it, not really. Besides, Milly was trying and she saved his life, came back for him when she didn't have to. Damned if he didn't trust the witch fully now. When he first met her, before he knew Rylee well, Milly had been nothing but trouble. His cop instincts knew she was up to no good. But now that they'd all been through so much together, not a single doubt resided in him. Milly was with them, for good or ill; she would stand with them against Orion.

That didn't make it any easier on him that Rylee smelled like her all the time—and it certainly wasn't helping him sleep.

But, underneath it was Rylee, the smell of his mate, and it was enough.

He tucked an arm behind his head and stared at the ceiling. The farmhouse was quiet except for the steady blow of wind against the building.

Erik's voice suddenly whispered along the floorboards. Without another thought, Liam slid out of bed and made his way through the house to the living room. A dying fire flickered shadows and light against the far wall.

"I wondered how good your hearing was."

Liam didn't answer, just stood there, waiting for the man—this Slayer—to say something.

Erik turned to face him, a smile on his lips. "I didn't know she was alive, not until this past year when you and your pack went trapeezing across Europe. You stirred up all kinds of shit with your passing."

"She has a tendency to do that." A smile twitched his lips.

"Yes, our family was not known for. . . subtlety."

There was nothing to say to that, so Liam just nodded.

"She needs to ride with my dragon, have a little girl chat, and I do believe that Blaz will not like this, much as he tries to act as though he would rather not have a rider. It would only be temporary of course. Long enough for Ophelia and Rylee to speak to one another," Erik said, his voice pitched low.

"Why are you telling me this?"

"Because you have her ear. Ophelia knows about the Blood of the Lost. My dragon is the last keeper of the knowledge of what Rylee truly is, a truth she needs to claim if she is to be the one to stop Orion. . . Unless you have the violet-skinned book of prophecies?"

Liam let out a slow breath, his mind working through this piece of new information. "No, the book is missing. You'd be better off telling Rylee yourself. She doesn't like games, nor does she play them well when forced to. More than likely she'll break something. Your face to begin with, your balls shortly after that."

The older man grinned at him. "Good. Then at least I know the blood runs true. I didn't want to approach her until I had a better feel for how she'd react. Then, of course, the hard part is going to be dealing with her pain in the ass lizard. He really doesn't want to be tied to my girl."

Liam tipped his head to one side. "You've already called Ophelia here, haven't you?"

Erik nodded. "She'll be here by morning light. And she truly can be a cranky bitch—all female dragons are—but she is loyal beyond the grave."

There was nothing to be done for it. "Is that all?"

"You don't trust me yet, wolf, but you will." Erik held out his right hand and it was the first time he noticed the last two fingers were missing.

Liam didn't offer his own hand back. "Missing appendages don't make me trust you any more, they only make me think you're weaker than you look."

Their eyes met and Liam expected a challenge, but Erik didn't seem to be looking for a fight. His eyes were full of questions, but no direct challenge.

"Well, goodnight then, Liam." Erik walked past him toward the guest room down the hall. Liam watched him go and waited until the sound of the bedroom door clicking shut reached his ears.

His voice low, he stared at the closed door. "I don't trust you. But I think we're going to have to."

Moving quietly, he slipped back into his own bedroom and shut the door. Rylee still slept, motionless on her belly, her breathing deep and even. Lying beside her, he pulled her gently into his arms. She murmured something unintelligible and buried her face against his chest. The long gold chain holding the pendant he'd given her when they'd bound their lives together warmed between them, reminding him of the promises he'd made.

Holding her tight, he closed his eyes and let out a long, slow breath.

Keeping Rylee safe, and in one piece, was his number one goal. And his wolf acknowledged, as he did, that if Erik was telling the truth, the Slayer would be able to help them do just that.

Of course, that was assuming Rylee wouldn't take exception to Erik bringing in Ophelia, or trying to tell her how to kill demons.

Another long, low breath escaped him. Yeah, it was going to be an interesting morning.

Waking up to a dragon roaring inside my skull was not what I'd call pleasant. I was on my feet and scrambling for clothes before I was fully awake.

"What the fuck is going on, Blaz?" I grabbed my new leather jacket as I bolted for the back door. I was still breaking it in; it only had a few stitched up spots from our stay in Europe, and the leather was still a bit squeaky. When I reached the door, a burst of cold air wrapped around my neck and face as Erik stepped in, blocking my path. He held up his hands, palms facing me. I hadn't noticed before that he was missing fingers on his right hand. Not that it mattered.

"Let them work it out. A tiff like this always looks worse than it is."

I narrowed my eyes. "Let who work it out?"

He tipped his head toward the window over the sink and I peered out. On the far side of the barn, in the fields, was a red and silver dragon beating the shit out of Blaz. Her wings buffeted him as she snaked her head forward, biting his shoulders.

"That doesn't look like they're working it out." And just how was I going to stop her? I mean really?

"You want get between them?" Erik laughed at me and headed to the coffee pot. He was wearing the same clothes as when we'd met him, minus the long fur-trimmed cloak.

"Not really. She won't kill him?"

"Nah, she's just pissed he's avoided her for so long." He sat with a thump and then I realized we were by ourselves. I Tracked the others in the household and found them either still asleep or, in Liam's case, out for a run with Alex.

I kept my back to him and watched the dueling dragons, seeing now they were both holding back.

Blaz was no longer yelling inside my head—hell, how did he think I was going to help anyway?

"How do I know you are really my uncle, or if you are my uncle, you're not some evil ass relative who's waited for years to get your revenge on my parents by trying to take me out?" Fuck, I felt like some twisted Disney princess saying that, but the possibility was there. Especially with my life.

The sound of someone choking came behind me and then a cup being set on the table. I turned to see a very amused Erik leaning back in his chair.

Before he said anything, a rather loud and peevish female dragon interrupted, her voice echoing inside my head loud enough that I knew I was not the only one hearing her words.

Tracker. Come and deal with your lily-assed blue boy; I cannot talk any sense into his pea brain head.

I didn't wait for Erik to follow me; I was pretty sure he would. Hell, I had no doubt he'd set this up, even though he'd said he wouldn't call Ophelia.

Which went to prove my distrust was well placed. Already I knew I needed whatever knowledge he had about demons and fighting them, but I was keeping him on the outskirts of my circle. No need to let the viper in the front door, even if you needed his venom to poison the bad guys.

Walking across the muddy farmyard, I circled to the back of the barn. Tracking Eve, I found her sound asleep too. It was like everyone was still on vacation, sleeping in, resting their bodies as much as possible. That we were all on the same page made me a bit jittery. Like we all knew the "big game" was coming and we were prepping. I didn't like it, not one bit.

Around the back of the barn I found the two dragons. Ophelia sat on her haunches, still as a statue, glaring at Blaz with his wings spread wide and his jaw open as if warning her off.

"You two kids having fun?" I stopped and put my hands on my hips. Blaz tipped one eye toward me.

This is not fucking funny, Tracker.

I lifted my hands overhead. "Look, you two big-assed lizards figure this the hell out. I'm not a negotiator and I don't relish the idea of trying to work out your breeding rights or who takes out the fucking garbage in your dragon relationship."

Ophelia's jaw dropped and her eyes widened, showing off the deep brown edging the purple of her iris. *I am not here for breeding rights. That is months away. I am here to help my rider. And quite frankly, I am here to help your scrawny ass, Tracker.*

Blaz snaked his head toward her going nose to nose. *Don't talk about my rider that way, bitch.*

Ophelia snarled and shoved him away. *So, you do have some spine in there after all.*

Again, I held up my hands. "Stuff it, both of you. I'm going to Portland; Blaz is taking Liam and me." I glanced at Erik leaning against the barn. "I suppose you and Ophelia are coming too?"

Erik nodded the same time Ophelia did. Though on him, it looked like he held back a laugh, and Ophelia just looked smug.

A black streak of fur ripped across the yard, mud flying in all directions. "Alex tooooooooooooo!"

Liam, in his wolf form, loped lazily along behind Alex, his tongue lolling out. He gave me a wink over one silvery golden eye as he stepped beside me, Alex right behind him. Alex pushed hard against my leg on one side, and Liam pressed against the other, heat from their bodies warming my legs in a split second. Submissive he was no more; Alex pressed harder, begging with his eyes as round as he could get them, his lips whispering "please, please, please."

"Fine, Alex, you can come too."

He leapt up and mud sprayed around him, splattering my pants and jacket. I wiped it off, but didn't bother to scold him.

Within fifteen minutes, we were ready to fly. Liam shifted and put on warmer clothes, and Blaz backed from Ophelia to give them both room to take off.

I cannot believe she is here. His voice was low and I knew he spoke just to me. I shrugged; nothing we could do about it.

I know that. His voice was resigned. Was it really that bad being with her? Hell, I'd be pissed if my mate avoided me for years.

I don't love her. It is that simple. A picture of a smaller dragon, tawny and cream colored, flickered from his mind to mine. Shit. And Ophelia no doubt knew Blaz felt something for this other dragon.

It was her cousin.

I didn't stop the groan that slipped out of me. A dragon love triangle? That was not going to be good. Wait, was?

Sorrow, thick and heavy, flowed into me. *Her cousin is dead. Gone for many years.*

What the hell was I to say to that? Nothing. If I lost Liam, no way I could just "move on" with someone else. Not even if someone paired us up and said it was for the best and we needed to be together.

I touched Blaz's back, pressed my hand into his scales. "I'm sorry."

He said nothing more, the feel of his long-buried sorrow enough to keep our thoughts to our own heads.

Liam and I tucked into the harness on Blaz's back, and Alex climbed behind us, wrapping himself into the leather. Though we planned to see Doran and Louisa first to ask about casting out the evil spirits, at the last minute I directed Blaz to head to Portland. I could always call Doran, or even Louisa, but the ogres had waited long enough.

Blaz didn't wait for Erik to mount on Ophelia before he spread his wings and launched into the air. A few short hours and we'd be in Portland, and I'd be facing ogres I wasn't a hundred percent sure were on my side anymore.

Peachy.

Ophelia's voice rippled across my mind, and by the way she spoke, she wasn't projecting to anyone else. Curious.

May we speak, Rylee? Apparently she could be polite when she wanted.

I gave her a nod.

I am the keeper of the knowledge, the last dragon to hold information about the Blood of the Lost. Of which you are the last. If you are anything like Erik, trouble will soon find you and I will lose my chance to speak with you.

My mind whirled. If Erik was related to me, how was it I was the last?

Erik is your father's brother. Your mother is the one whose bloodline carries the Blood of the Lost. They were an ancient supernatural, one who held much sway over the rest of the world of magic and wonder. It is why they were wiped out. They had too much power. They were the ones who created the Veil.

Son of a bitch, that did not sound like it was going to help me in the "making friends" department. A question formed inside my mind but I blocked it. I didn't do well with the whole speaking privately inside my head. Not when I would just have to fill Blaz and Liam in anyway.

"How many other supernaturals might remember this?"

Ophelia was ahead of us and she craned her head back and lifted her eyebrows at me as if to ask if I were sure.

"How many, Ophelia?" I repeated the words louder.

Her voice projected through us all, a booming echo where before it had been just above a whisper. *A few of the very old ones, this all happened thousands of years ago. The blood line was thinned to a few families, barely enough to keep it alive. Your kind was not always known as "The Lost."*

"Then what were we know as?" This was too damned weird of a conversation, but it had been a long time coming.

That is beyond even myself and I have all the information anyone could have. It was a part of the systematic destruction of your kind. If you didn't know what you were, how could you possibly return to it?

She seemed to let out a heavy sigh and a deep regret flowed through her and into me. *You need to know that your kind created the many levels of the Veil; your people ruled the supernatural world. And now it has come to you to bring that world together again, under your name to fight the darkness. To fight the demons. It will be the last act of the Blood of the Lost, to finish what they started, keeping the world safe from the demons who would rule it. That was why they created the Veil in the first place, a holding ground for demons.*

Her words stirred something deep within me and I recognized what she said for the truth it held, even if I didn't like it so much. Liam's hands tightened on my waist and I glanced over my shoulder. His eyes reflected what I already knew. Truth, when it came, was less likely to make us happy than we thought. Finding out who and what I really was didn't necessarily make life easier.

My fingers dug into the leather straps in front of me, but I wasn't really that freaked out. To be fair, in some ways this was just regurgitation of what I already knew via the prophecies I'd read. I had to pull off this coup and kill Orion or everyone was doomed. Did it really matter what my bloodline was when no one else knew or even gave half a shit. "Anything else? Any other skeletons bitching in my family closet?"

Ophelia blinked back at me, her eyes uncertain. *Perhaps you do not understand the severity of the situation, Tracker.*

Erik slapped her on the neck. "Spit it out, cranky."

Blaz snickered and Ophelia glared first at Erik, then Blaz.

Pushy dicks. Fine. There is only one thing you truly need to know, if Erik would have his way. Erik threw his hands into the air and she ignored him. *Seal the Veils; that is what you must do to stop Orion.*

Well damn, that was actually helpful. It was the first time anyone said *how* I was going to stop the demons. "Do you know how I'm going do that? You know, the details of this deed I'm supposed to perform?"

She shook her head, and I glanced at Blaz. "How about you?"

No, I don't know either. Has there been nothing in those ogre-skinned books of Jack's?

We flew through a bank of clouds while I mulled it over, moisture slicking any bare skin in seconds. I wiped my face and closed my eyes, thinking hard. When we'd been in Europe, I'd spent time reading through the remaining books of prophecy at Jack's manor. I'd done my best to decipher the meanings, but so much was written in cryptic old English, it was difficult at best to slog through.

"No. Just lots of 'you will be the one to stop him,' no how to actually stop him, or any helpful shit like that. Knowing my luck, that bit is in the violet-skinned book."

The two dragons kept pace with one another, their wings dipping and rising almost in tandem. Neither had anything else to add to that.

Liam leaned forward and put his mouth near my ear. "You okay?"

Surprised, I turned to face him. "What do you mean?"

His eyebrows rose high. "Just surprised you aren't freaking out. You don't tend to take information like that well on a good day."

"Just what is that supposed to mean?"

Means you explode first and think about the new info later, once you've caused a fair amount of chaos. Blaz didn't project to everyone, or I might have given them the explosion they expected.

Instead, I withdrew, pulling deep into myself. I didn't want to admit they were right. I wasn't feeling like myself lately; something was off and I couldn't pinpoint it. Maybe it was all the quiet hours and too much time to think, or maybe it was the fact I slept through the night consistently for a longer stretch than I ever have.

Even Berget's visits didn't disturb me. She made it a standing meeting that we saw each other at least once a week in my dreams, but they no longer left me shaking and pumping full of adrenaline. Now, they were like seeing her face to face, no more smoke and mirrors, no more wondering which Berget I was talking to—the sane one, or the one who wanted to see my head on the end of a pike.

I leaned against Liam's chest and closed my eyes. "I'm going to see if I can talk to Berget. Maybe her memories will hold a clue for us."

I wasn't sure if I could sleep while flying, the air cold on my face, legs strapped against Blaz, but it was an excuse to keep to myself.

And damned if I didn't slide into a light doze. I reached for Berget as she'd shown me, and she came into view, walking along the edge of Blaz's wing and sat beside me. She wore a long, full blue skirt and corseted top, very old school. The colors accentuated her bright blue eyes and long golden hair. Of course I knew she wasn't really here; her hair and skirt didn't move in the rushing wind and she walked just above Blaz, floating an inch over his skin.

"Rylee, is something wrong?" Her mouth turned downward in a sharp line.

"Yes and no. Don't use the castle, the doorways have all been destroyed with the exception of three and red caps are guarding the shit out of the place." My eyes drifted to half mast and I almost pulled out of the doze. Berget crouched beside me.

"Orion and his demons are making a bid?"

I nodded, still disturbed at times with how old she sounded when she spoke most times. Old and wise. The memories and power of her adoptive parents were held in check by the opal implanted into the side of her chest, but she could still access them when needed. And sometimes the years of playing the part of the thousand-year-old vampire came through in her speech patterns and behavior.

She rubbed her fingers over her side where the opal was buried. Fear sparked through me.

"Are you having problems?" I didn't need to be more specific; we both knew what that one problem was.

"They are . . . grumpy, for lack of a better term. Ir-ritated that I've bound them." She gave me a small smile "But that isn't here nor there. For the moment, they are fine. What is it you wanted to ask me?"

I looked her over, saw she wasn't trying to hide anything from me. Worry still trickled along my spine. The opal was a temporary stop, one that would eventually run out. I pushed that aside; I had to believe we had the time to figure out a better way to keep her safe. And to be honest, the help of vampires with a lot of years behind them was not a bad thing. At least, not right now.

"In their memories, is there anything about how to close the Veil?"

Her eyes widened and I quickly told her about Ophelia and Erik, and what Ophelia shared in regards to how to bind the demons.

Berget didn't ask if I trusted them; even though we'd spent most of our lifetime apart, she knew me well enough to know I wouldn't pursue this if I didn't think it was the truth.

"I will have to take some time to see what I can find. While I can access everything, it is delicate because they are bound. They are not always willing to share. I will come to you if I drag something out of them." She shrugged her pale, slim shoulders, and her lips tipped upward, though a current of sadness ran through her eyes. Then, she went a totally different direction, one I wouldn't have seen coming, not in a million years.

"Doran is in love with you, you know that, right?"

I couldn't hold onto the light doze, jerking awake with a gasp. Liam's arms tightened around me.

"Bad?"

My jaw dropped open and I coughed on the moist air. Doran was . . . nooooooo. That couldn't possibly be. Of course, I forgot to close my thoughts from Blaz so he chimed in.

Not surprised, you have intrigued him from the beginning. You two would actually make quite the pairing.

"Shut up!"

Alex from the "back seat" let out a howl. "Shutttttt uppppppppp!"

That was my boy, always backing me up.

Liam leaned forward and I shook my head. I was not going to discuss this with him with all this audience. Even if I whispered, Blaz would hear and right now I didn't want anyone to know.

I already know, you twit.

Hot embarrassment and even hotter anger arched along my spine. "Stay out of my head, Blaz." I snapped.

He had the gall to laugh, a deep rumble slipping through him and into me as he dove. I clenched the leather and Alex let out a series of excited yips and howls.

Liam said nothing. Smart man, he knew when to wait for me.

We dropped in large, lazy circles, the two dragons mirroring one another. From where we were I saw the city of Portland. I Tracked Sas and the ogres, felt them pulling me away from the city proper. My gut clenched. I knew where they were. Fuck it all, I did not want to visit the place where Orion had almost broken free. No choice, I had to speak to the ogres, had to see if they were with us or not.

Time to suck it up.

"All right, kiddos, we're going to Mt. Hood."

5

The ground was thick with cooled and blackened lava, and the mountain was bare of trees and wildlife. Ophelia and Blaz didn't seem bothered by it, landing on the edge of the lake where the flow was the thinnest, the surface cracking under their weight.

Erik slid off Ophelia's back and glanced around. "Let me guess, you had something to do with this? Untrained, you cause a lot of problems, don't you?" The second bit was not a question but a statement. Asshole.

I gritted my teeth against the flood of heat climbing into my face as I slid off Blaz's back. Embarrassment wasn't something I was used to and it irritated me. Which made me angry, a much more familiar emotion. Liam hopped off behind me and we stepped out in front to meet Sas head on.

"Not on purpose," I said.

Erik snorted and crossed his arms over his chest. "Rarely is with someone like you."

Damn, he was pissing me off. Screw it, I would ignore him, get him to show me what I needed and then send him on his merry fucking way. I Tracked Sas and felt her moving toward us. To say she was not happy was an understatement. A self-righteous fury slipped along her threads into me. Yeah, this was going to get interesting real fast. At least we wouldn't have to look for her.

Liam lifted his face to the breeze rolling down Mt. Hood. "The whole mountain is quiet now. Almost like it never tried to kill us."

"I wouldn't worry about the things that aren't ogre shaped and carrying weapons right now," I said, shifting my stance to face the oncoming ogress, and of course, she happened to be headed our way through the only clump of trees and bush left standing. Even if it was all dead. I saw her in the distance, her violet skin catching the light here and there. Or maybe that was a weapon the light danced off. That was more likely. Behind Sas was a veritable army of ogres, the colors of the different gangs' skin catching the light as they drew closer.

And it wasn't just Sas who was angry; the whole of the group was geared up for a fight. Suddenly I was very glad Ophelia had come along. Two dragons were a hell of a lot more intimidating than one.

Blaz glared at me.

I'm not intimidating enough for you?

"The more the merrier and all that shit." I pulled my sword from my back and uncoiled my whip with the other hand. A little bit of distance wasn't a bad thing with angry ogres.

Thirty seconds passed while we waited, weapons out and tension high.

Thirty-one and a half seconds, and Sas raged in front of us, battle axe raised high above her head, fury lighting her features. I didn't move, didn't even change my breathing, though my heart was pounding like an oversized jackhammer.

I tipped my chin up a fraction of an inch. "Hello, Sas."

"I can't believe you'd dare come here. You are stupid." She slowed her steps, her eyes only on me. Fortunately, the gang of ogres behind her wasn't quite as single-minded; they formed a long line, their eyes glued to the two dragons.

Hell yes for back up. I would never complain again about Blaz coming along.

About damn time.

I ignored him and struggled to find the right words, words I'd been working over for the last month. "Sla gave me his oath that the ogres would stand with me when the time comes. Does that still hold or are you as honorless as the rest of the supernaturals think?"

She let out a long, low hiss. "Sla is dead, and I lead the gangs now. All of them."

The ogres behind her, men and a few women, clanged their weapons, sending a bevy of birds into flight.

Ophelia snaked her neck out and grabbed two birds midair, gulping them down. The ogres went silent again—well, maybe that wasn't quite right. Still, except for a tremor here and there, their eyes darting to one another and then to the dragons. No shit, there wasn't a chance in hell I'd want to face down a dragon either.

Yet you already did, little idiot. Blaz's tone was full of humor; Erik and Ophelia let out a snicker as if it were some big joke.

Again, I did my best to ignore him. "And you won't stand by Sla's decree?"

"Fuck you, Tracker. You killed my men, led them into a trap. They were my mates, I felt their deaths and they were not good deaths. Slow and tortured, they broke at the end, screaming my name as they died." Tears slid down her cheeks but they did not soften the fury lighting her face.

The bile in my stomach jumped halfway up my throat and tears stung at my own eyes. I knew the boys had been skinned alive, knew it had been bad. But feeling their death, that was not something I could imagine. I didn't know ogres had that connection once mated.

I knew if I felt Liam die a horrid death, there would be no stemming my rage, especially if I thought someone I knew had done it, someone I trusted. I cleared my throat and pushed down my emotions as best I could.

"And you think I did it?" My voice was husky, filled with emotions I couldn't contain no matter how I tried.

With each word she stepped closer until we were nose to nose, her breath hot on my face. "Your stupidity did it. You thought you were all powerful, that you could change the world but you can't. You aren't the one the prophecies speak of. You are nothing but an interloper, a fucking twat filled with the idea of ruling the supernatural world like her ancestors did."

The pain of losing Dox was not done healing, but that didn't mean I would take this shit. The sympathy I had for her fled.

"You're a moron, Sas. That's what you are. I'm not here for power or prestige. You think I want to face down strongest demon this world has ever seen, and all that comes with him? You think I want to put the lives of those I love on the line to keep this piece of shit world safe?" I shoved her hard, tucking a foot behind her feet so she ended up on her ass in front of me. "You stay here on your bare-ass mountain and cower as the demons over run this world, and know that maybe your help would have tipped the scales and kept us safe."

She snarled and leapt to her feet, battle axe raised. "I am not the fool that the boys were. I see you for what you are, and I will not let my people be slaughtered and turned into petty pawns for your dreams of power."

The ogres behind her let out a low murmur, but I saw doubt on some faces.

"And you all agree with her? You think I'm here to rule you?"

I shook my head. "Dox was my friend, one of the few I had. He was shunned by his own because of his gentle nature, he was cast aside. And yet he fought at my side against Orion because he believed it was the right thing to do. He was a hero; he didn't shy away from danger, or the possibility of death. He knew, as did the triplets and Sla, this is *war*. Not a game, not a silly play. And they were willing to lay down their lives to try and stop the demons. The same as I am. The same as we are." I swept my hand back to encompass the dragons, Liam, Erik, and Alex. "Perhaps I was wrong thinking the ogres were strong enough to face the darkest hours this world will ever know."

Sas glared at me, but said nothing, only lifted her axe higher. Looked like I wasn't getting through to them. Not that I really expected to, I wasn't much of a motivational speaker.

Erik stepped to my side to speak with me, careful to keep me between him and the ogres. "You won't ever convince them, but as Orion unleashes his demons, he very well may do it for you."

I clenched my whip handle, the leather digging into my palm. "And by then it may be too late."

"Yes, but you can't force them to see. When the blind refuse the gift of sight, you only anger them by describing what the world around them offers."

I glanced at him. "Damn, that was downright poetic."

He gave a shrug and a wry grin. "I have my moments."

Blaz dropped his head close to us and Sas took several large steps back, her eyes widening and her hand tightening on her axe handle.

I agree with Erik, it is time to go. There are more pressing matters.

Fuck it all, what could be more pressing than trying to get allies on our side?

Ophelia stretched her wings, her eyes locking with mine. *There has been a break in the Veil; we must attend to that now.*

"And you waited 'til now to tell me?" I yelled as I ran for Blaz's back.

Blaz let out a big snort, a spurt of flame with it. *We just sensed it. It just happened.*

I yanked myself onto Blaz's back, Liam behind me. Alex lifted his eyes and cracked a yawn; the lazy sod slept the whole time.

"Home now?"

"No. Not yet."

From the ground Sas let out a laugh. "So now you would run away, without even finishing our conversation?"

"What more is there to say? You would let the world die for your pride and your grief; I don't have that luxury. No need to be proper—you're an idiot and I have work to do. Piss on you and your gangs. I hope Orion bleeds you dry showing you the error of your ways." There, how was that for poetic?

The ogres sucked in a collective breath, as did Liam.

"That was necessary because . . . "

"Because this world is black and white. We have no room for grey anymore and I can't damn well coddle them. They are with us, or against us." And that was the truth of it; there was no leeway anymore.

Liam didn't touch me, didn't wrap his arms around me as Blaz took off. The dragon's wings sent up a spiral plume of ash, for a brief second obscuring the ogres below. I wished to hell things had gone better.

Could have gone much worse, Rylee. We might have had to kill them if they'd attacked. Besides, this way they might come around. You never know with ogres, they love fighting almost as much as they love fucking.

Blaz had a point. "For now, it doesn't matter. Where is this breach in the Veil and what the fuck are we going to do about it? Better yet, how did you know?"

Ophelia spoke loud and clear. *Perhaps the better question would be 'What is a breach in the Veil?' Let us start with that.*

Liam ground his teeth behind me. "What the hell is a breach in the Veil, then?"

It is a true tear in the fabric between the worlds, not a doorway, but a spill over from too much power bearing down on that which keeps the human and the supernatural world apart. They happened in the early days when the Veil was first created, before the levels were instituted to keep those most dangerous farthest from the surface.

"Shit, that sounds like a dandy time," I grumbled.

Blaz kicked in, *Dragons sense a tear in the Veil, an actual tear, not an opening. The ability is hardwired into us, part of why the Slayers took to pairing with us back in the day. Made it easier to contain the demons.*

In that moment, I didn't need to ask where the tear in the Veil was. I could find out myself. Swallowing hard, I Tracked demons as a whole.

"Don't do it, Rylee," Erik called back to me, turning in his seat to face me. "Tracking demons is beyond dangerous, they can lock onto you and pull you through to them." How did he know I was going to Track demons? Shit, could I be read that easily? I guess I'd have to ask after all.

"Blaz, Ophelia, where is the tear in the Veil?" I yelled to be heard over the wind whipping past us.

Blaz's words rocked me. *The farm.* No, no, no, that couldn't be right. It couldn't.

Feeling a steady beat of panic rising through me, I Tracked Pamela and Milly and nearly swallowed my tongue.

Liam grabbed my arms. "What is it? Your heart rate is into light speed."

"They broke through at the farm and Milly and Pamela are fighting them."

He didn't let go of me. "How bad is it?"

I shuddered as something hit Milly, and a shard of pain rippled from her to me and then the same thing happened to Pamela.

Not again, I couldn't lose the kid again.

I whispered the words, feeling them pierce me.

"As bad as it could be."

6

Tracking Pamela and Milly, I felt them both fall unconscious, and then they disappeared in the way only the Veil can affect my Tracking ability. They were alive, but somewhere within the Veil where I couldn't pinpoint them. We were only half way home and there wasn't a damn thing I could do. I Tracked Eve and Frank, they weren't anywhere near the farm; they were somewhere east of Bismarck. Too far to be of help, but also out of harm's way. I wasn't sure that the young necromancer or the young Harpy would be of any help against demons anyway.

Shit, I wasn't sure I could be any help against demons.

I glanced at Erik. If he could teach me to fight demons, then he was damn well teaching all of us. It was the only way to keep our asses safe from Orion and his lackeys.

Even with the two dragons flying at top speed, and as close to the ground as they dared, it took over three hours to get to the farm. We didn't land right away, though.

We need to find the breach first and any demons waiting on us. Blaz's voice rumbled loudly through my mind and I turned in time to see Liam nod; I frowned at him.

He frowned back. "What, you want to see if one of us can get snatched by a demon too? We make sure it's safe, then we land. And not a damn second sooner."

Alex peeked over Liam's shoulder, his golden eyes wide and serious. "Boss is right."

Oh for fuck's sake.

I gritted my teeth and waited while Ophelia and Blaz circled the farm. Ten minutes they floated and spun in thermals, but there was nothing to see.

Finally they descended to the ground, landing to one side of the barn, their feet sinking into the slurry of mud and snow.

Keep Rylee close, Erik, Ophelia said, her head dropping low to look Erik in the face. As if he was deaf.

"I know my job, ugly lizard." He batted her nose and drew one of his swords. With it he traced a symbol in the air, what looked like a figure eight that burned in front of him for a split second before fading.

He motioned for me. "You do the same, kid. It will help your blade bite hard into the demons."

"My blades are already spelled." And I refrained from saying it looked like a pretty damn simple thing to do. "If that's all it took to be a demon hunter, anyone should be able to do it." Okay, so that last part slipped out.

Erik laughed. "Yeah, you would think that was all. It's in your blood; that's what kindles the spell. No words, just you."

I let out a slow breath, pulled my right hand blade and whipped it through the air in an elaborate figure eight. The air burned a bright red, the same as Erik's, before fading.

"Happy?"

He nodded. "Yup."

Alex snickered and waved one paw mimicking the figure eight. "Yuppy doody."

Of course, I didn't expect anything, so when the air in front of Alex burned I was, to say the least, shocked.

Nothing compared to Erik's reaction. His eyes went wide and he stumbled forward, dropping to one knee in front of Alex.

"What the fuck is this? Is he related to us?"

"Not that I'm aware of. Were we the only line of demon hunters?" I put a hand on Alex's head, and he glanced up at me, a grin on his muzzle.

"No, no of course not. It's just that everyone thought the others had been killed or died without any knowledge. Of course, that could be what happened, his family might have some long lost history they stopped believing. That wouldn't stop the blood from running true." Erik pointed to Alex's other paw. "Do the same with that one."

Alex obliged and again, the air burned.

A funny feeling rolled through my stomach. We'd all faced demons at one point or another, and we'd all survived. Fate had a funny way of showing her favor sometimes, and I wondered if Alex was the only one.

"Liam, use your sword and do the same thing."

His eyebrows went up but he pulled his short sword and whipped it through the air, following the pattern. I wasn't surprised when the air burned. In fact, I was betting that everyone within our group had some demon hunter blood running through them. Erik's eyes, I didn't think they could get any wider, but they did.

"Mother of the gods, this is a miracle I did not expect."

I pulled my other sword out and drove it through the air so that it had its own little burning lines.

"Erik, I think this is something that needs to be discussed after we find the breach, and after we pull Milly and Pamela back from where ever they were taken." I was already striding forward, knowing if we couldn't see the breach from the sky, it was likely inside one of the buildings.

Most likely the house. It would make a perfect ambush.

I trotted up the steps to the farmhouse, the glass in the kitchen door was shattered, shards everywhere. "Alex, watch your step."

"Yupsy." He moved sideways, carefully avoiding the broken bits of glass. Erik and Liam pulled up the rear and the dragons drew close, giving us what back up they could without tearing down the house.

I pushed the door open and stepped inside. A putrid scent of shit and ammonia filled the air, gagging my throat closed. Liam and Alex both let out low growls, and I was betting it was the scent of the demons, and not the shit, that irritated them.

"These don't smell like hoarfrost demons," Liam said, his voice pitched low.

Once Liam and I were through the door, Erik followed, moving beside me. "I told you, there are only so many of those bastards." He glanced around, took in the scorch marks on the walls, the stains going part way up that had the look of piss marks, only normal piss didn't tend to burn.

I put the tip of my sword out, touching the marks on the wall closest to me. "You know what kind of demon we're facing?"

"Looks like hounds and their masters. The hounds love to mark territory, pissing and shitting on everything. The masters are not very big, about the size of a large monkey, but they're fast and mean and have no sense of pain. So you can cut them into pieces and they're still alive, so they'll still come after you."

I let out a snort, gagged on the intake of air. "Gah. Sounds like fun."

We made our way deeper into the house. The bedrooms were clear, as was the living room. That left the bathroom on the first floor to check.

Erik put a hand out, stopping us, his eyes flicking to Liam and then back to me. "The hallway is a perfect funnel for them, and if they're in the shitter, they've got the high ground."

Liam shook his head. "Worse than that, they already know we're here; if they have hounds there is no way they haven't heard us talking."

Erik let out a loud, booming laugh, making the three of us jump. "Those bastards sleep like the dead, and coming through a breach in the Veil will leave them exhausted. So we go in careful, but I'm betting whoever is on guard is asleep. They would have come out after us if they'd been awake."

Blaz spoke softly to me. *Eve and Frank are here, do you want them inside?*

"No, keep them outside and out of our way." Not that Eve would have fit well at her height, but she would have tried if I'd asked her.

From outside the house Eve let out an irritated squawk. Liam lifted an eyebrow at me, and I shook my head.

Erik moved to the side of the bathroom door. Very slowly, he put his hand to the knob and turned it. The waft of air that rushed out of the room would have knocked me to my knees if I hadn't been already exposed to the shit smell through the rest of the house.

He pushed the door open and it swung inward on silent hinges. My bathroom looked the same, so I squinted and used my second sight. Nope, still nothing but a toilet, sink, and shower.

Mind you, the shower curtain was pulled shut.

I pointed at it and Erik nodded. With the tip of his sword he pulled the shower curtain back, the plastic crinkling with the pull of the rings across the metal rod.

Bingo.

The back wall of the shower was no longer the old, yellow tile that was a throwback to the seventies when the house was built. Nope, I had a lovely, deep violet swirling mass that took up the entire wall and seemed to be belching farts. Awesome, just what I wanted for the new year, a bathroom renovation complete with demons sleeping in the tub.

A mass of light-brown fur rumbled with a snore as it shifted in the clawfoot tub.

How the hell could something so small, and so obviously stupid, have taken not only Pamela, but Milly too?

The rather non-imposing ball of fur rolled over, its eye sockets empty of any actual eyes, its mouth open and three spiked tongues swirling out toward us.

"Fucking hell!" I was closest to it, and I whipped my swords forward, lopping off the tongues reaching for me.

"Rylee, don't!"

Too late.

The thing let out a screech that drove all sense from me, and I couldn't move. My body remained unmoving as the demon rose out of the tub, a vague shape of a hound underneath the muscle and writhing hunks of tongue. Its eyes, or the sockets where its eye were supposed to be, snared mine and I knew I was done in.

"Do you think to stop us, little demon hunter? You have waited too long." It licked its jaws with its stumps, pulling tufts of fur out of its own face. "We will rule this world, and the humans will bow to us."

The thing was breathing heavily in my face, so close I could have kissed it if so inclined, why couldn't I move, why couldn't I get away? Some demon hunter I was.

Hands grabbed me and pulled me out of the bathroom as the demon made a lunge for my head, and the door slammed shut behind us.

Someone threw me over their shoulder and ran toward the dragons.

Blaz and Ophelia fought to be heard inside my head, but there was nothing I could do at that particular moment. Nothing at all. Weirder yet, I wasn't scared, or even worried, I felt detached, as if I wasn't really there.

Distantly I heard Eve squawk, Liam said something to her and she was quiet.

Then Erik's voice argued with Liam and I was handed off and we were airborne and after that nothing made sense. A jumble of voices, and colors, red and blue, and the sound of the demon keening, and even that faded into nothing.

I don't know how long we flew, or where we were going, or even why.

Best part was, I no longer cared.

Rylee lay limp in his arms, her face pale, but breathing steady; they hadn't been able to rouse her though and if Erik was right they needed to get her help. Even though there wasn't a mark on her.

"Blaz, what is going on with her?"

Her soul has been detached. I am holding it tight to her, it is one of my jobs as her dragon to help her face the demons, but I had no idea it would be holding the little idiot together in such a literal way.

"It wasn't her fault. Erik let us walk in on the demon."

Ophelia let out a long snort ahead of them but said nothing.

"Will she be all right?"

I think so. Erik and Ophelia both seem confident. I would be more worried if they were having a meltdown. But they aren't. Keep her warm; I will keep her soul close. That is all we can do until we reach the shamans. They have ways to bring her back to herself.

Liam gritted his teeth and held tighter to her body. Anger and fear warred within him. "I think we need to bring one of the shamans along with us. It seems we're always needing them to patch her up, or give us a hand anyway."

You would never convince them to leave their territories. They are not the kind that wander far from their homes. Blaz tipped his head to look back with one eye. *But perhaps we could convince a druid to stay close. It is something to consider.*

That would mean bringing Deanna, most likely, which would mean Will. And Will wanted to make Rylee his mate. A growl slipped out of him just thinking about the cocky panther shifter, then slowly faded. There would come a day when he wouldn't be there for her. Will *could* be the one who looked after her. The thought clutched hard at his gut, digging in with nails of truth he wished he didn't have to know.

Be easy, she loves no one but you. I do not think her heart has it in it to love anyone but you. She is not like other women I have known. She gives her heart freely to her friends and those she would protect, but you . . . you hold the keys to her deepest pieces, and she loves you beyond her own life. I do believe she would die for you, without a question, without a thought.

Liam stared down at her face, soft with unconsciousness. She was his world, and she kept coming so close to dying that he knew at some point fate would catch up to her and that would be it.

He could only hope he was there in that moment and could trade his life for hers.

A prayer slipped from his lips. "Let it be done that way, or not at all."

The flight was smooth, mostly because I recalled none of it. With seemingly no transition, we were on the ground and I was packed into an adobe house I distantly recognized, but I couldn't remember who owned the house. Someone, I knew the person. Maybe. Did it belong to a Daywalker?

Vampire. He was a vampire now.

Hands hovered over my face. How did I get on my back? Fingers snapped and the fog shrouding me cleared. I jerked up to a sitting position, gasping and choking as if I'd been running a fucking marathon.

"Oh, well, welcome back, Tracker. Nice of you to join us."

Doran sat across from me, knees apart, elbows resting on them. Berget stood to one side of him, her eyes on me. Louisa was behind them both.

"All your favors are used up, Rylee. There will be no more freebies," Louisa said and then walked out. No goodbye, no see you later. But then, that was a typical shaman for you.

Doran, on the other hand, was not so typical. In any way. He leaned forward, eyes intense. "How are you feeling?"

I ran a hand over my face, closed my eyes for a brief second. "Fine. I think. What the hell happened?"

Footsteps, the sound of lowered voices, then Erik stepped into the room with a more-than-agitated Liam right on his heels. "I told you she'd be fine, ease down, wolf man."

"It's not about her being fine, I never doubted that. You knew going in, and you let her do something stupid without—"

Erik rounded on him. "I did try to stop her, but if you haven't noticed, she's faster than a human, faster than she should be even as a Tracker or a demon hunter. I won't make that mistake again. Trust me on that, there will be no more demon hunts until she's had at least the rudiments of training."

"That ain't going to fucking well happen. We have to get Milly and Pamela out. I can't leave them there." I pushed myself to my feet and was pleased to see I wasn't unsteady in the least. "Why the hell did you bring me all the way here if I wasn't in trouble?"

Blaz reached out to me. *Erik is lying; your spirit was being bound. You were alive and wouldn't have died, but who you are was being eaten. Your bond to me staved it off long enough for Doran and Louisa to break the bond between you and the soul sucker demon.*

My eyes darted to Doran of their own volition. "Thanks. Seems you saved my ass again."

"My pleasure; after all it is such a nice ass to be saving." He gave me a grin and a wink, his green eyes full of life and so very different from the eyes I'd seen in other vampires. Even Berget didn't have the spark I saw in his emerald depths. Unlike other vampires, his soul remained intact when he'd become a night-walking blood sucker. Apparently it had something to do with my blood being the catalyst in the spell that turned him. I shook my head.

"Whatever. You need to get laid, vampire."

He let out a laugh and held out his hand to me. "You offering?"

Berget's words came back to me full force and I shot a glance her way. She lifted an eyebrow and one pale shoulder.

"Thanks, but my dance card is full."

I hoped that would get the point across; I really didn't want to be a bitch to him. He was a friend and an ally, and it looked like Berget was staying with him, which was good for her. He wouldn't hurt her, or take advantage of her, and the memories trapped inside her head could help him lead the vampires better than if he was doing it on his own.

Doran stepped toward me, one hand out as if to touch my cheek. "You sure about that?"

Instead of continuing that thread of conversation I turned my back on him and changed the subject.

"Berget, anything on your end of things?"

She shook her head, soft blond hair shimmering. "Not yet, but I think I am making some progress."

"Okay." I reached out and pulled her into my arms, gave her a hug. "Thanks."

She grinned at me. "We're family, you don't have to thank me."

"Just be careful."

"Of course."

Doran's eyes whipped from me to her and back again. "What are you two up to now?"

"Nothing you can do anything about." I let go of Berget and then kept my eyes down as I checked my weapons. They were all there; that at least was an upside to this mess.

Doran stopped me with a hand on my arm, and very gently pulled me aside. "There is a betrayal coming your way, Rylee. One I can't see clearly, but it is there nonetheless."

I went still. Was he buzzing on the blood I'd fed him in order to turn him into a fully-blooded vampire? Damn, he must have gotten more than I'd thought at the time. It was the only time he could Read my future.

"What kind of betrayal?"

His brows crinkled, tugging the silver piercing downward over his right eye. "Your life and your wolf's will be on the line, but it will be up to Liam and another to stop it from happening. It's muddled because your blood runs thin in my veins. I should have thought to do a reading sooner, but I've been busy." No doubt that was true, taking over the vampire nation was no small task.

Great, just what I needed. That meant it would be me and Alex in trouble. Awesome sauce. "Any idea of time frame?"

"Soon. Within the next few days. Death will be heavy with the one who betrays you."

That made no sense, but it was all he was able to give me. At least it was something. I thanked him and turned to leave, almost running into Erik. Bouncing off his chest I grimaced. Time to get back on track.

"I'm not leaving Milly and Pamela in that freaking purple hole in my bathroom wall, Erik. So how are we going to get them out?" I didn't wait for him to answer, but started down the hallway. Liam caught my eye and slid in behind me.

"Alex is already with Blaz."

"Good, we're already so far behind we're in fucking first place," I muttered under my breath, half pissed that they'd brought me here, so far from home. But also knowing that if they hadn't, there wouldn't be anything of me left. What a hot shitty mess.

"Where do you think you're going? I was not kidding when I said that hunting demons is a bad idea until you know more," Erik shouted after us as we strode through the night-darkened courtyard and past the koi pond to the two dragons waiting for us. They barely fit in the front yard, but it didn't matter that this was a suburban area. Doran's house sat within a fold of the Veil, or a wrinkle, if you will. He used the Veil to hide his whereabouts from the humans and anything within that fold couldn't be seen by human eyes.

So much disbelief in the world of magic kept them blind to all the wonder—and horror—that surrounded them.

More horror than wonder. Blaz said softly, and I had to agree. There was far more horror in our world than I liked to admit. Yet I knew very little else.

I was up on Blaz in a matter of seconds, Liam behind me.

"Erik, either you're coming with me or I'm damn well going in on my own. My friends need me, that's all there is to this."

Erik scrambled onto Ophelia's back. "You are no different than your mother, running headlong into danger for your friends." He shook his head. "Fine. But you will listen to me the whole damn way back, not a word out of you. Understood? It is the only way it will work if we're going to go into the deep levels of the Veil to bring them back."

I nodded, ignoring his comment about my mother, my heart pounding with something akin to excitement. Shit, I was terrified for my two girls, but I was excited to learn I finally had an ability that would give me an offense instead of a defense. Blaz leapt into the sky, his wings stirring up the surface of the pond, lifting Berget's curls back from her face. I lifted a hand to Berget and Doran who waved back to me in return. They watched until I could see them no more, and I had the feeling they watched still, long after we were out of sight.

Yet there was no time to ponder what the hell I was supposed to do with Doran's affections. Nope, I had a couple short hours to learn about being a demon hunter before going into the deep levels of the Veil.

Oh, I had to believe that we could do it, that we would be able to walk in, slaughter a few demons and pull both witches out intact.

Yet a small part of me knew it was going to be much harder than that. I only hoped that small part of me was wrong.

Listen to that small part of you, Rylee. It is what has kept you alive all these years.

Blaz words resonated truth within me.

That's what I was so very afraid of.

7

The farm was still, the fields black and reflecting light only here and there on the patches of snow. If the clouds surrounding us were any indication, we were in for another big dump of snow that would cover the fields in a matter of hours.

However, the weather was the least of my concerns.

Ancient words still rang inside my head, two hours of memorization with Erik and I wasn't positive I would be able to deal with the demons after all. To me the words didn't feel like magic, or strength, or even anything important. They sounded like nonsense, gibberish words that would do dipshit. Would I use them? Yup, even if I thought I sounded like a fool. I had no choice. I was going in after Milly and Pamela. Just meant it was going to be a bitch of a rescue. Liam grasped the words quicker than I did, and Alex, though he didn't recall any of the words, listened to everything Erik taught us via Ophelia. She projected his words to us along the flight home.

Standing in front of the dark farmhouse, I knew at least the rudiments of how to tangle with the lesser demons.

A loud screech turned us around to see Eve and Frank bursting out of the barn. Frank was downright tiny next to the Harpy, but it looked like he'd finally gotten used to her.

Eve skidded to a stop, her wings flapping, right in front of me. "What happened? Did you find Pamela and Milly?"

"Not yet," I shook my head, "we're going in after them now." No need to point out that I'd blown it the first time.

Frank cleared his throat and pushed his glasses up on his pimpled nose. "Umm. That might not be possible."

Liam put a hand on the kid's shoulder. "Why not, Frank?"

Frank gave a tiny shrug. "I can feel the . . . Veil . . . when it opens. And when it closes. I think they closed this one."

"Why the fuck would they do that?" But I knew the answer to my own question. I really had blown it, we'd had our chance to go in after Milly and Pamela and because I didn't listen to Erik those demons had closed the breach.

Of course, no one answered my question. They all knew as well as I did the why of it.

"Doesn't matter, you still need to go in and check it out." Erik didn't pull his weapons out, instead looked at me expectantly. And maybe with more than an ounce of disappointment in his eyes. I blushed under his recriminating gaze. I didn't need the less than subtle reminder that I'd screwed this up. "Mark your blades," he instructed. Liam swung his sword in the figure eight and the blade burned, Alex followed suit with his claws, and I reluctantly did the same with my weapon.

Something didn't sit well with me, but fuck if I could figure it out.

"If anything shows up," Erik said, "that doesn't fit the descriptions I've given you, run back out and I will deal with it."

"You're a human with a few words and a few hand gestures. You really believe you can do this better than me?" I wasn't being cocky. I'd seen more than one human go down in flames because they tangled with the supernatural with the belief they 'had it in them' to do so.

"It's unlikely, but if anything does show up, Rylee, this is what I do. It's always been humans trained for hunting demons." He pointed at the door and I started forward. Stopping when a question caught me off guard. One I didn't want to wait on.

"Why the humans?"

"Because the demons expect to be able to control a human with hardly a flick of their claws, a tip of their eyes in our direction. Which for the most part is true. But," he stepped up and held the door open for me, "when a human finally sees the truth, and knows what they are facing, they become an unknown quantity in some ways."

"A wild card." I stepped softly into the house, avoiding the broken glass as best I could.

"Yes. Exactly. Even now, they don't think a Slayer has much ability against them, not understanding the fates gave us the words to stop the demonic in their tracks. At least, if you are one of the few families blessed to have the blood that will kindle the words."

I left him there, Liam and Alex following me through the shit and piss marking the demon hounds' passing, down the hallway, and to the closed bathroom door. But I already knew it would be too late, the breach would be closed.

I pushed the door open and the inside of the bathroom held exactly what I was expecting.

Nothing.

"Motherfuckers," I snarled. The floor was splattered with blood where I'd cut off the creature's tongues, and the back wall was no longer the swirling violet of the Veil. The yellow tile was scorched, chipped, and hanging from the wall in pieces.

But no breach in the Veil.

A low groan drew me to the tub and I raised my blade, whispering, "*Adonani*" before actually stepping closer. The word would still my soul, keep it attached to me and keep the demon from sucking me down again. Supposedly.

Another groan and I leapt forward, my blade sailing downward toward the face of . . . Eagle. Shit on a stick. Twisting hard, I drove my blade into the side of the tub, just missing Eagle's face. The porcelain shattered around my blade and Eagle, and what looked like all of his blood spilled out onto the floor. He was a Guardian, but more than that, he had been Eve's mentor, helping her control herself and her harpy tendencies. And I suspected she was more than half in love with him which was only going to make this that much harder on her.

Ignoring the blood, I dropped to my knees, put one hand on his chest and the other behind his head. "Eagle, what the hell are you doing here, what happened?" As a Guardian, there was no way injuries like this should have hurt him so badly. Never mind the fact he was supposed to be in New Mexico with his shaman. Not here bleeding out in the remnants of my tub.

His silver eyes rolled up to mine. "Tracker. Demons and evil spirits everywhere. Must stop them." A shudder rippled the length of his body, a single breath gurgled from his mouth with a bubble of blood, and then nothing. I swallowed hard, my mind and heart racing.

"They shouldn't have been able to kill him." I lifted my eyes to Liam's, fear clenching my gut tight. We'd been acting like Liam was invincible, that he was immune to any kind of trauma except decapitation.

Looked like we were wrong. And at the worst possible time.

Alex slipped closer, his nose quivering, but he said nothing. He just watched, his golden eyes taking it all in.

"Rylee, I don't hear any fighting," Erik called from the front of the house. "If there are no demons, I suggest you get your ass out here and we continue to train."

"Doesn't know you too well, does he?" Liam squatted beside me, his eyes sorrowful. I doubted it had to do with just Eagle's untimely death.

"Talk to me, Liam. You know what this is; you spent time with Peter talking about guardians and werewolves. You know what's going on, don't you?"

His eyes slid closed and he slowly shook his head. "Maybe, I don't know."

Well, that was an improvement. When we'd been in Europe, he and Peter had gone off on their own for days at a time. He hadn't spoken to me about what he'd learned, and I wasn't sure he ever would. More and more, he was keeping things from me, and it killed me to know he didn't fully trust me.

More likely that he can't tell you, Rylee. Blaz whispered to me. *Every species has its secrets they are not supposed to share. He will be no different.*

Ignoring Blaz, I let the subject drop between me and Liam, stood, and strode to my bedroom. Even in there, the demons had done their job of marking territory, shredding my bed, shitting on the pillows. There was nothing to be saved. Beside the bed was my mother's journal, the only thing I had connecting me to her and my father. Shredded into pieces, I was glad I'd read it through once. I thought about what my mother had written about Erik, about how bold he was, about his willingness to jump into danger. He sure changed a lot since his younger years if his standing outside and waiting for me to do the dirty work was any evidence. A long coiled pile of feces sat on the front cover of the journal; I pushed the book with my toe.

"Nasty shit heads," Alex muttered, rubbing at his nose.

"Yeah, that they are." I backed out of the room.

I only hoped the demons hadn't gone into the root cellar, that somehow they'd missed it. I headed out of the house, Alex trotting beside me.

"Boss is sad. Rylee is sad. Everyone is sad." He shook his head, the silver tips of his fur catching the scattered moonlight.

"You aren't sad, Alex?"

He shook his head. "Nope. Alex has Rylee. Has Boss. Has Evie and Pamie. Alex has love."

My feet stilled and I dropped a hand to his head. "You are pretty damn smart, you know that?"

He snickered and sat in a patch of snow. "Nope. Alex just loves back."

Such a simple truth. Just love back. I wished it could be that easy when it came to facing demons.

Behind us, Liam's footsteps on the porch reached my ears. "Did they take the book?"

He didn't have to say what book; there was only one book the demons would have been after. The black-skinned book of prophecies.

Around the side of the house I went, my heart sinking to my boots when I saw the busted open door of the root cellar.

"We are so fucked," I whispered as I carefully made my way down the broken and slippery stairs. The weapons, remarkably, were left untouched for the most part, and there was no marking going on. But the lock box I kept the book in was missing.

Not surprised, I headed back out.

Liam took one look at me. "Gone?"

I gave him a sharp nod. "Help me get the weapons out."

With everyone helping, it didn't take long to empty the root cellar and put all the weapons into the barn.

Once that was done, the house no longer had a purpose.

"Blaz, burn it down."

Frank sucked in a sharp breath. "Why would you do that?"

"You can't salvage it, kid," Liam said. "The house has been destroyed and anything of value taken."

Are you sure, Rylee?

"Yes. Do it."

He lifted his head and inhaled, his body expanding, belly rumbling with fire, burning hot. I gave him a nod and he exhaled a brilliant shot of flame that sparkled and danced in the air.

Eve stepped over a half-frozen mud puddle to my side as snow began to fall. Shit, I had to tell her that her mentor was dead. I glanced at Liam and he shook his head. I let out a slow, disheartened breath.

"Eve, someone died in there. Someone you know better than anyone else. He was very important to you."

Her beak clacked together, and her eyes filled with fear and grief. "Please, don't say his name. I know, I felt him die."

I clamped my lips shut and put a hand on her trembling wing. "I'm sorry, Eve. I don't know how they did it, but the demons know how to kill guardians." A sudden thought flashed through my mind. "Will you take this news to his shaman and warn the others?"

Sure, I could have phoned them, but Eve needed something to do with her grief. Something constructive or I was afraid she would resort to her natural inclination of Harpy destruction and terror.

"I'll go with you, if you want," Frank said, looking from Eve to me. "I'm not much use here anyway."

In a way he was right. He was young and inexperienced, both in life and as a necromancer. But if he could get a little training he could jump the Veil easier than anyone else. I Tracked necromancers as a species, and felt a hit in the deep south.

"Go to Louisa and the other shamans, then see if you can convince them to help you pinpoint another necromancer. I'm getting pings off one in the deep south, feels like Louisiana."

Frank nodded, but Eve didn't react.

The fire behind us warmed the air and sent shadows dancing across her body. She stared into the flames, tears trickling down her feathers. I wished I could spare her this kind of pain; grief was something I knew all too well.

"Eve, can you do this, can you help Frank find the necromancer?"

A deep breath escaped her in a long exhalation. "It will help stop the demons?"

Best to keep it simple. "Yes."

"You aren't sending me away? To keep me and Frank safe?"

"Eve," I tugged on one of her long, tawny pinion feathers. "Look at me."

She slowly turned her face to mine, tears scorching across her cheeks.

I touched my hands to the tears. "No one is safe, it wouldn't matter where I sent you; I expect there to be danger. But together, you and Frank have a chance at accomplishing two things I don't have time for. That doesn't mean they aren't important, nor does it mean they will be safe."

"I'll look out for her." Frank stepped beside me, scuffing the dirt with his worn sneakers.

"More likely she'll end up saving your ass; that's the way it's always been with her and me." I laughed softly.

"You like Blaz better than me." Ah, here we were at the crux. I'd been waiting for this, knowing it was only a matter of time before the teenage harpy finally said it. But seriously, did it have to be right now? I restrained the bitchy side of me that wanted to tell her to take her insecurities and stuff them until this was all said and done. Only there was no guarantee there would ever be a time when it was all said and done. So now it was.

"Not true. You are part of my family, part of my and Liam's pack. Blaz is more like . . ." How to find the words to describe my relationship with Blaz?

We are partners, and we work well together. But her heart does not lie with me as it does with you and those she deems family. Blaz's tone wasn't snarky or even upset. Just matter of fact. All and all, it was the truth.

Eve's eyes flickered in the light. "Truly?"

I nodded. "Yes, he kind of nailed it on the head. I didn't want to say it out loud, he can be a fucking crybaby, you know."

Blaz snorted, a gout of flame shooting out his nostrils toward the house. As if he'd meant to do it.

Eve's eyes crinkled with a half smile that quickly slipped from her face. "I will come whenever you need me. You know that."

I didn't say anything. I didn't have to. Frank stepped up and swung his leg over her back and settled into the harness. "Where should we meet you when we're done?"

That was a good question. Who could keep them safe, who did I trust that was still alive? There were only a few people left now.

"Go to Doran's. Wait for us there."

Eve nodded, spread her wings and took off, the downdraft fanning the flames and sending up a shower of sparks. As they left, I finally Tracked Pamela and Milly, nearly slumping with relief. They were alive, and though they were either asleep or unconscious, they weren't being hurt. Only thing better would be if they'd been brought to this side of the Veil.

Erik watched me from where he leaned against Ophelia's side. I was actually surprised she'd been as quiet as she had.

She feels responsible for what happened. Apparently she told Erik he needed to give you at least a few words of protection, and he didn't listen to her. At least we know the stubbornness is inherent in your family.

"He fucking well should have given us something. We could have gone in and gotten them both without this damn mess." A part of me wondered if he'd done it on purpose, but what advantage would he have, taking my family from me? I put my hands on my hips, for the first time truly stumped as to how to go about a salvage. I felt them, knew they were alive, knew they were in the Veil, but how did we get to the deep levels?

And that was the question of the day.

One I had no answer to.

8

Watching Rylee, the flames throwing light and dark against her face, made his heart tighten. There was nothing he could do at the moment, and he knew her well enough to let her mull this situation over before he said anything. So he waited, knowing she would find him soon enough. He leaned against the barn, Alex tucked up against him, though he doubted it was for warmth.

"Boss."

"What?"

The formerly submissive werewolf looked up, making direct eye contact. "Rylee smells funny. Not right."

Liam's heart tightened more. Fuck, Alex would blurt out what Liam already suspected but didn't say out loud. The only thing he could do was stall the werewolf at his feet and hope to hell he said nothing. "She's sick. Don't tell anyone."

Alex let out a gasp, his clawed paws clamping down on his muzzle. Through his clenched teeth he whispered, "Sick? Dying?"

Liam shook his head. "Keep it down. And no, she isn't dying. Just . . . a little bit sick. She'll get better."

"Promise?" He wobbled to his back legs so he could look Liam in the face.

Damn it all. Liam nodded. "Yes, I promise. But say nothing. Understand? Not even to Rylee. Not to anyone."

Alex dropped to his haunches, sitting back to cross his heart with the tip of one claw. "Promises."

Promises. He'd made so many. To himself, to Rylee. To Peter, the old wolf, who'd told him what he really was and where he stood within the prophecies. He couldn't keep all the promises, as several stood at odds with one another.

Death was coming for him, he felt it drawing closer each day, and if the old wolf was right, it was the prophecies coming into play. His life and death would not be in vain, but it would mean breaking his promises to Rylee.

It meant keeping the truth from her until the last possible second. He closed his eyes and leaned his head back, not moving even when he heard her footsteps. Rylee put her head against his chest, a tremor rippling through her.

"How do I find them? Tell me how to fix this, Liam. Blaz doesn't know, Ophelia doesn't know, Erik can't help though he should know better than anyone else." Her hands curled up on his chest and he wrapped his arms around her, rubbed her back and held her tightly against him.

"Something will show us the way. It always does. We wouldn't have come this far only to lose now."

She lifted her head and stared at him, her tri-colored eyes searching his. "How do you know that?"

He gave her a smile, lips barely moving. "Because that is your life, Rylee. No matter how bad the shit gets, something or someone always pulls through. The help will be there when you need it. And we need it now. So I believe. I hope. You taught me that." Even though his heart didn't believe it, not for a second. Sure, things had worked out so far, but he had a feeling those days were over.

Tears swam in her eyes, spilling over her cheeks. "Thank you."

He rubbed a thumb under her eyes, wiping away her tears. A few months ago she wouldn't have broken down like this. But things were changing for them all, and Rylee more than anyone else.

"Who do you know with knowledge, who has an understanding of the Veil?" he asked.

She took several breaths before answering. "Doran and the other shamans might but it's a long shot, and Berget, I suppose, if she could access the memories easier."

"No one else?" Shit, there had to be someone, something they hadn't tried.

Her eyes flicked up to his. "Maybe there is someone who would know, but I might have to kick his ass to get him to help." She stepped back from him, a spark lighting her up. She had an idea that likely involved some level of danger; he saw it written all over her face.

He stifled a groan. Rylee and her ideas or hunches were usually right on, but that didn't mean they were easy—ever.

Nor did it mean he would let her go on her own.

Alex let out a yip and pushed his way between them, so he could face Rylee. "Alex too. Rylee not leaving Alex." He let out a low growl to punctuate.

Rylee let out a small laugh. "Yeah, of course you can come too." She looked at Liam, put a hand on his cheek, resting it lightly. "Thank you."

He smiled, leaned in and took her mouth in a kiss that he'd been waiting on a chance for all day. These moments were too few, but it made them all the more sweet.

"I'm going to find us something to eat in your barn stash."

Her eyelids fluttered back open. "You know, you trained pretty good for a stuffy FBI agent."

Laughing, she walked away and he watched her go, the sway of her body, the tumble of auburn hair down her back, her weapons so much a part of her he barely noticed them anymore. There was never a moment he regretted this life, even knowing it was coming to an end sooner than he liked.

"Come on, Alex. Let's get the boss lady something to eat."

Alex took off with a mad scramble, nearly breaking down the barn door in his excitement.

Shaking his head, he followed Alex into the barn. No, he would never regret the way his life turned out, no matter how it might end.

I knew it was a long shot, what I was planning, but I didn't have much choice but to at least try. I couldn't recall the symbols on the steel reinforced door in the castle, but if they were close enough to the ones Erik knew, I'd bet every last dollar I had that the doorway led into the deeper Veils.

Getting to the doorway and getting in would be a matter of navigating the castle, finding the captain of the red caps, and then convincing him we should be allowed to use it. Simple, right?

Yeah, probably not so much.

I found Erik standing apart from the two dragons, who seemed to be having a heated conversation if their snaking heads and snapping teeth were any indication. I ignored them and headed for my uncle. Damn, that sounded weird, even inside my head. "What symbol would you put on something to keep a demon locked inside?"

He turned to face me, his eyebrows near his hairline. "And you want to know this why?"

"Don't answer me with a question, just tell me what it looks like." Damn it, I had to bite my tongue to keep from cussing him out.

"You aren't a Slayer yet, Rylee. You don't get all the tools until you've earned them." His voice was even, but his eyes flashed and I swore there was a spark of fear in there.

"Oh fuck off." So much for not cussing him out. "I don't want to have all the tools, I don't want the title, I don't even want to be a freaking Slayer. I want to know what the symbol to keep a demon trapped would look like. Is that too fucking much to ask?"

His jaw twitched, but I couldn't tell if he was angry or trying not to laugh at me.

He pulled a short dagger from his waist and the breath in my chest seized. There was no way he'd challenge me to a fight . . . was there?

He dropped to one knee and with the dagger drew a symbol in the mud. "Here, it looks like this." He drew two squares, one inside the other, and inside the smaller square was a starburst. Simple, clean. Now it was a matter of matching it to what was on the doorway in the castle.

"What are you thinking?" Erik stood and wiped his dagger on his pants before putting it away.

"I have to see if that," I pointed to the dirt at our feet, "matches what I think it does. Are you in?"

A snort escaped him, followed closely by a laugh. "I knew you were going to be difficult, hell, I even expected it. But I had no idea what I was getting into when I set off to find you."

I didn't know whether or not to take offense, so I ignored him. Hell, I knew I was a pain in the ass, knew it was only a matter of time before I pissed off every person in my circle. Didn't make me any less right though when I followed my gut.

I put my hands on my hips. "You in or not, old man?"

The two dragons behind us went absolutely still and silent, their snarls cut off in mid snap.

"Old man?"

"That's what I called you. Seeing as you're old." Okay, so I was pushing, but I still wasn't a hundred percent in when it came to him. He showed up out of nowhere, and while Blaz vouched for him, my uncle hadn't been exactly forthcoming with how to deal with demons until it had been essentially forced on him.

"Well, since I'm so gods-be-damned old, I guess I'll stay here and tend the fire."

I shrugged. "Fine." Hell, it wasn't fine, but I wondered if he'd be any real help anyway. Or if he would let us get hurt and then try to fix it.

I walked away, paused and turned back. "If that's all you've got in the way of being *helpful*, maybe you and Ophelia should leave."

The air grew heavy and Erik kept his back to me for a split second before spinning, anger etched on his face. "You think you can do this alone? You think you've got it in you to finish this without anyone else? You're as blind as your idiotic parents."

I faced him, all the years of anger and hurt, all the betrayal and loss I'd dealt with on my own finally getting a voice. "Where were you when I needed you, *uncle*? Where were you when my parents died, when I needed my family? Where were you? Oh, that's right, you were a drunk who couldn't be relied on when they needed you the most. You think my parents were idiotic? Well, maybe to you they seemed like it, but how would you have known when you were always sauced to the gills? Ophelia isn't even your dragon, is she?"

He flushed and Ophelia sucked in a sharp breath, purple in her eyes flooding the iris.

"Yeah, that's right, I read my mother's journal. Ophelia was my father's dragon, not yours. She was his companion. Your dragon was killed, wasn't she? What, were you too out of it to realize your own dragon was being killed?"

Erik didn't say anything, hell, he couldn't.

What did you say when the truth was flung into your face? The worst part was, I wanted him to be a real part of my family, of my life. But he was proving as unreliable as my mother made him out to be in her journal. I'd wanted her to be wrong.

What a fucking disappointment.

I turned my back on him and strode toward the barn, but Liam and Alex were standing beside Blaz, a bag on Liam's back.

"Blaz, can you give us a lift?"

Of course. You know, they could follow us.

"They won't follow. That would take balls." I pulled myself onto his back. Liam strapped himself second, and Alex behind him. Blaz took off as soon as the last buckle was clicked.

"That's why you weren't sold on him, isn't it?" Liam asked as he handed me a sandwich.

I took a bite, chewed, and swallowed. "Yeah. I read all about him, and there was even a picture of him in her book. He was an ass to them both, was jealous that my father was a demon hunter of the first order. Erik did all the training, was a Slayer, but my dad was better."

"So he could still help you."

"If he didn't let me get caught by each demon first to teach me a lesson. Maybe he hates me, because of who my parents are, and who he was to them. It doesn't matter now, I'm done with him." I took another bite, grateful for the food. How long since we'd last eaten? Shit, I could barely remember but my body was suddenly craving the peanut butter and jelly. I downed the last of the sandwich and Liam handed me another without being asked.

"You aren't taking me with you, are you?" Liam asked and I felt Blaz stutter underneath us.

You're taking the wolf. There is no other way.

"Milly can't jump him out. Which means he can't come with me and Alex."

Then we go back for Erik. You bloody well cannot go by yourself.

"We aren't going back for Erik. He's proven quite freaking nicely that I can't trust him. He's too busy trying to rewrite the past."

Liam grabbed my arms, squeezing them hard. "Rylee, don't be stupid about this. I realize I can't go. I get it. But Erik can. And even if he hated your parents, even if he is on a vendetta of his own, he can help you in there, he can be the person at your back while you face down demons."

I twisted in my seat. "Yeah, and when he puts his blade between my shoulders and hands me over to the demons in exchange for his own skin, what then?"

I can't believe he'd do that, Rylee. I can't.

"Have you been in his head, Blaz?" I snapped. Anger and fear for Pamela and Milly made me less than tolerant. "You don't know him. You hardly even know Ophelia, but I would trust her over him. My father . . ." The words choked in my throat for some stupid reason.

He loved her dearly, didn't he?

I nodded, took a breath, and finally got the words out. "He died before my mother, and Ophelia nearly died with him of a broken heart. My mother's journal said Ophelia was never the same after he died, that something broke within her. I'm surprised she's as cognizant as she is, considering what my mother wrote."

Regret flowed from Blaz into me, and I realized he knew very little about Ophelia, that he'd made snap judgments about her because his heart was tied elsewhere. He back drafted his wings so our forward progress stilled and he tread the air. My jaw ticked.

I will speak to her before we go farther. If she vouches for him, will you take Erik?

Shit, I'd just said I trusted her over him. And I did trust Blaz. "Fine. If she will vouch for him, if she would trust him with me, then I will take him."

Blaz gave a nod and his eyes half closed. Minutes passed and several times he shook his head, letting out long low growls. Finally, he turned his head back to me.

She will vouch for him, she says he has changed, and she knows he is not the man he once was. If he was still that man she would have killed him herself.

"And she speaks truly?"

For all her faults that I see now were my own, yes, she speaks the truth. He started off again toward the badlands, heading to the mineshaft.

"Is he going to help?"

No. He's not.

Fuck a duck, why was I not surprised?

9

Standing with Rylee and Alex in front of the doorway within the mineshaft that led into the castle where red caps waited was one of the hardest moments of his life.

"You still trust me to do what I have to?" Rylee lifted her eyes to his in the flickering light, an eyebrow arched in query.

"I said I did. I stand by it. Doesn't mean I damn well like this plan of yours." Actually, his gut was churning with fear for her. The red caps were one thing, but going into the deeper levels of the Veil, which neither of them knew anything about, with no one to guide her. . . the thought pulled at his soul. Going with her through the doorway wasn't an option and it killed him.

"Thanks." She leaned up and kissed him, pressing her lips hard to his before backing away. "I don't know how long we'll be."

"How long do I wait before I come after you?" Because that was a distinct possibility.

She shook her head. "You don't. Because if I'm wrong and I get killed, then I'm not the one the prophecies speak of, and you will be one of the last few who has an ability to face demons."

He sucked in a sharp breath. "That does not help me let you go."

"But it's the truth."

Alex's tail thumped the ground and he tugged at Liam's pant leg. "I take care of Rylee."

Liam looked from Rylee—her jaw hanging open—to Alex and back again. He didn't want to change the subject but . . . "Did you hear that?"

She sputtered, "He used 'I' instead of 'Alex.'"

"Shit, he really is coming around."

Alex grinned at them and even winked at Rylee. "I keeps her safe, Boss, no worries."

Without any thought other than to hold her one last time, Liam wrapped his arms around her and held her against his chest. "Come back to me, Tracker."

She clung to him for two breaths before pushing back. "I always do."

With that, she stepped back, put her hand on the door and she and Alex slipped through.

He saw a glimmer of the castle walls within the lower dungeon levels and then nothing as the door shut behind them. In the quiet of the old mineshaft Liam waited. Hating he'd lied to her.

"Blaz, can you hear me?"

Ah. Yes. Why, is something wrong already?

"I don't care what you have to do, but you get Ophelia to get Erik's ass here pronto."

Sweet mother of the gods, I didn't think you'd let her go without a fight. I'll make it happen.

Liam stared at the closed doorway. There was no way he was letting her go on her own.

She just didn't know it yet.

The walls were splattered with blood from the red caps where the hoarfrost demons had gone through them. Except for the distant sputter of torches, the place was quiet, even more so than usual. Like a tomb. A shudder rippled through me.

"Fucking creepy," I muttered, and glanced at Alex. Crap, I stifled a laugh.

He was walking on the tip toes of his front paws, very cartoon like, his lower lip drawn down in an exaggerated frown, mumbling, "Stupid red caps, dumber demons," under his breath.

I pulled my swords from their sheaths and drew the symbols Erik taught us. Tapping Alex on the shoulder with a clenched fist, I pointed at the tip of my sword while I drew the symbol again. He nodded and did the same with his claws. But no flash of light this time, no burning of the blades. Maybe it was only the first few times? Didn't matter. We were in and going, we couldn't look back.

A swell of nerves rose in me; why would the symbols work when Erik was around, but not now?

I swallowed hard, tried to convince my brain we were ready to rumble with any demons we might face. Though I doubted we'd face those first. Red caps now, demons later.

We made our way up the first flight of stairs and at the top I peered out a window. It was early in the night here, the crescent moon giving off a bare shiver of light.

That would help cover us, as long as we kept to the shadows. The most direct route to the barricaded doorway was to cross the courtyard. Of course, I was assuming that not only could I get through the door, but it indeed led to the deep levels of the Veil. And that I wouldn't let anything nasty out when I opened the door.

I had to trust my gut on this one; everything brought me back to this doorway.

At the edge of the courtyard we stilled and I stared into the open space. An ocean of red caps lay between us and the other side of the courtyard.

Literally.

They camped, sleeping soundly, weapons within easy reach. Lazy bastards, hadn't even bothered to set a guard. They just plunked down and went to sleep.

"Stinky dead caps," Alex said, his voice echoing across the open space. I clamped a hand over his muzzle, but it was too late.

I balanced on my toes, waiting for the first rush, trying to see where we might dodge and get to the other side. Deliberately not thinking about having to retreat like a fucking coward. But they didn't jump up to charge us, hell, they didn't move a muscle. Not even a breath. "Wait, dead caps?"

"Yuppy doody. Red caps are dead caps." He waved a paw in front of his nose and then let out a big sneeze. "Damn stinky."

Alex trotted to the closest red cap, cocked his leg, and peed on his face. "See? Dead caps."

"Stop that," I snapped. Alex dropped his leg and shrunk a little.

"Sorry."

They might not have been my friends, or even allies, but something had destroyed them like matchsticks snapped in half for fun. My chest tightened as I walked amongst the strewn bodies.

Limbs and heads twisted the wrong direction, weapons broken and, now that I was closer, I could see the pale moonlight gleaming off pools of blood. I bent and touched my fingers to the red cap closest to me.

He was still warm.

This was bad. I stood and beckoned to Alex. "We gotta move."

He trotted to my side, snapping his knees up high to miss touching the bodies of the red caps, like a prancing pony.

Another time I would have laughed, or at least smiled. But not tonight. Whatever killed the red caps was close.

"Fuck this shit." My nerve endings jangled, dancing with the knowledge something big, bad, and probably really ugly could be watching us. And if the hair on the back of my neck was any indication, I wasn't far off the mark.

Breaking into a jog, I wove through the bodies until we were on the far side of the courtyard. I paused at the open, dark doorway and put a hand out, stopping Alex. We couldn't go in blind, that was just stupid.

"What do you smell?"

He lifted his nose, then dropped it to the ground. "Red caps. And a monster."

"Do you know what kind of monster?" He was usually good at identifying the things he smelled, even the ones he'd never met before.

With a shake of his head he took another long sniff. "I sees it, but I don't know what it is."

I clenched my weapons. "See it in your head?" Shit, I hoped that was what he meant.

A quick nod and he tapped his head with the tip of one claw, and my nerves slowed a half beat. That was only a small consolation prize.

"Is it in there?" I pointed into the dark entryway.

Alex gave a long slow nod. "Yes."

Fuckity fuck fuck. This could not get any worse.

"Traaaaaacker."

I spun on my heel, dropping into a crouch. A hand lifted amongst the red caps, the fingers bending to draw me close. Breathing hard, I made my way to his side and crouched near his head. He was the captain who spoke with me in the mineshaft.

"Tracker. You are either braver than any man I know, or dumber than a troll." His jaw was broken and words were slurred, messy, and pain filled, but I understood him.

"Combination of the two. You have to be to do my job." I wasn't sure what to do for him. He was dying and we both knew it. He flopped his hand over and dropped it on my shoulder.

"I've never seen a thing like this before. We had no chance."

Chills swept up and down my spine, the skin on my arms tingling. "Can you tell me anything?"

His eyes flickered, the light in them fading and then he let out a cough. "Alex, help me!" We rolled him onto his side as blood and bile poured out. Carefully, I rolled him back.

"It moved like the wind, a shape that could not be seen, a monster that had no form but killed with ease."

"A demon?"

His eyes stared up at me. "It wants the sealed door open. Don't open the door, Tracker. The world will cease to be if you do. Orion waits for you on the other side."

My jaw clenched and tears threatened at the back of my eyes. "My friends are in the deep Veils, and I have no other way to get them."

"One other way. Always another way."

My fingers found his and I clenched his hand hard. "Tell me. Please." I would beg on my knees, give him anything he wanted. I would put on his bloody cap if it would make him tell me.

A long low boom filled the air and his hand gripped my shoulder. "It tries to break the door. It cannot. Blessed gods, let it not be able to."

I shook his shoulder, demanding his attention. "The other way into the deep Veils. Please, I can't leave them there."

He took a sudden, sharp breath and let it out in a final word.

"Necromancerrrrrrr."

His hand fell limp on my shoulder and I slid it off, placing it across his chest.

Another castle-shaking boom rattled the air. Whatever it was, even I wasn't brassy enough to try and find it. I stood and backed away from the captain's body.

"Alex, we are leaving."

"Goody good."

We jogged to the doorway and I looked over my shoulder, regret for the lives lost heavy on me. Even if they were red caps.

There was no way to honor them, to honor their sacrifice to keep the deep levels from opening. And they did deserve that honor, even if they'd tried to kill us. Twice. I knew it wasn't personal; they were doing what they'd been trained to do.

Protect the castle.

"Boss is here," Alex said and I whipped around to stare into the dark stairwell leading to the dungeon.

"Are you sure?"

"Smells him."

I didn't dare call out, hell, there was no way I wanted to draw the thing's attention to us.

"Give a soft woof, Alex."

He did, but there was nothing from below. A slow burning fuse of fear wrapped itself up my legs and buried deep in my belly. There were two ways to get to the upper levels on the other side of the castle. I'd gone for the more direct route.

But Liam . . . he would take the long way so I wouldn't see him. Which meant he'd be closing in on the doorway.

"Oh, shit."

I ran across the courtyard, Alex behind me. We'd never beat him to the sealed doorway.

I knew why he'd come; hell, I even wondered at how easy he'd let me go. But I was too blind to see he had no intention of letting me go by myself.

None at all.

We bolted up the dark stairway and another boom rattled the walls, dust falling around our ears. We had to stop and steady ourselves or fall back the way we'd came.

"I no likes this shaking shit," Alex grumbled, his body pressed into the side of the stairwell.

"Me either." Fuck, I didn't know whether or not to call out to Liam. It would draw the attention of the thing at the doorway, which was one problem. Another shake dropped me to my knees. There was no way we'd make it up the stairwell before Liam . . .

A yell erupted from above us.

Liam.

The shaking stopped and we scrambled to our feet, running up the final few flights. Once on the upper level, I didn't pause, just turned to the right and ran through the hall.

"Liam. Don't open the door!" I screamed the words, and what came back was not Liam's voice.

Alex and I rounded the corner and there was the sealed doorway, bite and claw marks etched into the steel. And a ghostly figure hovered in front of it. Seriously, it was like a ghost; I saw through him, and yet the figure flexed and reformed several times within those first few seconds. A red cap, then a troll, then an ogre, and then human again.

Behind him huddled a tiny figure, a woman with crazy, bright white hair and a young face. Very young, like maybe my age if she was showing her true age. Her eyes were wide and wild with terror and power.

The ghost image turned to me and I knew what I was looking at.

We were fucking dead.

Orion stared at me, his figure solidifying for a split second. Tall, brawny, bald, and seriously bad ass. "Ah, I thought you would come if you believed your mate was in trouble. So predictable. "

"How'd you manage this, douche canoe?" I snapped, my fear making me stupid.

"Ah, well, it seems Milly has a fondness for that little witch of yours. She traded her services to me in order to keep the young one safe. For a few moments at least."

"She wouldn't do that, you're a fucking liar!"

He smiled. "When the blind refuse the gift of sight, you only anger them by describing what the world around them offers."

A chill swept through me. I'd heard those words before. What did Erik have to do with this?

Orion shifted, drawing my attention back to him.

I had to stall him. Try to figure out how to send him back, minus the availability of a volcano at my fingertips.

"If having Milly at your beck and call was all it took, you'd have done this long ago."

He gave me a slow nod. "True. I needed a necromancer. Do you know they are notoriously hard to find, train and . . . bend . . . to one's will? I've been working with Talia here for years. Years." He shook his head and the image shattered into a swirling mass of energy.

I held my ground. I would not bow to this piece of shit even though he scared me to my core.

"Good for you. But you still don't have a body, do you? And it's awfully hard to rule without that."

He snarled and the castle shook. "I have that taken care of. Finally. You know, it is easier to take over the soul of an infant than an adult. Surely a," he let out a laugh that made the hair on my arms stand up, "Slayer such as yourself would know that."

I wanted to vomit as his words hit my heart. Milly's baby. Son of a bitch, let him mean something else. Yet what else was there?

He shimmered and an ogre looked at me now. "Her child will have a natural ability like no other witch ever born. I will have him. He will be my vessel."

I lifted my swords, rage like no other coursing through me, so hot and sweet I thought I would cry with the poignancy.

"Never. We end this now."

Alex was at my side, but I knew it wasn't enough. That didn't matter. There was no going back.

"You would try and best me? After you saw the carnage of the red caps, you think you could do better, you and your pet?"

Alex let out a long low growl. "There is no try."

Of all the times for him to quote *Star Wars*, of course this would be it.

"You heard the wolf. Come on, bitch. Let's see what you've got." I beckoned to him, every part of me knowing it was too soon, this wasn't the time. But I couldn't let him take Milly's baby.

With a roar he came at us and I bent my knees, the wind pushing me back along the stairwell. Alex dodged around the floating mass and Orion ignored him.

Alex dove into the mass with flailing claws, the symbols he'd etched into the air coming to life in a blast of white fire that slammed Orion against the wall. "No hurts Ryleeeeee!"

The wind died, I leapt forward, and the demon disappeared.

"What the fucking damn shit is this?" All the rage, anger, and fear poured out of me in a breath, and I had nowhere to direct it. Orion was gone. Just like that? No, it couldn't be that easy.

Alex puffed up his chest and lifted his lips up, exposing his teeth. "Bad-ass demon scared of me."

I wasn't so sure, in fact, I was damn sure Orion wasn't scared. But something Alex had done was enough to throw him back. Maybe Erik hadn't been full of shit after all.

"He didn't expect you to know the rules. The werewolf's heart and intent are pure."

We turned to face the crumpled necromancer. Her eyes were as colorless as her hair, rimmed in red. Her skin pulled tightly over her face like she'd been starved.

"What?" Yeah, I couldn't come up with anything more pithy than that with the raging emotions dancing along my nerve endings. In fact, she was lucky I wasn't ramming my sword down her throat. She was helping Orion. Maybe I should kill her. I stepped forward as she spoke, my hand tightening around my blade.

"Orion is a coward. He will only fight when he believes he will win. But he will be back for this doorway. It is how he will take over the world." Her eyes slipped closed, but her chest rose and fell with life.

"Why would you tell me this?"

"Because I hate him and want him dead. I cannot do it. You can. You are the only one. Kill him. Save us all. He is here in spirit only, not in form. He can't last long on this side of the Veil without a body, none of the powerful demons can."

"And you?" I lifted my sword and pressed the tip into her chest over her heart. "If he no longer has you to help him?"

Her eyes flickered. "He will find another if he hasn't already begun training one on the off chance I am killed. I wish this on no one, but my death would be a release. I will not fight you."

I gripped my handle, indecision rocketing through me. "It will buy us time if I kill you, even if there is another necromancer in the wings."

She gave me a half smile. "Yes. He needs me, but he needs the door open more. Not all demons can cross the Veil as I open it."

Like with Liam—my mind grasped onto that. Some demons needed the physical crossing. Maybe that would help stall them.

I loosened my hand on my weapon. Shit, I didn't have it in me. Not when I knew she was right. Orion would find another and another. I would have to kill every necromancer in the world to keep this power from him. I dropped the tip of my sword.

"Your heart rules you," she whispered. "That is as it should be. I will do what I can to stall him. I must go."

A spark of light bloomed behind her, the wall disappeared, and she fell through, the slash in the Veil closing as soon as she was immersed in the darkness on the other side. The black that she fell into was so deep I knew in my heart it was the last point of the Veil. The seventh level. Nothing would be deeper, and that was where Orion was.

Where Milly and Pamela were.

Shit.

10

On the first floor of the castle, I stopped in front of the doorway to the room where India had almost been possessed. We'd rescued two other children that night. One alive, and one very much not.

I couldn't even remember their names. I put a hand to my forehead. If I couldn't remember them, what the hell was I fighting for?

"Rylee."

I lifted my head. Liam and Erik stood in the doorway to the mine, one looking pissed, the other looking relieved.

"We have to make other arrangements. We can't use the sealed door." I stepped forward.

"I scared a demon," Alex said, his golden eyes serious.

Erik laughed, but Liam didn't as his eyes searched my face. "How bad was it?"

"Could have been worse. The red caps are all dead."

Erik stopped laughing. "What?"

"They're all dead."

Silence for a heartbeat then I finally asked, "Why are you two here?"

"Came to save the helpless princess," Erik said. "And maybe try to make things right that went so very wrong in the past."

Liam gave a sharp nod. "Very touching, but I think this would be better discussed not in a castle full of dead red caps."

We filed down the hallway and while a small part of me knew I should be upset that Liam intended on coming after me, the majority of me wasn't. I'd been on my own for years, it was pretty damn nice to know someone gave a shit.

Didn't matter now; it was a moot point.

Erik was first to the doorway and he tugged on the handle. "Sticky-assed doors."

"Sticky?" That didn't sound good.

"Won't open. What have you got us into now, Rylee?" Erik did not sound happy. If I didn't know better, I'd think he was scared. I wanted to groan from the irony. I was supposed to be trained by a Slayer, and I got the cowardly one. Fucking hell, that was just peachy.

I thought about the red caps, what the captain said when the hoarfrost demons had come through.

"Damn, they blocked it. You can only come in I bet. Which means we need to find another way out."

"The only way out," Liam said, "Is through the front gate. Assuming any other doors we find within the castle are blocked like this one."

I led the way back up the stairs and into the courtyard. The two men froze when the dead red caps came into view. The slice of moon took that moment to peer out from the clouds and illuminate the ugliness of the scene, the horror of it etched in blood and gore.

"This is a massacre." Erik said, barely breathing the words.

"This was Orion."

Erik's eyes went wide and under the moonlight he paled. "Please tell me you're joking."

"He's got a necromancer," I said and Erik groaned. Apparently Orion's pet, Talia, hadn't been kidding.

"That's the worst news. Means if he's broken her he can make forays into the world to wreak havoc in spirit, even if that means just for a short time, it is enough to do shit like this." He swept his hand out wide to take in the scene at our feet. Not that I needed it pointed out.

"Yeah, things just get better and better." I walked into the courtyard, aiming toward the main gates that were blocked. They opened into the English countryside.

"Erik, can you still reach Ophelia?"

"No, too far."

Liam jogged ahead of me and put his hands on the gate. "You think it will open?"

"Only one way to find out."

The four of us pushed and while the gate was heavy, it slowly slid open.

"You know," Erik said, "those two dragons are going to be pissed when we don't show back up."

The thing was, dragons were the least of my worries. They would survive without us. Milly and Pamela, and worse, Milly's baby, needed us desperately.

There was no gentle way to say what I'd learned so I blurted it out, the words like bile on my lips. "I'm not worried about the dragons. Orion is going to possess Milly's baby."

The countryside beckoned to us, but none of us moved, my words freezing everyone to the spot as if I'd spelled them.

Erik grabbed my arm, his fingers digging into me, and I jerked away from him. "I'm not going anywhere, you don't have to get all Grabby Mcfeely."

He stared into my face, his eyebrows drawn low with a pain I almost felt against my skin. "That's why your parents died, Rylee. A demon threatened to possess you as a baby and they died to protect you, to allow you to live. You have to stop him. You have to find a way into the deep level of the Veil."

What the hell was I supposed to say to that? "That's been the plan all along, smart ass. Stop the demon, save the world."

Yeah, that was easier to spit out than what I really wanted to say. That I was terrified we wouldn't be able to get to them, that Orion would possess the baby, and Milly and Pamela would be tortured and killed, or worse yet, tortured and forced to serve Orion.

Liam took a step out and then held up his hand. "Be quiet. You'll wake the giant."

Oh for fuck's sake. I peered around Liam to see the giant sound asleep on his side, his bare ass peeking at us from under his dirty loincloth.

"You shift," I said softly. "Take Alex and get Will or Deanna to meet us at the trail head with a car."

He nodded and stripped out of his clothes, then handed them to me. "I'll head to Jack's."

I took his clothes and tucked them into my jacket, his smell easing some of the anxiety in the pit of my stomach. At the rate I was going, I was going to have some seriously massive ulcers by the time I was thirty.

Of course, that was assuming I'd make it to thirty.

Naked, Liam shifted into his wolf form and without a backward glance, took off, Alex tailing behind.

No words were exchanged between me and Erik. We jogged through the gate, down around the feet of the sleeping behemoth, and into the open field. Roughly a mile of wide, open space stood between us and the relative sanctuary of the forest. A mile. Easy as peach pie.

The thing was, the last time I'd crossed this, things hadn't gone so well, in large part due to the big ass sleeping in front of the castle.

Halfway across the field, it happened. A loud grunt, and the ground rumbled as the big bastard woke. I didn't have to see to know he'd spotted us. We were moving fast but still in full view of him. Shit sticks.

A roar lifted the hairs on the back of my neck and I found a burst of speed I didn't know I had in me. Erik was breathing hard beside me, but he managed to keep up. I glanced at him, saw his face pale and the sweat beads roll down his cheeks. Terror did not look good on him.

The thunder of the giant's feet hitting the ground rippled toward us in waves that threw me to my knees once, and Erik twice. But we scrambled our way into the dense forest as the giant closed in.

"Here," I snapped, grabbing Erik and tugging him around a large tree. I pushed his back against it and then did the same. "Quiet."

Erik closed his eyes and I saw him trying to even his breathing. I didn't close my eyes. Around us trees shuddered as the giant slowed to a stop and let out another roar. Trying to flush us.

Beside me, Erik shook and I saw him tense up. I slapped a hand out across his chest, stopping him. I needed him in one piece, needed him to actually help me, and him getting eaten by a rampaging giant wasn't going to further my cause.

With a low grumble of what sounded like "screw it all" the giant backed away and retreated toward the castle. I took another thirty seconds before I peered around the edge of the tree.

The giant schlepped, slow and lumbering, scratching his bare ass cheek with overly long dirty fingernails. Disgusting to think I'd been trapped in one of those hands not so long ago.

Dirty fucker.

"Come on. We'll go slow." I stepped away from the tree.

"You sure?" Erik's tone was calm, but I saw the fear in his eyes.

"You don't deal with the supernatural much, do you?" I weaved through the trees, stopping every ten feet or so to check the giant continued to move away.

"Just demons. Nothing else." He paused and then went on. "Are you going to let me help you with Orion?"

Wasn't that the question of the day, one I had only another question for: "I don't know, are you going to get me killed, or are you actually going to help me?"

"I wouldn't have come all this way to see you die." The sadness in his voice struck me and I did something I didn't often employ. I Tracked Erik, right where he was. His threads were heavy with sorrow, true sorrow that flowed from his soul, and a heavy dose of fear.

From what I could tell, there was no malice in his intentions.

I let out a long sigh. "Erik, I protect those I love and trust above all else. I've lost too many people and been betrayed too many times not to. If I could do it on my own, I would. But I can't. I'm not fucking delusional. I need to know—are you in this with me, really with me? No more holding back."

He nodded slowly and held out his hand to me and I bit the inside of my cheek. I was not a public display of affections kind of girl. But he was my uncle and we were trying to make this right. I reached out and gave him a hug. Quick, very quick. I stepped back—his eyebrows were high with an unspoken question.

"You're my uncle. It would just be weird to shake your hand, I think."

With nothing else to say, I continued on the path as the skies above opened up and welcomed us back to Britain.

Alex followed him the whole way to Jack's manor, running right at his hip where the second in command in a pack would run. It both amused and pleased him that the formerly submissive werewolf would willingly take the place.

Jack's manor looked fairly silent. Liam knew there would be clothes and a working phone; Rylee and he had spent a little time there only a few weeks past. His bigger concern was booby traps and uglies might be waiting for them. Or worse, for Rylee.

He let out a low growl at the thought of someone trying to ambush her, but he knew that was more likely than people waiting with cake and cookies to welcome her.

They circled the manor twice and smelling nothing other than Will, Deanna, and a faint hint of Jack, Liam made his way to the back door and shifted. As a wolf he hadn't noticed the misting rain, but buck naked . . . he let out a shiver and tested the door knob.

Locked.

With a sharp push of his shoulder, he popped the lock. One of the perks of being a shifter, he didn't have to use much force to make things happen. Alex trotted in behind him and pushed the door shut with a hind foot.

"Dusty." He let out a loud, fake sneeze as if to make sure Liam understood him.

"Yeah, a little."

Liam wasted no time, going to the closest phone in the library. He lifted the old-school receiver, relieved to hear a dial tone beeping even if it was a bit scratchy with his proximity to it. Dialing Deanna, he wondered how his wolf would deal with Will now. Now that he knew he didn't have long to live.

His hand tightened over the phone, creaking the old plastic.

Of course, Deanna didn't pick up, Will did. Liam could tell just from the sound of his breathing.

"Will, Rylee needs a ride from the castle trail head."

"Nice to hear from you too, old chap," Will grunted. "Is she there now?"

"If she isn't, she will be soon. Bring her to Jack's place."

"Of course, anything for you, O' Mighty One." Will hung up and Liam let out a breath as he put the receiver down.

Will loves her; he will keep her safe after you're gone. Truth, though it might be, was not welcome in his head. The worst part was how quiet his wolf was. Above all else, he wanted to protect Rylee, and if that meant allowing Will to be a part of her life, then so be it.

He grabbed the phone and threw it against the wall, a snarl ripping out of him.

Alex cringed and stared up at him, licking his lips. "Boss?"

"It's not you." He stalked out of the room to find clothes. "It's me."

11

We didn't have to wait long at the trail before the sound of a vehicle reached our ears. But long enough that we were soaked. The only good thing was Liam's clothes insulated me and kept me warm, despite the wet. Even gone, he looked out for me. The thought made me smile, and then cringe. Lovestruck was not something I thought I'd be in my life. Yet every once in a while I realized that's exactly what I was.

Such a weird, weird world.

"You got friends everywhere." Erik's hand went to his sword as the vehicle drew close, and I shook my head.

"Not everywhere, but I have a few here. No need to get all freaky protective, not with . . ." I stood a little taller, straining to see who was driving the coming vehicle. I couldn't help the surprise that colored my voice. "Will."

"Not who you thought?"

"Liam hates him and the feeling is fairly mutual." Deanna was the one I expected. But maybe she wasn't answering her phone. Who the hell knew?

Will slowed to a stop and rolled his window down. "Hello, beautiful, you need a ride?"

My eyebrows shot up and I slid into the front seat. "I look like a fucking drowned rat, so keep your pretty words for the pretty girls."

Erik slid into the back, behind Will. I had to admit, at least he was taking his role of protector and teacher seriously now. From where he sat, and the length of his sword, he could run Will through in a split second. Not that he would need to.

Will tried to grab my hand and I slapped him away. Hard. "What the hell, you think because Liam isn't here you can make a move on me? Idiot."

From the back seat, Erik tried, and failed, to stifle a laugh. Will's jaw ticked and I just shook my head.

I pointed at Erik. "Will, meet my Uncle Erik. He's a Slayer, so treat him with respect."

Will gave him a nod, and a slight widening of his eyes, but said nothing. Hell, I was surprised he didn't ask what a Slayer was. Then again, he probably knew. I seemed to be the only one lacking in the "know your supernaturals" department. If you didn't count Erik, that was.

"Where are we headed?" I assumed Liam gave Will instructions to meet up and I could tell by our direction we weren't headed to Jack's.

"The police station."

I frowned, surprised that Liam would have run all the way into London proper after going to Jack's place. Or maybe he was headed that way to meet us. Yeah, that was more likely. I slid down in my seat and closed my eyes, Tracking Pamela and Milly.

Milly was awake, Pamela was unconscious. I had a feeling Milly kept her knocked out on purpose. The more the kid's mind was protected, the better. I was betting the less Pamela saw in the deepest level of the Veil, the easier her life would be after. And yes, I did think she would come out of this; I had to believe. There was no other way to do a salvage like this.

The thing I couldn't figure out was why Milly didn't jump them both out of there. Or even herself. Not that I wanted her to leave Pamela, but couldn't she even open the Veil up to us, so we could come through? Fuck, this was one of those moments where the ability to Track frustrated the hell out of me. I could find them, know what they felt, even know if they died, but I couldn't communicate with them.

"How long are you here for this time?" Will's voice snapped me out of my thoughts.

"I don't know." I tried not to snap at him; he was helping after all. "Sorry, you just interrupted a flow of thoughts."

He laughed softly. "I know who and what you are, Rylee. You don't need to apologize to me."

From the back seat, Erik let out a grunt and leaned back, lacing his fingers behind his head. "I see why Liam doesn't like him. Does your friend here act like this around your wolf?"

"Yes." I rubbed my head. "Is Deanna at the police station?"

"No. She's out of town, on some sort of druid business." Will's hands flexed on the steering wheel and I wondered what kind of business a druid could have. Not that it really mattered unless she was trying to unite her people against me. Which she might very well be with her ridiculous ideas of peace.

"Will she side with us? When the time comes, will she actually fight?"

His eyes slid to mine then back to the road. "I don't know. I'm trying to bring her around. All the shifters here will, and of course my cats, the destruction, is with you. I don't have much connection with other supernaturals, which is where Deanna comes in. And she wants this to end peacefully."

So we had help in the form of Will's destruction, a pack of cat shape shifters and not much else.

That was exactly what I was worried about.

"She's an idiot." I struggled not to cuss his sister out. I wanted to, but I didn't. How could she be so blind as to not see we needed all the help we could get to fight Orion and his demons?

"All the prophecies I read," I said, "talk about how Orion will break through, that it is just a matter of when and where. It's that point we have to take him out."

Erik leaned forward, putting his arms on the edge of the bench seat. "You mean to let him come through?"

"Shit no. I will stall him as long as I can because we need time to get our own allies together. You saw the ogres. Orion isn't fucking stupid, though I wish he was. He's dividing us so I will stand alone, or close to it, when he finally breaks free." The words were harsh and they were the first time I'd said them out loud. The weight of them wrapped around me and made it hard to breathe. All the prophecies, all the things I'd learned, finally came together in one big swoosh inside my brain. Divide and conquer, that was Orion's game. And it was working.

"We are in deep shit; I had no idea how bad it was," Erik said.

"Are you telling me you don't know this? You don't know any of the prophecies?" I twisted in my seat, and he shook his head.

"I'm taught how to fight demons, not prophecies. Big difference."

Will shot a glance at Erik in the rear view mirror. "No history lessons about the creatures you were learning to kill at the academy? My understanding was that it was one of the most important parts of being a Slayer. Learning what had happened, and what was coming."

Erik's face paled, and then went bright red. But he said nothing. And I knew then he truly wasn't trained as a proper Slayer. Fuck, just my luck to get a second-rate trainer when it came to saving the world from demons.

Still, he was all I had.

"Lay the fuck off, Will. Unless you suddenly have a degree in demon hunting."

The two men sat silently and I tucked myself deeper into my seat. There wasn't anything I could do about Erik. I needed him and every scrap of knowledge he had. I hugged Liam's clothes to me. His scent wafted up, soothing, and Will wrinkled his nose.

I didn't care; he could damn well suck it up. I only wished Liam was with me now; just being there would be enough to help with the fears boiling inside my head. ·

The police station came into view and my anxiety rolled back full force. Last few times I'd been here, things had not gone well. Zombie outbreak, big-ass panther guardian trying to kill me, Liam trapped by Milly. Yeah, not much good ever happened here.

Will went in first but I found myself dragging my heels.

"Bad memories? Get locked up as a kid?"

I glanced at Erik and saw he wasn't teasing, he was serious.

"Bad memories, yes. Locked up as a kid, only once." I walked forward, not really afraid, more apprehensive. But then, Liam would be inside, waiting for me. Yeah, that helped. I jogged up the steps and opened the door.

Inside, the SOCA agents worked diligently, in fact not one looked up. That was a bit odd. Then I saw Denning. The biggest douche in Britain, if not the world. His eyes flicked to me and I saw the glimmer in them, a flash of red, and something shimmered around him. I squinted, using my second sight, my eyes widening when I saw confirmation of what I suspected. Motherfucker, I would take his head right now.

I straightened my shoulders and strode toward him, loosening my swords. The world seemed to slow as Erik strode behind me, somewhat oblivious. How could he not have seen what I'd seen?

Denning was demon possessed. Which explained why he wanted the world to know about the supernatural—it would only forward Orion's position.

From the corner of my eye, I saw Will, saw him nod. The asshole kitty cat knew about his boss.

And had brought me here to clean up the mess. Lightning fast anger zipped through my synapses.

I would deal with Will soon enough. Denning saw us, raised an eyebrow, and then opened his mouth. I expected him to yell at us, to try and bluff his way out.

Nope, not this time. Black vomit flecked with pieces of what I knew was intestine spewed out of his mouth as the demon broke free of its human prison.

"Come on, bitch!" I wove my blade in the air, making it burn. Prepping it to drive into the demon who pulled himself out of Denning like taking off a Halloween costume.

Slimy with Denning's remains, the demon unfolded itself, head touching the ceiling. Like a stick bug on steroids, the thing was long and gangly, joints all over the place so when it reached to drive a long pointy stick leg through a SOCA agent sitting stunned at her desk, I wasn't surprised.

"Erik." I moved to one side, and he flanked the demon on the other.

"It's a Stick demon. We like to keep it simple. Slow it down by taking its head."

Sure, that was going to be simple. More and more long, dangerous stick legs unfolded from the fucker's body and I was through waiting. The more legs he had out, the harder he would be to deal with.

I leapt in, swinging both swords, reverberation going through the tough exoskeleton running up my arms and down my spine. The demon didn't screech, didn't even moan.

It laughed, multiple eyes blinking at me, all at different times. "Little girl, little girl, I will love to eat your heart and hand your soul to my master." It swung a leg toward me and I deflected it. From the other side

I caught glimpses of Erik battling with his fair share of legs, ducking and slashing, but unable to actually hit the bastard. Backing up too fast, he tripped over a desk and disappeared. Great. Some help he was.

"Creepy fucker." I spun, driving my right hand sword down through its body, pinning it to the floor like the bug it was. A spurt of pale yellow fluid bled out around my blade, coating the floor with a hissing burn.

"Watch the blood," I said, raising my second sword and grabbing my whip with my empty right hand.

Now the demon wasn't so happy. I smiled up at him. "Little girl, this, shit head."

"Wait. Do you not wish to interrogate me?" Its eyes rolled and blinked and I didn't dare look away. Too many legs still flailing about.

"Wrong person. I don't interrogate. I kill." I snapped my whip forward, curling it around the demon's neck, and yanked it forward. The whip didn't hurt it, but it brought the bastard within range.

My blade bit through the demon's neck, the head rolling forward, yellow bile pouring out of its neck hole. In a rush, the body slumped down, melting into the bile, bubbling and burning a hole through the floor. Chunks of concrete fell into the lower levels along with the dripping body.

Erik clapped a hand on my shoulder and I tensed. He didn't seem to notice. "Not even trained and you are a better Slayer than me. Not surprised; your father was the best of the best."

There was no malice or jealousy in his voice, but I had no doubt at one point, there had been.

I gave him a nod and looked into the hole. At the bottom, I could just see the glimmer of my sword. Swinging my whip, I snapped it into the hole and with it grabbed the handle of my sword. A sharp tug and the weapon sailed up to where I could snatch it out of the air.

"Fancy," Will said. "You practice that move?"

"I work with all my weapons, asshole. You know that."

"Why am I the asshole?"

Erik snorted and tucked his weapons away. "You have to ask that and then wonder why she picked Liam over you? Shit, man, even I know that answer and I've only known her a few days."

"Liam isn't here, is he?" I looked around for something to wipe my blades off and settled for someone's coat slung over a chair. The demon blood burned right through it, so I threw what was left down the hole.

"He's at Jack's manor."

I glanced around and really looked at the SOCA agents surrounding us. Oh, fuck a duck. There were a dozen—as in twelve—and every single one flashed me some seriously red eyes.

We were in for a fight.

"Will."

"What?"

"You think that Denning wasn't busy recruiting the whole time he was here?" Will's body stiffened. Yeah, that a boy, let that thought sink through your thick stupid skull.

Erik let out a sigh. "Bah. There can never be just *one* demon. Always has to be a bloody damn herd of them."

The "agents" were shifting closer and closer, tightening the ring around us. Will's eyes were wide. "I didn't think there would be more."

"There's always more," Erik said. "Nature of the beasts, as it were."

I didn't wait for the "agents" to completely shift. I lifted my two swords and ran at those closest, swinging hard. They didn't fight, couldn't, when caught between their two forms.

Will followed my lead and we'd downed ten of the twelve before the last two broke through their human shells.

Upside, they were small, young demons. Downside, they were fast little bastards. And they didn't wait to fight us. They ran.

"Rylee, they breed like rabbits," Erik yelled, running after them. They were headed for the stairs leading to the roof.

With a grunt I bolted after them, knowing if we didn't catch them it would only be a matter of time before London was overrun with breeding red-eyed human demons.

I burst through the door to the roof to see Erik standing over one of the young demons. He lunged and tried to drive his sword through the demon's neck. He missed, nicking the demon on the shoulder instead. Shit, he had bad aim. The young demon scampered in front of me and I swung my sword hard, driving it right through the little fuckers neck. But that left us one more to deal with.

"Where?" I yelled, searching the rooftop, feeling more than a little frantic.

"Gone." Erik slowly stood, his blade dripping yellow goop. Worse, as I watched, it was eaten away, the steel unable to hold up, even after being prepped. We needed to get him a weapon that Milly or Pamela had spelled.

I moved to the edge of the roof and peered out on the street. There was no sign of a demon. No doubt it would go into hiding.

"Please tell me they need each other to breed."

Erik's footsteps drew close. "No. They have eggs that are already fertilized. Handy for them."

I turned in time to see him throw his sword to the ground. "Piece of shit."

Reluctantly, I handed him the larger of my two swords. "It's spelled to withstand that kind of damage. Until we get you one of your own, use mine."

He gave me a surprised nod, took the sword and tucked it into his sheath. "Thanks."

I had my whip, and I could always pick Erik up another weapon at Jack's. There might even be a few weapons there already spelled. I Tracked Liam, felt him in the general direction of Jack's place. Of course, that was where he said he'd meet us. Damn Will for his motherfuckery.

"Come on, let's get Will and get our asses out of here."

Erik was quiet a moment but I could see he wanted to talk. "Ophelia is a real treat when she's angry. I almost feel bad for Blaz." We walked side by side down the stairs.

"You think they have any idea where we've gone? I don't think they should come here; the plan is to go home, not cross paths with them mid Atlantic."

"Blaz can probably sense you, but that doesn't mean he'll realize how far we've gone. Ophelia can't sense me as we aren't paired in the proper sense. I'd bet we have a few days before they start looking for us."

A few days. I planned to be home that night if I could. Planned.

Yeah, my plans always went exactly as I hoped.

Right.

12

Jack's manor was dark except for a single light in what I knew was the library. I also knew Liam was going to be pissed. Didn't matter that we'd taken out a few more demons, what would matter is that Will defied him and had taken me into danger without Liam at my side. Saying the two alphas did not get along was the fucking understatement of the century.

"Will, you can't come in," I said, stepping out of his car.

"I'm not afraid of him," Will said, his green eyes far too intimate in the way they traced my face.

"It's not about fear. He'll kill you for this stunt. You don't get it; you don't have a shot with me. End of story." There we go, spitting it out and probably breaking his heart. A part of me hoped it worked; the other part knew Will was stubborn enough to ignore my blunt, mean words.

Erik ignored us both and headed in. "I'm tired and hungry. You two figure this out."

The door slammed behind him. Shit, it would only be moments before Liam came out ready to strangle Will. I had to speed this up.

"Thanks for the ride." I slammed the car door shut and headed for the house. Will was right behind me.

"Rylee, I love—"

I spun on him and smacked him in the chest with the palm of my hand. "NO. That is not coming out of your mouth. Ever. You are my friend. And not a very good one right now. You let me walk into a fucking nest of demons without even a simple warning! Why would you do that?"

Will's hands fisted at his sides. "Because I knew what he was, but there was no way for me to kill him! When you said your uncle was a Slayer I knew it was a shot. Maybe the only shot to get Denning out."

I pushed him back. "You are a supernatural. You're telling me you didn't talk to Deanna about this? Didn't consult your destruction about making a full-scale attack on the station?"

"And do what, Tracker?" He snarled at me, his eyes shifting to his kitty cat green. Oh yeah, now he was getting angry. About fucking time.

"Something. Anything. We can't hide in a corner anymore. We have to face this together or no one will survive."

"How would I survive getting covered in that bile that spewed out of him? It ate Erik's sword. Damn. Well. Ate. It." He shoved me, I stumbled back, and I had to give him props. There was some tough shit coming our way. He needed to be tough too. He needed to be angry enough to fight.

"There's got to be a way. That's why I'm pissed at you. You didn't even try; you just set me up and hoped to hell I could handle it." I turned my back on him and walked away. Shit, I was going to alienate our current allies before we ever got to a battle with Orion.

Damn, I could almost hear Jack's voice. *Good job, Rylee, good fucking job, you little idiot.*

But I was doing things the only way I knew how. Straight forward, no games, kill or be killed. I slammed the door behind me and locked it for good measure. Without thinking, I stormed toward the library where Liam and Erik sat across from each other, digging into what smelled like stew.

"Hungry?" Alex held up a bowl, balanced carefully between his claws.

"Yes. No. Shit, I don't know." I wanted to rant and rail, to throw things around. Instead I stomped to the kitchen and swung open the freezer. There was a half tub of cookies 'n cream ice cream from when we'd last been here. My stomach growled and I yanked it out of the freezer, grabbed a spoon, and headed to the library. Good for me? No, but I wanted something that would make me feel better. The top of it was covered in ice crystals I scraped off to reveal sweet, sweet ice cream and cookie chunks below.

I slumped into Jack's chair and dug into the ice cream. Around a mouthful I said, "Did Erik tell you what happened?"

"Yes." Liam kept his eyes on his bowl. "Will is gone?"

I nodded. "Yes." I pulled his clothes out of my jacket and tossed them at him. "Here. I kept them warm for you."

He caught them and put them on the table. The silence in the room was rife with an uncomfortable tension I hadn't felt in a long time. Not since before Liam and I were together as a mated pair. "Aren't you going to say anything?"

Liam turned to me. "About what?"

"Will, the demons, I don't know. Getting the wool pulled over our eyes by our pussy cat friend?"

His lips quirked. "I know you can take care of yourself, hell, you did for a lot of years without my help."

And just like that I knew something was wrong. Sure, Liam had been doing his best to not be over protective, to let me do what I had to do, but this was a step too far.

"You don't care that Will made a move on me?"

His shoulders tightened and his breathing changed. "I don't like it. But I'm not going to kill one of our allies because he makes a pass at you. Blaz flirts with you, Alex climbs into bed with you whenever I'm not looking, Doran grabs your ass on a regular basis. You want me to kill them too?" His eyes flicked over me and while there was heat in his voice, nothing matched it in his eyes. No, his eyes were tired. Resigned.

"That isn't how it was last time we were here. Every move Will made you were ready to pull his balls up through his throat." What the hell was going on with him? If there was a logical reason he was no longer a jealous wolf, fan-fucking-tastic. But there didn't seem to be any logic here, just a sudden change of feelings and that was not like Liam. There was always a reason for what he did, for how he acted. Which told me again that something was being kept from me. A reason he didn't want to share.

Like the pro he was, he changed the subject. "Have you tried Tracking a necromancer here? Isn't that the person we need to get to Pamela and Milly?"

It was a good idea and for that moment I let him move on. "We aren't done talking about this."

"I wouldn't for a minute expect you to let me have any secrets," Liam said, his voice dry as a popcorn fart. Ass.

I drew in a deep breath, then took another bite of ice cream, getting a good chunk of cookie in the process.

With very little belief that I would get anything back, I tried to find a necromancer, Tracking them as a group. I sucked in a sharp breath and a half mouthful of cookie crumbs as I got two strong threads. One to the north of us and one way to the southeast, on the tip of the island. Both were about the same distance from us, a few hours away regardless of which direction we took.

"Shit, there are two living here."

Liam gave a nod and winked at me, though his face was tired. "See, there's always a reason for the crap that gets thrown at you."

I checked the clock. Six at night. I didn't want to wait another second. Milly and Pamela had been trapped with demons in the deep levels of the Veil for too long as it was. Everything just seemed to be pushing us away from getting them out, and I couldn't stand it.

"I'm going." I jammed one more spoonful of ice cream in my mouth and stood.

Liam pushed his chair back. "How are you going to get there? No Blaz, no Eve. No cars in the garage."

My jaw twitched. Shit, and I'd just pissed Will off and I doubted he would drive back out here. "I'll walk. Hitchhike, or steal a car. I've done it all before."

Without a backward glance I left the library, though the footsteps told me both Erik and Alex were following. Liam was not.

Erik caught up to me. "Rylee, you said there were weapons here. I'd like to load up before we're off again."

I nodded and at the next hallway intersection I took a left toward the armory.

Caught up in my own thoughts, I clung to the feel of the necromancer in the north. That was the one I'd go after. That one was incrementally closer, maybe two hundred miles, when the one to the southeast felt closer to three hundred. And if I was on foot and hitchhiking, closer was better. Shit, I hoped it wasn't a young, inexperienced necromancer like Frank.

The armory was locked, the heavy wooden double doors identical to the library's. On both sides of the door stood waist-high blue vases with cracks and chips around the lips. One had a cactus in it, the other a dead tree that was mostly sticks and few barely-there leaves.

At the base of the cactus I scraped away the sandy dirt.

"Not a good place to hide a key," Erik said.

I didn't say anything. Jack had always said if someone wanted in badly enough, they would break his doors, and he hated fixing locks and hinges more than anything else. But I didn't feel like explaining my dead mentor to Erik. Besides, half the time Jack wasn't mentoring me, he was just pissing me off.

The key turned with a smooth click and the doors opened into complete darkness. No windows in the room, nothing but the lights overhead. I flicked the switch and they came on with a low buzz that only crappy bulbs could do. The smell of leather, well-oiled steel, and a tang of blood crept up my nose. I rubbed my face and headed to the back wall where the swords hung.

None of them were spelled, I could tell right away. I'd been hoping maybe Jack had Deanna do something to help him out.

Erik rumbled under his breath as he picked through the weapons. Alex sat in the middle of the room and stared at me, watching.

"What is it?" Did I expect anything profound or deep. Not really. But his words slithered around what was left of my hope and faith and squeezed them until they were blue in the face.

"Your heart sounds funny."

Beside me, Erik's breath caught in his throat. "What do you mean by 'funny'?"

Alex tipped his head and one floppy ear stood straight up. "Different. Funny." He shrugged then put a claw tip to his muzzle. "Don't tell Boss."

Fuck, there was no way I was telling Liam my heart sounded funny. Alex's hearing and sense of smell were better than Liam's. Maybe not by a lot, but enough that I trusted Alex.

So if he said my heart sounded funny, then I believed him. The last thing I needed was to get sick. My mind raced. Was that why I'd been so much more fatigued? My heart began to hammer in response and

I listened to the pulse roaring in my ears for the sound of a tick or tremble.

"Nothing we can do about it now," I said, but even I heard the shake in my voice. "We'll get Milly and Pamela out and Milly can heal me from whatever this is. She can do that."

Erik nodded and Alex gave me a big grin and two "thumbs" up. "Yuppy doody, let's rescue the witchy witches."

The truth was, I didn't know if Milly could heal something that was a sickness. Injuries that had you on the brink of death, you bet. But sickness I wasn't so sure. To keep my mind from dwelling on the possibility that something was seriously wrong with me, I Tracked the necromancers. I couldn't Track them individually, because I didn't know them or their names, but I could focus more on the one to the north for some reason. There was more of a pull to him for the threads I followed.

He, and I called him a *he* for simplicity's sake, was pretty calm, relaxed. There was no stress in his life that I could tell.

That made me smile. Erik noticed.

"What's got you grinning now?"

"That necromancer has no idea what's coming for him. I feel a little bit bad." I reached for a beautiful crossbow hanging on the wall, one that I'd shot a few times during practice.

"Really? You feel bad for someone who can raise the dead?"

"Not because of that, because I picked him to be our mark. He has no idea what's coming for him."

From the doorway, a swirl of air swept in with Liam. "I think I've got an idea."

Now, when I said stuff like that, everyone cringed.

When Liam said it, no one cringed. But we should have.

13

I clung to Erik as he drove the rickety old motorcycle across the English countryside in the dead of night as the rain poured. Yeah, it was a fucking tea party. The old engine sputtered once with me on the back, so I was grateful for that small mercy.

Teeth gritted, I kept my head down and eyes closed. The jarring of the bike bouncing off the ruts in the ground felt like I'd driven my spine deep into the back of my head. Not pleasant.

Beside us, Liam and Alex loped along, having no difficulty keeping up. As if to emphasize how easy it was for them, twice they started a wrestling match mid-stride, tumbling over one another, through puddles and mud. To be fair though, I saw the way Alex would cock his head a split second before he'd pounce on Liam. Liam tolerated him, like he would a young wolf in the pack.

"North?" Erik hollered over the wind and rain. I tapped his back once for "yes," a system we'd worked out starting this miserable-ass journey. Twice meant "no" and he would question the direction until I tapped once.

From what I felt of the threads of the necromancer, we were about halfway there. I Tracked Pamela and Milly, felt Milly's concern and fear. Pamela was not yet awake and that was starting to freak me out.

There had been another child I'd sought out, a young boy who'd remained "asleep" the entire time I'd Tracked him.

Only he hadn't been asleep, he'd been dead and a spell used to make me think he was still alive. I shivered and found myself clinging tighter to my uncle.

He patted my clenched hands where they tightened around his middle. "You'll find them."

Funny thing was, that was the first "uncle" type thing he'd done or said and I was strangely comforted.

Four hours into our ride, Erik pulled over at the end of a long driveway. "We're almost out of fuel, and we've hours to go yet." He flicked the engine off and I stepped away from the bike, stretching my legs. Comfort was not what this particular machine was made for; torture was more like it.

Erik glanced down the driveway. The sign in front of us read "FIELDING'S DAIRY." "They will have fuel. Wait here."

I didn't argue with him. Fuck, I was cold, it was dark out, the rain seemed to be coming down harder, and while I wouldn't have minded going with him, I could let him do this on his own with very little fear that he couldn't manage.

Alex grabbed my pant leg and shook it. "Alex sooooo hungry." He pointed to his mouth as if I wouldn't understand otherwise.

"You have to wait." I rubbed behind one of his soaking wet, muddy ears. "I'm hungry too, but I'm not whining."

He let out a grunt and then threw himself backwards, landing in a puddle that sprayed up muddy water all around him. Laughing, I could do nothing but shake my head at him.

Liam stepped beside me, his back standing just above my waist. Hell, he was big enough he could probably pack me across the countryside if we had too, not that I'd ask him.

"Do you think we'll find them?" I whispered as we watched Alex take off in circles, chasing his tail, freezing in place, and then taking off again.

Liam cocked his head at me, but his liquid eyes said it all. There was fear in him too. Maybe this time we weren't going to be able to save the day. We would lose Milly and Pamela to Orion.

I closed my eyes, fighting the hot scalding tears that would weaken me. Now was not the time. "Not yet, we haven't lost them yet."

There was a distant sound of barking and then a holler. Liam and Alex took off down the driveway. Of course, a farm would have dogs, but the boys could take care of that.

A mad scramble ensued as Erik ran into sight, lugging a beaten-up old gas can. I spun open the bike's gas cap and he poured as the sound of the dogs drew closer, then stopped altogether.

A high-pitched screaming bark erupted and Erik slopped the fuel. "Pay attention," I said. "The boys won't really hurt the dogs."

"Not the dogs I'm worried about, but the farmer with the gun."

"He can't hurt them either." But I knew Alex could easily spread the werewolf virus with a single bite. There was nothing for it now, whatever happened, happened.

Erik shook the gas can for the last few drops and I screwed the cap on and hopped onto the back of the bike. Erik jumped on the kick start and the engine rolled over perfectly.

"LIAM!" I yelled as we sped away from the driveway. Within moments Liam and Alex were again running beside us.

And deeper into the night we drove looking for the necromancer who would either help us save Milly and Pamela, or help us bring back what was left of them if we took too long.

Please let it be the first and let the second be decades away.

The dark of the night didn't bother him, nor did the engine spitting out stinking fumes, or even Alex tackling him from time to time out of sheer boredom.

No, he was more bothered by the sound of Rylee's heart beat, completely out of whack, sounding more like a hummingbird than a human. It only made his own heart clench harder. He would have to tell her soon; she had to know what was going on so she could deal with it. Especially if he wasn't there by her side.

He let out a long, mournful whine at the thought, unable to keep his emotions in check. Alex bumped up beside him, pressing the length of his body against Liam's.

"I here. Don't be sad," he panted as they ran, and amazingly, Liam did feel better. This was not the time for sad, this was the time to make things right, so when he was finally gone, Rylee wouldn't be alone.

She would still be safe.

They ran so long that even he began to tire, so long that the rain eased and finally stopped. And that fatigue caught him off guard, leaving him unaware of his surroundings. The scent of rot and death was heavy in his nostrils before he realized what he was scenting. And where they were.

"Stinky rotterrrrrrsssssss!" Alex howled out as the first zombie dove toward them. The dead bastard was fast, grabbing Alex by the tail and jerking the were-wolf to a sudden stop. Alex snarled and turned, his teeth clamping down on the zombie's hand and biting it off. Spitting and gagging, he ran to catch up.

Liam had more pressing concerns though. A wall of zombies stood ahead of them.

"You've got to be fucking kidding me," Rylee snapped as Erik slowed the bike. Erik's voice wavered.

"Are those . . ."

"Yes, they're zombies. They can't turn you with a bite, that's an old-ass wives tale full of shit. But, their bites hurt like a son of bitch and they will take chunks out of you." She slipped off the bike and took swords from her back, and Liam caught a glimmer of a smile on her lips. "At least they aren't demons."

Beyond the wall of not-yet-moving zombies sat a house on top of a rolling hill. Lights lit the home, making it a beacon. Yet it was surrounded by zombies. He didn't need Rylee to tell him where the necromancer lived.

"What do you think, we rush them and try to break through?" Erik asked, though to Liam's ears, the man did not sound all that willing. More like he wanted them to break through and he would follow them.

"No, there are too many, at least a hundred." Her eyes scanned the group ahead. "I'll try to call him out. See if he'll talk to us."

She took two strides closer and the zombies began to groan and shift. Apparently that was close enough.

Liam scented the air, picking up only zombies. Nothing else waited for him that he could tell.

"Necromancer." Rylee's voice rang clear on the air that still clung to the night. "I need your help. Will you talk with me or are you going to make me burn through your fucking pets?"

Liam cringed. For her, that was down right polite. But for everyone else on the planet, not so much.

No answer. Wait, not quite true. The answer came in the form of the zombies shambling and running toward them.

"Ah, fuck." Rylee bolted forward and he knew what she planned. He ran beside her. If they could break through a thin part of the ranks, they might be able to make it to the house. But like always, Rylee wasn't thinking too far ahead. She only saw surviving this instant, not what would happen when the necromancer saw her charging up the hill with her swords and two wolves at her side.

There was nothing for it.

They hit the line of zombies hard. Rylee's blades flashed and he barreled into those coming from her right flank. Teeth and claw slashed into the dead flesh, skin and bones busting with ease. But there were so many of them. A set of teeth sunk into his hip and he spun, shaking the zombie off, but not before it took a piece of him with it.

Growling and snarling, he fought, his wolf loving the rawness of the battle, the sheer love of being by his mate's side and keeping her safe. Of fighting for her and protecting her.

The zombies didn't break, they kept coming, but from one breath to the next, they were through the line.

"Erik, run!" Rylee shouted, blood dripping from a deep scratch down her neck, and what looked like teeth marks scraping her arm. The older man didn't question her, just bolted for the house. His eyes, so reminiscent of Rylee's, were wide with a fear hard-wired into every human. Finding out the dead could truly walk and were a hazard to your health when controlled by a less-than-friendly necromancer were something of a blow to the human psyche. Even one who rode a dragon.

Liam loped behind them, keeping himself between Rylee and the zombies, who were only now figuring out they'd lost their prey. Alex, seeing where he was, dropped back beside him.

That was when the ground rumbled and a hand shot out of it. A hand big enough to grab them both

and squeeze the life out of them without even trying.

There was no warning, just an explosion of dirt behind
us. I spun mid stride to see Liam and Alex caught up
in a dead, rotting hand that could only be a giant's.

A zombie giant. My brain stuttered over the image
and I didn't know if it was even possible. Yet, here it
was, happening.

"Holy hell," Erik breathed out, stumbling backward, fear clinging to his words.

Yeah, those were my thoughts exactly. I ran down the
hill, slipping and sliding as the earth continued to shift
and the giant fought to emerge from the dirt that had
held it for who the fuck only knew how many years.

Alex screamed a high-pitched shriek that hurt my
soul, but Liam was quiet. All I saw was black fur,
legs and one tail sticking out between fingers. They
weren't far above ground and I jumped, driving my
sword up through the wrist of the dead giant. Pain
wasn't going to work here. I had to cut the hand off.

"Erik, help me!" I screamed and moments later he
was at my side. Below us, the smaller and suddenly
harmless seeming zombies continued up the slope. A
minute, maybe two, was all we had before we were
surrounded and the giant was fully out of the ground.

Erik stood on the uphill side of the wrist and cut
downward as I stood on the downhill side and slashed
up. The wrist began to tip as we hacked, and my breath
came in sharp bursts as fear and panic drove me.

Screaming, I gave a final furious slash and the wrist dropped off, the fingers relaxing enough for Liam and Alex to wriggle out. A hand grabbed me from behind and I spun, driving my elbow into rotting teeth.

"Get off me, you dead motherfuckers!"

I bolted forward, taking in the way Alex limped, the crooked angle of his front leg. "To the house! Now!"

The giant was pulling itself out of the ground with a draining, slimy stump and a hand; its head finally broke the surface.

Fuckity fuck fuck. This was not going to end well. The four of us ran, each dragging in air as if that breath would be our last. At the top of the hill the house lights flicked off, all at once.

I didn't give a shit; we were going in.

One way or another.

The front door opened with one kick, and I stepped inside, the three boys following me closely.

"Shut the door, bar it with a chair. That'll keep them out for a minute or two."

Liam shifted and let out a groan. I handed him clothes that were tucked inside my jacket. He dressed quickly. "I understand how bad the rib crushing you took was now."

I put a hand to him, worry streaking through me. "How bad?"

"They're healing already."

That was enough for me. I checked Alex's leg. The break was clean and though he whimpered when I touched him, like Liam he was healing. Perks for being a werewolf.

"Erik, you okay?"

"For standing in the pitch-black house of necromancer, a horde of zombies outside, and a dead giant wanting to grind my bones, I'm doing bloody peachy."

"Good. Because we aren't done yet." I took in a slow breath. "You two smell anything?"

Alex grunted and snapped his teeth together before answering. "Stupid necromancer."

"Nothing but the one person." Liam said, his voice low.

But I wasn't about to be quiet. "Necromancer, we need your help."

The floorboards upstairs creaked and then a man shouted down to us, but his voice echoed and bounced around, like a ventriloquist throwing it.

"So explain to me why you are such a rude little bitch? Hmmm? You ask for help and then a foulness of cursing flows out of your lips. That does not seem to be a smart move when begging for help."

"I'm a Tracker. Foul language isn't personal. I didn't tell you to fuck off or kiss my ass. That would be personal." I stepped closer to the stairs. I could see better in the dim light. I took a chance, hoping that blunt honesty and begging would get our point across. "Please. Our friends are trapped within the deep Veil and Orion is going to kill them. Or worse, he will take possession of the baby my one friend is carrying. Damn it all to hell and back, we are desperate. You think we would face down a zombie horde for nothing?"

The wood above us creaked again and there was a scuffle of a footstep, and then front door knob rattled. I spun as did Liam, Alex, and Erik. In the windows along the house stood zombies. Waiting for the signal to come in and finish us off.

The necromancer's voice boomed, though his tone was slightly less threatening. "I should have known you were a Tracker. Do you know Jack? We worked together once, many years ago."

I gritted my teeth and took a slow breath before answering. If he wanted to reminisce, I would play along. Anything that might help us win his help.

"Yes. I knew Jack. He got cancer and died." I didn't really want to mention he'd been brought back to life and was a vampire. Doran told me necromancers and vampires didn't like each other. I could only guess the reason and didn't want to stir things up.

"Pity. He was a fun chap to have around." More protesting wooden stairs and then a figure limped into view. Tall and thin, he seemed as skeletal as some of the zombies outside and I wondered if perhaps he was like Anna, living for hundreds of years past his natural time. "Perhaps I will help you. But there is a price to pay for the help of the oldest living necromancer."

"Done."

"You agree so easily to a deal you know nothing of," he said, his head tipping to one side, reminding me of Eve when she was contemplating. And indeed, he had a bird-like quality about him, like a stork strutting about on the upper landing watching us.

"I would do anything to save my friends. To spare them." I spread my hands. "Tell me what you want, what you'd have of us, and I will make it happen." Fuck, I had to. There was no other choice.

Erik leaned into me. "What about the other one, the necromancer in the south?"

Above us, the necromancer laughed. "That one, a mere child in ability. He would not be able to open the Veil that deep. He would lose his mind. If you hadn't killed Anna, she could have opened the Veil for you."

Wait, if he didn't know who I was, how did he know I killed Anna?

"You knew who I was when we called out to you, didn't you? Otherwise, how do you know about Anna?"

He chuckled. "You have caught me. I do not do well at deception."

My face warmed. "Is that why you thought I meant you harm, because I took her head?"

"I am not yet convinced you do not mean me harm, Tracker. But yes, it seems an obvious connection. Besides, I'm not particularly fond of company. Most people want something for nothing. Particularly when they show up late at night."

Again, my face warmed and I felt the need to defend myself. "Anna asked me to end it for her. I was ready to spare her life."

He let out long, blowing sigh and the lights flicked on. "That sounds like Anna. She was always my favorite student." With a limping, slow gait he walked to the edge of the stairs and then slowly down. "She had great talent; if her mind had not broken at the loss of her child she would have surpassed even me in ability."

The tension settled and Liam touched my elbow, turning me to the window. The zombies were gone. I gave a slow nod and turned back to the necromancer. "She was free of the madness for a little while at the end. That was all I could do for her; all she wanted from me."

He took the last few steps and then stood in front of me. He towered over me; he had to be almost seven feet tall. His pale brown hair was slicked back over his skull, accentuating every line. I stared into his eyes—they were a startling indigo, a blue so dark that in the right light you might call it black. My impression of a stork held firm as he held out his hand, his long fingers extended to me. "You may call me Thomas."

I put my hand out, covered in dirt and blood and zombie bits, and grasped his fingers, unashamed. "I'm Rylee. This is Liam, Erik, and Alex."

"You hold an eclectic company, Rylee. A werewolf trapped in his shape, a guardian who is more than a guardian, and you." He faced Erik. "I am not sure what to make of you just yet. Your aura hides from me."

Erik frowned at him. "Human and Slayer. That's all I am."

Thomas gave a slow nod. "Perhaps."

I didn't like the direction he was going, but I held back my comments.

Thomas tucked his hands behind his back and led the way into what I assumed was the parlor. He snapped his fingers and candles bloomed on nearly every surface, giving the room a warm and welcoming look. I wasn't fooled though. This was a negotiation; he would give us nothing if we did not find for him what he wanted. Or give to him what he wanted.

He motioned to the chairs, but none of us sat. "We're covered in filth," Erik said. "I'd not like to add a cleaning bill to whatever it is you'd have us do in exchange for your help. Where Rylee goes, we all go."

I shot him a glance and his eyes crinkled up at the edges. My heart thumped hard, and I felt for the first time he really was with us. He was my uncle and here to help, not just be an ass.

"Touching. There is only one thing I want that I cannot find, and I have searched all of Europe."

Oh, shit, that did not sound good.

"Does it exist?" Liam asked, "Or is it a wild goose chase you would send us on?"

Thomas lowered himself into an oversized chair obviously custom made for him, the soft cushions barely giving under his minimal weight. "I do believe it exists, I do not have the energy any longer to find it. I am old, coming to the end of my days and there is only one thing I don't have. I did have it, but you, Rylee, ended her life."

I swallowed hard and guessed that Anna was more to him than just a pupil. "You want a new wife?"

He threw back his head and laughed, his Adam's apple huge and bulging in his scrawny neck. "Ah, no. I need no 'love connection.'" His deep indigo blue eyes sparkled as he looked me in the face.

"No, Anna was my best pupil and nothing else. She was to be my heir, if you will. That is the only way we are ever remembered, by the ones we leave behind."

I glanced at Liam and lifted my eyebrows. If what I thought Thomas was asking for in exchange for getting Milly and Pamela out was what he wanted, we fucking well scored.

"You want an heir? Someone to teach?" Liam squinted his eyes. "That's it?"

Thomas gripped his chair, and he snorted. "That's it? Guardian of the lands you might be, but you are blind. Do you know how rare it is for necromancers to be born and then survive past the age of twelve? They cannot control the dead they call forth by their very blood and most are killed by their own zombies by accident."

"Let me be very clear." I held up my hands, stalling them both. No need for Liam to blow the very lovely, big fat ace we had up our sleeves. "We find you a young necromancer to teach, bring him here, and you will bring our two friends out of the deep levels of the Veil?"

Thomas's eyes drooped. "For every young necromancer you bring me, I will bring one of your friends back. And to be sure you mean no harm, one of you will stay with me here as insurance."

I didn't even hesitate. "Done."

Erik let out a strangled squawk. "And who do you propose we leave behind?"

Thomas looked me straight in the eye, holding me with his gaze. There was only one person he would allow to stay with him. Fuck, might as well get it over with.

I shifted my weight, cocking one knee and crossing my arms. "That's simple. I'll stay."

14

A chorus of 'no's' ripped out of all three boys at the same time. I ignored them, staring at Thomas. "That's what you want, isn't it?"

His lips quirked up. "You read me very well, Tracker. Why is that?"

Truth was, I was good at reading people and had a knack for knowing what they wanted. Maybe not always the why, but I could usually dredge at least the 'what' out of them. "You won't settle for anyone else. You want to know what I know."

Erik and Liam argued behind me but I ignored them. Thomas continued to hold my gaze. "You hold the prophecies in your head. The books that Jack would never share with me. I want to know what you know now that he is gone, and the books are destroyed."

I stared at him, and my jaw dropped.

"Wait, they're destroyed? No, I saw them—"

"They were destroyed upon his death being discovered. That was a task he left to the druid girl. And while it is not the way I would have done things, I do understand. In the wrong hands, the books are deadly." Thomas drummed his fingers along his thighs twice, and then laced them in his lap. Waiting for me to say something.

I wracked my brain—did we tell Deanna that I'd taken the black-skinned book, that we'd left a dummy in its place? Shit, I didn't think we had. And then of course there was the violet book, the Book of the Lost. Orion had it. So there were two books left, but we had no access to either of them. Orion had them both.

"You have thought of something important, I see the way the colors in your eyes spin and dance. Just like Jack, your eyes will always give you away." Thomas gave a long shiver through his lanky body and let out a low moan that had my skin quivering with goose bumps.

"What the fuck are you doing?" I stepped back, my hands going to my weapons without another thought. I would kill him if I had to, which would be the shits since I needed him. He didn't answer, just continued to moan and sway, increasing in intensity with each second.

Liam slid between me and Thomas, a low growl rumbling through his chest; I felt his wolf just under the surface, ready to explode. Alex was only a step behind, all the hair along his back standing at attention, mimicking Liam. Their growls filled the room, but over them Thomas spoke.

Swaying from side to side he said, "Someone is trying to rip the Veil wide open. That would be . . . unfortunate for everyone."

I swallowed the bile that rose in my throat, knowing exactly who it was. "What can we do?"

The necromancer's body shivered and then went quiet, his long chin lowering to his chest. He barely seemed to breathe. "Nothing. His time is coming and there is nothing we can do to stop him. The rip is incomplete."

Silence echoed through the room. He didn't say who 'he' was, but we all knew.

Orion was trying again to break through the Veil.

That was not what I wanted to hear, not by a long shot. Yet I knew there was nothing I could do, not right then.

Back to the task at hand.

I stepped around Liam and Alex, waving them to ease back. "I'll bring you a young necromancer, but I want you to bring both women out of the deep levels of the Veil. That's the deal. A two for one. And I'll stay here and answer all your questions, everything I can when it comes to the books of prophecy that I've read."

Thomas's head remained lowered against his chest. "No. One for one."

I ground my teeth and shot a look to Liam.

"We can get them both out. We're going to need help from someone who can jump the Veil. I hate to say it, but there's only one person we know who can do that now that Milly is trapped."

My blood pressure went up another notch. I did not want to bring Faris in on this. I didn't need to owe that bloodsucker anything. Even if we had worked out our differences.

Kinda.

It was Erik who cleared the air. "Thomas, we'll get you your young ones to train, but we need to know that our friends are alive, otherwise there is no point to getting you what we want. Can you at least show them to us, allow us to speak to them?" I was shocked at his subservience, but it seemed to stir Thomas. Perhaps I needed Erik more than I thought. He was a level head where Liam and I tended to act first, think later. Ok, maybe that was just me, but Liam wasn't much better, especially lately.

"Yes, that would be fair. Only I am no Tracker and do not have the ability to pinpoint people as such." Thomas finally lifted his eyes, and they were heavily bloodshot, as if he'd been awake for days. "Bring me the two necromancers and I will allow one of you to go into the deep levels to bring your friends out."

More and more restrictions he laid, and I wondered if he wanted to help us at all. "What the hell, you can't keep changing the rules." I clenched my hands hard to keep from grabbing my swords.

Erik touched my arm. "Let's get what we need first." His eyes pleaded with me to listen to him.

"Can I use your phone?" I ground out between teeth that really would rather say, fuck you asshole. But I didn't. See, I could mature a little too.

Thomas gave a start. "I suppose. You wish to call the Necromancers-R-Us hotline?"

I glared at him while a smile tipped his lips up. Fucking necromancer thought he was a comedian now.

"You'll find it in the kitchen. Though I do not know if it is connected or even works, I have not used it in many years." He slumped deeper into his seat. I motioned at Erik and Alex to stay with him, as I strode out of the room. Liam grabbed my arm as we hit the foyer, stopping me in my tracks.

"Talk to me, Rylee, what are you planning?"

"You're right, we need Faris to jump Frank here. That would be faster than anything else. But necromancers and vampires do not get along. Like hated enemies, *kill each other on sight* not get along. So I have to find a way to keep Faris from killing Frank to start with. That's problem number one—and that's just the start; then we have Faris and Thomas to deal with." I waved my hand in the air several times to make my point. Bringing Faris here was going to be difficult at best. And potentially deadly for Frank. It had been sheer luck they hadn't run into each other over the last month. Then again, Faris hadn't stuck around once Doran claimed the vampire throne.

Liam's eyes drooped and I saw him mulling it over. "We'll meet him in the graveyard. Faris can stay there until we get Milly and Pamela out."

"And Frank?"

His jaw ticked several times. "You'll just have to work your charm on the fanged one and make him see Frank is harmless. And that you need the kid to save Milly and Pamela."

I nodded, feeling the worry climb my spine, sticking its spikes deep into my body. As far as plans went, it wasn't much. But considering the number of times I flew by the seat of my jeans, it was a damn miracle we had even that much mapped out.

It would have to be enough. We headed into the kitchen and I was thrown back in time for a moment.

Everything was old school. Circa 1950s old school. Older too, if the wood burning stove was any indication. Everything was in muted pastels that made me ill looking at their sickly, pale tones.

"Gag me, hire a decorator," I muttered, walking to the black rotary phone hanging on the wall. It was freaking huge, at least two feet tall and a foot wide, black with the white numbers nearly rubbed completely away.

I held my breath as I picked up the receiver. A steady beep, beep, beep sent a flood of relief down me.

Liam stepped closer and the beeping faded. I pushed him back. "Too much of you apparently is not a good thing."

He laughed softly and he trailed his fingers along my collarbone. "You sure about that?"

My eyes flicked to his and I shook my head. Now was not the time for *that* kind of discussion.

"Ease up. Work first, play later."

He gave me a salute and stepped back, dropping into an awful green pleather chair that made me cringe. I dialed Doran's number.

There was a click, a buzz, and finally the other end rang. "Come on, be awake, be awake."

"Hello?" The hesitant voice was not Doran's or even Berget's.

"Frank?"

"Yeahhhhh. Who is this?" The fear in him was palatable. Shit, had something gone wrong?

"It's Rylee. What time is it there?" Hell, I didn't even know what time it was here.

"Early afternoon I guess. I just woke up."

I squeezed the receiver. "Is everything okay?"

"Yeah, I just, I don't like it here with Doran. Something about him is freaking me out."

Ah, that explained it. Nature trying to assert itself and force their hands to each other's throat. "Don't worry, you're leaving in a bit. We need you here."

"Where are you?"

I ignored his question, feeling the bite of timing running out nipping at my heels. "Just listen. Did you find the other necromancer?"

He cleared his throat. "Yes, she was very pretty. I mean . . . smart . . . and . . . um."

"Spit it out, kid."

Again he cleared his throat and if one could hear a blush, it was all over his voice. "But she couldn't help me, she's far too young to know anything either."

I wanted to shout for joy. Fuck yeah, we were getting both Milly and Pamela out! The fates were looking kindly on us finally and sending help our way.

"Get a hold of her and get her to meet you at Dox's bar. Do you understand?"

"Yeah, but I don't know she will, and why at the bar?"

"I've got someone to teach you both, an old necromancer. He's the best in the business. Don't worry about why I'm having you meet us at the bar." I didn't want to tell him the reason he was uncomfortable at Doran's. I didn't want to compound that with a second necromancer. Last thing I needed was an inexperienced necromancer freaking out and raising zombies.

That was all it took. He was off the phone and I stood listening to the empty dial tone.

Liam hung up the phone. "How are you going to contact Faris?"

I ran a hand through my hair, my brain trying to tell me something, a tease of a hint I could grasp if I worked at it hard enough.

"He has ties to those he bites, can find them pretty much anywhere, right?"

Liam gave a slow nod. "But that wears off with you, doesn't it?"

"Yes, but he bit someone else with us. Alex."

"You think he would come if Alex called him? I doubt it. There's nothing in it for Faris to show up at the beck and call of a werewolf he thinks is submissive." Liam leaned back in the chair, his eyes calculating.

"But Faris knows Alex is always with me. Alex would never call Faris on his own."

He nodded several times. "True. Is there a distance factor, like with your Tracking?"

"I don't know."

And there was no way to know until we tried. "You think Thomas would open the Veil to pick up his two new pupils?"

"Good question."

So, back to the living room we went. Erik stood at the edge of a large, bay window, peering out through the curtains. "The zombies are still out there."

Well that was just great. Peachy. "Thomas, we have located two young necromancers for you. Are you willing to open the Veil to bring them here?"

Thomas sat up, as if he pressed each vertebrae into his chair individually before he finally lifted his head.

"That was rather quick. I find it hard to believe you have more ability to find a necromancer than I do."

I shrugged. "Do you really care if I have more connections than you? Now, will you bring them across or not?" If I could have done so without him seeing, I would have crossed my fingers. As it was, I held my breath.

"There are two reasons I will not," Thomas said and my stomach sank, breath knocked out of me. "The first is you could be lying and just trying to find a way out for yourself." I sucked in a sharp, very angry breath but he plowed on ignoring me. "The other is if I open the Veil now, after raising so many dead to keep you out of my home, I will not be able to open the deep level of the Veil to the friends you wish to save. For days, perhaps. I am at the end of my strength now. I must rest while you bring the new young necromancers to me. Once they are here I can tap into their strength and we will open the deep levels for you."

Shit. That was not good news on any front.

"Then I may not be able to stay with you. The only way to get them here will be . . . difficult." There, that was a nice way of putting it.

Thomas waved both hands at me. "If you get them both here, a task I did not think and still do not think is possible, I will forgo the knowledge you have 'til another time. That being said, I will keep one of your men here, just to be sure you will come back, Tracker."

Asshat, he'd deliberately made a request he thought we couldn't achieve. And I wanted nothing more than to shove it up his nose that he was so very wrong.

Erik let out a growl. "I'll stay." At the same time Liam said, "It will have to be me."

Fucking hell, Liam was right. He couldn't cross the Veil unless it was a physical entrance like the doorway in the mineshaft, or the exit out the front doors of the castle.

"Erik. You come with me." My heart clenched knowing that once again, Liam and I would be apart. I clamped down on the tears suddenly there. Seriously, I was far too tied to him; it was making me vulnerable. But I didn't care. He caught me up in a quick hug, brushing his lips across mine.

"Don't take long."

"I won't."

Alex gave a whine. "I stays with Boss this time."

Shit, I hadn't expected that. "I need you, Alex. I need you to come with me."

He gave a low shiver. "Stinkers outside. I don't like them." He shook his head several times, his whole body shaking. Shit—getting caught up by the giant zombie affected him more than I realized. This was not the time for the scaredy-cat werewolf to show back up.

"Alex, they aren't bad anymore. They aren't going to hurt us. You have to trust me."

He licked his lips several times, looking first at me, then at Liam.

"Boss?"

"Go with her."

"Okee dokee." And that was that. The little shit was waiting on Liam to give him the word.

"He needs it to be okay with both of us. He doesn't have just one alpha, Rylee," Liam said, brushing a finger along the frown I knew was etched over my eyes.

"Fine, let's go." I ran my hands over my weapons, testing each sheath that held blades. A shot of anxiety zinged through me. Yeah, Alex was smart to not want to go out there. A flick of Thomas's hand and the zombies would be on us, and we'd be in the midst of them waiting to be torn apart.

Sweet mother of the gods, this was a bad idea.

15

Standing outside the front door I almost swallowed my tongue. The giant had pulled itself out of its grave and stood about fifteen feet from the porch. Alex pressed into my leg. "Don't like this, nopes."

"Just don't touch any of them." I took a step forward, and then another and another, weaving my way between the smaller and yet just as threatening zombies scattered everywhere.

"Rylee, I had no idea you dealt with this much shit," Erik said. I didn't look back at him, just kept moving as I answered.

"Yeah, well, stick around. You'll see a lot more than you bargained for before we're done."

He laughed, but it was shaky and Alex mimicked him. The zombies' heads turned to follow us, the hollow spots where their eyes should have been, black, and yet I knew they could see us. And if they saw us . . . I gave them a wave. "Thomas is watching us, I think."

"Ready to unleash the horde if we misbehave?"

"I'm guessing."

We slid and slipped down the long slope, the morning sun not yet rising. "We've got to hurry. Faris won't be able to help us if the sun is shining fully."

Picking up speed while trying not to touch rotting bodies did not work as well as I'd hoped. The whole thing ended up reminiscent of a pinball machine gone terribly wrong. My shoulder banged into a zombie and I bounced off, slamming face first into another's chest.

I peeled myself off, spit, and wiped the goo from my eyes but kept going. There was a flat spot to the left of the hill, not far beyond where we left the motorbike. I pointed it out. "That's where we're headed."

"Gots it!" Alex yipped and zipped off ahead of me, dodging and ducking around the dead bodies, turning the hike downhill into a game. He managed to avoid the worst of the zombies. Me and Erik, not so much.

By the time we reached the bottom, I was covered in filth and viscera.

"Fuck, that is nasty shit." I broke into a jog to cover the last twenty feet or so, Erik grumbled along behind me.

"I'll have to get new clothes, this is never coming out."

I couldn't help laughing. "Troll shit is worse."

"I don't want to know then."

Sliding to a stop, I called Alex to me. "Okay, this is important. I want you to think about Faris."

Alex frowned up at me. "I don't like him."

"I know, but we need his help. Can you think about him?"

Alex squinted his eyes shut and pressed the tips of his claws against his head. "Yuppy doody, thinking about fang face."

Erik laughed again, this time it was more solid. "I like him more and more."

I glanced at the house on the hill. I hoped Thomas wouldn't be able to tell the kind of supernatural we were calling for help. No, the zombies closest to us weren't even looking our way.

"Alex, call him, call Faris to you."

Tipping his head back, he let out a long, full-throated howl. "Faaaaaaaaaarrrrrrriiiiiiis."

The zombies closest to us shivered, and then as a unit their heads snapped to focus on me and Alex. Shit, shit, shit. Surely Thomas wouldn't know the vampire by name, would he?

One of the zombies stepped forward, its mouth opening, Thomas's voice erupted from its mouth with a booming roar.

"YOU WOULD CALL A VAMPIRE HERE TO KILL ME. TRAITEROUS BITCH."

Apparently he did know the vampires. Shit, we were in trouble.

Erik and I backed as the zombies lurched toward us, and I felt something shift and shimmer to the left of us. Faris, it had to be, and even if it wasn't him we were going. We had to. "Alex, run!" I yelled and pushed Erik toward the spot where Faris was suddenly standing. There was no time. We rushed him as the zombies rushed us. His blue eyes flashed wide and his mouth dropped open as we tackled him through the Veil.

"Shut it, Faris, shut it!"

He slammed it shut, but not before several zombies made it through. Without hesitation he killed them with a ferocity I'd never seen. Their bodies pulled apart, heads first and then limbs in under a minute. All four of them.

I lay on the floor and stared. "Why do I get the feeling you've done that before?"

"Rylee." Faris turned his blue eyed, icy gaze on me. "What are you doing calling me out to a necromancer's territory?"

"Long story. Short version is—"

He held up his hands and closed his eyes. "Let me guess, you're in trouble?"

Erik, splayed out beside me, let out a deep shuddering breath. "Gods, yes. She's in trouble."

"Not surprised." Faris let out a deep sigh and held a hand to me. I took it and he helped me to my feet, his eyes flickering over my body and a frown twisting his lips.

"Are you well, Rylee? You seem different."

I took my hand back; with him I never knew what to expect, and hoped he wasn't hearing what was wrong with my heart like Alex. He'd use my weakness against me for sure. "Fine. Can you help us?"

"No, 'how have you been?' or maybe 'lovely to see you when we needed you to save our asses, thank you so much'?" His eyebrows rose over glacial blue eyes that roved my body. Not in a sexual manner, more like something puzzled him.

I didn't like it. "Stop looking at me like that. And thank you for pulling us out of there."

"Better," he grumbled, his eyes flicking to Alex. "It is a good thing I recalled this wolf was yours or I never would have bothered."

I knew that was bullshit, he wouldn't suddenly forget Alex and knew damn well he was my wolf. But I'd let him have his illusions.

"Yeah. Good luck for us. Listen. We're on a time crunch. Orion has stolen Milly and Pamela and if we don't get them back—"

Again he stopped me. "They'll die, isn't that the usual threat? And really, would Milly be much of a loss?"

I glared at him. "It's worse than that."

Faris's eyes flicked up to mine. "How can it be worse than that?"

"Orion is taking Milly's baby to possess it. And her child will have more magic naturally coursing through it than any other witch ever born, including Pamela. And Pamela, I don't think he'll let her go, or even kill her. He'll turn her like he did Milly." As I said the words, I knew they were true. Death was not the worst thing that could happen to them; no, Orion would make sure he had far worse for them both.

I saw the flicker in Faris's left eye, just a twitch, but I knew it for what it was. Fear.

"What do you need from me?"

A part of me wanted to stare around, see what place he'd brought us to, where he considered home. But a quick glance showed me we were in an average house, probably somewhere in the suburbs that held no decoration to it. Nothing that stood out from anything, just white walls, basic furniture and no knickknacks. The blinds were drawn and no light came through. I shook off my curiosity. "I need you to jump the Veil for me, we need to pick up Frank and his friend and bring them back to the necromancer we just left. And for the record, Frank and his friend are young necromancers. Can you handle that without killing them?"

Erik stood quietly, watching me and Faris. I had a flash of understanding that solidified into fact inside my brain. Erik knew next to nothing about the supernatural world; he was a human with the rudimentary knowledge of how to kill demons and, while he might be able to teach me, I was also teaching him.

Faris clasped his hands in front of himself. "First of all, I don't hate necromancers the way other vampires do; how do you think I learned to jump the Veil when no other vampires have?"

"You're telling me you don't want to kill them? If that is true, why did Thomas know your name? Why did he react so strongly to it?"

He shook his head. "The past is filled with stories and lives you can only imagine, Rylee. Thomas and I go way back." He paused and shook his head again, this time as if trying to clear some of those stories. "Besides that, while there will always be a built-in animosity between vampires and necromancers, I can easily control it. You don't know me, Rylee. Maybe it would be best if you don't make assumptions about me and how I might react."

Hell, there was truth in that. I didn't know him, or his past.

Faris cleared his throat. "Tell me though, why do you not use the castle?"

He didn't know. Shit. I filled him in as quickly as I could. Red caps, Orion, the doorways all busted up and blocked.

"Have you spoken to Doran of this yet?" Faris leaned over and grabbed the white phone that blended into the wall so well I hadn't seen it.

I thought about our quick visit to Doran to re-attach my soul. "No time, everything has been going to the toilet too fast."

Without looking at me he dialed what I assumed was Doran's place. Apparently Faris took his job as second in command to the vampire throne very seriously. I paced the room while he was on the phone. I got one pass in before he hung up.

"I didn't hear you say anything." I stopped in the middle of the room and looked over my shoulder at him, a bad feeling swelling up.

"No answer." Faris strode across the room. "We will wait and try again. I have not sensed his death, and I would. So we wait."

"Waiting isn't an option," I said, thinking he would listen. Nope wrong.

"Then leave. I don't have to jump the Veil for you, you'd be best to remember that."

Oh, how the four letter words wanted to spill off my tongue. Mostly because he was right. Saying nothing, I walked to the couch and slumped onto it. I leaned my head back. Maybe he only would mean a few minutes. Fifteen or twenty. I could do that.

Nope, wrong again. Four hours passed with Faris making phone calls at short intervals. Believe it or not, I managed to keep my mouth shut for most of it, only grumbling a time or two under my breath.

"Seriously, why are you not just opening the Veil for us?" I snapped somewhere near the end of the fourth hour.

"Because, jumping into situations that are unknown are bound to get you killed. And since you are the savior of the world, I'd like to keep you around until your job is done," Faris snapped back at me, the tension in his shoulders visible. I eased back into the cushions. Faris was trying to keep me alive. Again, I wasn't sure if I could trust him or not, but there was no other choice for me at that point.

He finally gave up when the line on Doran's end went dead.

"Someone's ripped out the phone," Faris said, setting his own phone down.

Without any warning, he swung his hand. The Veil sliced open ten feet away from him and then I understood why. Bright sunlight filtered in, the splash of Doran's koi pond echoing back to us. Doran's courtyard, but no one was there.

"You aren't coming with us? I know you can open the Veil into his dark room."

"And since we know there are intruders, do you want to stumble directly on them, or sneak up and remove their heads before they even know you are there?" His eyes flashed with anger.

"Fine." I hated when he was right, mostly because he'd been a pain in my ass for so damn long. He might want to keep me alive, but when push came to shove, he would rather put me on the line than himself.

Faris couldn't go and check on Doran himself, but this would work for me. Close enough to Frank and his little necromancer friend that I wouldn't need him to move us around. I'd just borrow Doran's car and get them.

"Make sure he isn't hurt." True worry in Faris's voice surprised me. "Do not fail in this, Rylee; the vampire nation has never been stronger than since he took the reins. We do not want to lose him."

I snorted and headed toward the sunlight. "He's my friend, Faris. If something or someone is trying to hurt him I will do everything I can. You fucking well know that."

Alex snorted, his words betraying him again as he gained more humanity back every day. "Doran is good. Worth saving." But he ruined the serious tone by prancing across the room with his front knees firing up around his ears.

He and I stepped through, Erik behind us.

"Have your wolf call me when you are ready," Faris said, and the Veil shut, closing us off.

Not that I was worried.

But I should have been.

"What the hell are you doing?" He tackled Thomas to the floor, not caring if he broke the old man's ribs, head, or any other body part. The necromancer's eyes glazed the second the Veil opened and then all hell broke loose.

Thomas snarled and tried to buck him off. The front door rattled as a zombie no doubt threw itself at it.

"Get off me, Guardian. I know how to end your life. I have no qualms about piecing you out to my pets."

Liam didn't move, fury and true fear racing through him. Not for himself, never for himself. Rylee had better have made it through the Veil. His muscles clenched and he fought to keep from snapping the necromancer's neck. They needed him for a while yet. "You sent her to bring back your protégés, how did you think she was going to get them?"

Thomas stared up at him and slowly the mania faded from his eyes, and the thumping against the door stilled. "Get off. I am myself again."

He waited a half breath before moving, then pushed to his feet. But he did not offer his hand to the necromancer.

With great difficulty, Thomas got to his knees, then his feet, his whole body shaking. "It has been many years since I last came across a vampire. The memories are too strong for me to deal with. Do you know the story of why the vampires and the necromancers hate one another?"

"No." Liam wasn't sure he cared either, but then again, maybe there was information that would help them later. Or maybe not. But the FBI agent in him knew all the knowledge he could gather couldn't hurt.

His body trembling, Thomas slid into his chair, and then lowered his head into his hands.

"Necromancers created vampires. An experiment with the dead to see if we could truly return life to those we'd lost. At first we ruled them, controlled them and their thirst for blood."

Thomas swallowed hard. "But in the end, they revolted and killed most of our people, taking us to the brink of extinction. From that moment forward, it is bred into our very being that we must kill one another."

"And you can't control it?"

The necromancer shrugged. "When I was young, yes. But I was a captive of a vampire for many years. He had been held by a vindictive necromancer and he returned the favor to me. I learned much, but . . ."

Liam didn't want to feel sorry for the necromancer who'd just tried to kill Rylee, but he understood all too well the feeling of being held captive. How would he have dealt with Milly if he'd been bound by her for years? No, there would have been no coming back from that; even Pamela wouldn't have been able to win him over.

"Rylee will have to use the vampire to bring her back."

"My zombies are cued to recognize a vampire and kill it if it steps foot onto our land." Thomas finally lifted his head. "I will not remove that from them."

Not that he couldn't, but he wouldn't. Liam wanted to pull his hair out. There was no way to contact her, no way to tell Rylee to have Faris drop them off further away.

He moved into the kitchen and picked up the phone, the line hissing at him but it didn't go out. Without another second wasted, he called Doran's number.

The phone on the other end rang a dozen times before he hung up. He waited a minute and called again. Nothing.

Damn.

Doing his best not to give into his inclination to smash the phone into tiny plastic pieces, he hung it up rather hard. There was nothing he could do.

Back in the living room he stood with his hands on his hips staring out the window at the zombies swaying ever so slightly in the early morning light.

Perhaps he could get more information out of Thomas, find a way to make this time pass and be of value. He dove in without preamble.

"There are demons coming through the Veil, and they are possessing supernaturals."

"Yes and no. Evil spirits are coming through; they're not the same as demons. Like shadows of a demon."

Liam frowned. "Why yes and no then?"

"Some demons are being drawn through as well. I don't know who is doing it but I have felt that through the Veil. They are being called forth with magic. The Veil has not ripped wide open, though there are attempts being made." Thomas placed his fingers under his chin, propping his head up. "It is a precursor to the final break. Most likely whoever Orion has working for him on this side has the capability to bring forth demons and then allow them to possess others. It is a slow process, which is why they are freeing the evil spirits to possess the weaker-willed supernaturals as well. They are covering all their bases, whoever is doing this."

Liam thought of India, and the black coven, how close they had come to having their first victim in that little girl. She'd been inside a pentagram and a hoarfrost demon would have possessed her if Rylee hadn't stopped the ceremony.

"Witches, black witches are doing it," he said, sure of himself.

"They would have the power and access to the knowledge. It takes more than a desire to pull a demon through the Veil."

He turned toward the old necromancer. "Can we send the demons back?"

"Yes. There are ways; that is what the Slayers were for. But there are none left but your Tracker."

"Erik—"

"Is a faint imitation. Years ago, he would have been lucky to be a teacher in the school that educated demon slayers. It is only because he is a brother to the greatest Slayer our world has known that he is even tolerated. Slayers are not human."

Liam closed his eyes. "And Erik is."

"Yes." Thomas frowned. "There is something about him I can't put my finger on, but I do believe he can teach her. If she will learn. I do not think it will be enough to stop Orion in the end, though."

That was not what Liam wanted to hear. Not for a second.

"The demons loose now—"

Again Thomas cut him off. "I know what you do, wolf. You try to gain knowledge through me. I see it in you, but I truly have little dealing with demons. What I know, I have gleaned from many years on this earth, not from direct contact. Necromancers are not demon dealers. We like them no better than the rest of the supernatural world. If those who were lost had truly done their job, the demons would have been sealed off forever."

"You mean the Blood of the Lost?" Oh, Thomas had his interest now.

"Ah, you know of them?" Thomas lifted an eyebrow. "They are all gone now. And with them the last of our hope."

Liam took a chance. "They are not gone. One is left."

Thomas slowly brought his head around to stare at him. "Do you speak of yourself, wolf? Guardian and werewolf, you are a strange mix, one that has not been called upon for many, many years."

"No, I don't mean me." Perhaps he'd said too much. Yet, his wolf seemed to be inclined to trust this man. Much as he'd tried to kill them, it had been in self defense, of a sort.

"Then you must mean the Tracker." Slowly, the necromancer bobbed his head. "Yes, I see it in her now. The confidence, the brash behavior, the belief everything will turn out in the end. It never does, you know. The darkness is always stronger than the light, snuffing out candles and hope with a single sweep of its hand."

"I pity you, if you truly believe that."

The silence stretched after Liam's words, the ticking of some distant clock in the house the only sound and he doubted Thomas could even hear it. But he could. He heard the way the necromancer's heart beat, a funny hitch every third or fourth 'lub, lub.' Liam shook his head; so what if the old man had a twitchy heart?

"And I pity you, wolf, for you will follow her down all the dark paths she takes, and in the end, it will kill you." Thomas's eyes pinned him.

Liam didn't turn from him, didn't blink, just met his stare with his own.

"I know. But I wouldn't leave her, not for an extra hundred years of life."

Thomas laughed softly, lacing his fingers together under his chin. "Then it seems we pity one another, for I would not follow her, not for all the love in the world."

His eyes narrowing ever so slightly, he turned from the necromancer. Not so long ago, he might have agreed with Thomas. But not now.

Not now that he had Rylee.

16

I stood on the threshold of Doran's home and very softly said, "Alex."

He slunk forward, breathing in the air deeply, and just as softly answered me. "Ogres."

Oh fuck. There was a shuffle of feet deeper in the house. A grumble of voices. Berget and Doran were not helpless, but they would be bound to stay in the dark rooms and spaces of the house. I wished it were night and Faris had been able to come with us.

Putting a hand on Erik's arm, I tugged him close. "Ogres are big, fast, and all they really know is fucking and fighting. And right now, they hate me with the heat of a thousand burning suns."

"Poetic," Erik whispered, "but I did manage to figure that out the last time I saw you interact with them."

I shrugged and gave him a tight smile. "Thanks. I don't know how you'll fare against them, but stick close to me."

He stilled. "I'll wait outside."

Again, he was going to leave me to do this on my own. Hell, he was really not much help at all. What a tool.

"Try not to get killed." I pulled my sword free of its sheath and headed into the house. I aimed for the kitchen, keeping my footsteps quiet, knowing the ogres might already know we were here. Their sense of smell was, in some ways, better than Alex's.

"Steak," Alex whispered and I caught a whiff of meat being roasted, setting off my saliva glands. Apparently they were good cooks, just like Dox.

We inched closer until I could peer around the corner into Doran's kitchen. Except for the two ogres screwing each other's brains out on the huge butcher slab that acted as an island in the middle of the kitchen, everything was the same as I remembered. One ogre was green, the other red. Like a seriously perverted Christmas scene. Never mind catching mommy kissing Santa Claus.

Their moans and cries were starting to fill the room, the slap of flesh against flesh sounding more painful than pleasurable. I'd lay down good money even if we weren't so quiet, they'd never notice us.

Using hand gestures, I relayed to Alex what I wanted. I'd slip in and put my blades to their throats mid-hump. Carefully, I slid my second blade from its sheath, the bare whisper of steel on leather the only sound.

Alex nodded and we swept in, as fast as we could. Fucking hell, it worked.

I had my blade on the throat of the one on the bottom for a good three seconds before he felt the pressure of the blade. Pressing hard, I tucked my short blade against the throat of the green female, her breath hitching to a stop as her eyes rolled to mine.

And it was definitely a her. She reminded me of Sas in the way her sensuality rolled off. Alex had his claws wrapped around the male's legs, ready to hamstring him if necessary.

A shuffle of feet behind me made me freeze. Alex grunted, "Uncle here."

So, Erik decided to creep in after us.

"Get over here and help me."

Erik moved to my side and I tipped my head at the female. "Hold the knife tight against her." Erik swallowed hard and I glared at him. "Don't let it slip. We need them alive for the moment."

The red ogre glared at me, then blinked a couple of times. "You're Rylee."

I nodded. "I am. And you are?"

"Raw."

I couldn't help the laugh. "I'll bet you are. But what's your name?"

His lips twitched. "My name is Raw. And not all of us hate you, Tracker. Ogres die all the time, but Sas can't see that. Your words stirred those of us who knew she was fighting her grief."

"Why are you here then?"

Footsteps came toward us and I pressed harder into his neck, drawing blood. "Tell me."

"She struck a deal with someone, someone else who hates you."

"Fuck. Let me guess, his name is Orion."

Raw's eyes went wide. "How do you know that?"

"He's a demon. And he means to take over the world." I stepped back and motioned for Erik to do the same. Raw sat up and gently pushed the green

ogre off him. She slid down, all suppleness and sensuality, unashamed she was bare-assed naked. But her
eyes were hard and full of intelligence, and I didn't
discount her for a second.

"I knew she was going to get us killed. She is blind."
She spat on the ground. "I will not follow her if she is
so stupid as to take orders from a demon."

"Mer. This needs to be discussed," Raw said, as the
footsteps I'd been hearing stopped in the doorway.
Three very large, very black ogres stared at us (though
to be fair, they didn't all fit in the doorway; I counted
the legs and did the math) before launching into the
room, weapons flailing. There wasn't enough space to
accommodate them. As the first ogre in line caught
his sword in the iron hanging pot rack in a downward
sweep that would have taken the green ogre's head, I
drove my sword toward the exposed, black belly.

"ENOUGH!" Raw bellowed, his voice rocking
through the room. He lifted his hands and everyone
literally froze, held with magic that affected them
all. No one could move. Except me of course—score
another one for being Immune. I pulled back from
my sword thrust, sparing the ogre at the last second.
I stood straight and let out a breath. That had been
close. I walked toward Raw. "Can you convince them
Sas is wrong?"

Raw shook his head slowly. "Some will believe you,
some already do. You killed the Roc, you are the
one our prophecies speak of, and for many, that is
enough." His dark, nearly black eyes searched mine.
"Sas sent us here to kill your allies. To set them against
you so you would lose the vampires at your back."

Shit, I wasn't surprised, just pissed I hadn't thought this far ahead. "Where do you and your friends stand on the subject?"

Raw and Mer exchanged a glance and she blinked once. He turned to face me. "We are with you, Tracker."

The three black-skinned ogres struggled, the one in the front finally speaking. "Traitor! Sas will kill your pansy asses for this, after she strings up the Tracker and peels her hide from her body."

"Will they ever be convinced?" I walked toward them, but my question was for Raw.

He hesitated, then slowly said, "No. They will not."

That was all the answer I needed, though I'd hoped it would not be this way. The more enemies dead before the final battle between us and Orion, the better. Three quick swipes and the black ogre's heads rolled to the ground, blood bubbling up and spewing out their neck holes. Raw dropped everyone and he then stepped around the bodies. "You could have been an ogre."

"I could have been a lot of things," I said, trying not to feel sorrow for killing them. They were the enemy; they would have killed us.

Mer slid into a pale green dress that offset her darker skin. "We could not find the new vampire leader, or his young sidekick, though we searched the house several times."

I let out a slow breath. That at least was good news. "Raw, you and Mer gather those ogres who would side with me against the demons. Do it quietly, do not draw attention to yourself."

Raw nodded and took Mer's hand. "We will do what we can. I do not think there will be many. Where should we meet you?"

This was as good a place as any with the farmhouse destroyed and the demons popping through doorways they were creating. "Here, bring them all here."

"And the vampire?" Mer asked, fluffing her hair back, then tying it into a loose ponytail to one side. Doran wouldn't be mad—at least, I didn't think he would be.

"I will find him and talk to him. He will agree to this being the central command." I thought of Frank and knew he would be happy there finally was a central command.

There were no goodbyes; I didn't tell them where we were going. Nor did I think we had time to find Doran, though I felt him sleeping deep below the house. A hidden bunker no doubt. But I knew how to contact Berget and I was tired enough that a nap was in order.

Doran's sleek, silver Mustang was parked in the garage, keys in the ignition. "Erik, you drive. I'm going to nap."

Alex woofed. "Sleeping helps sick people."

I froze mid stride and looked back at him. "I'm not sick, Alex. Just tired." His big golden eyes went soft and serious as he grabbed me around the waist.

"Rylee goes, I goes."

It was an echo of Giselle's last words for him. That he would be with me to the end.

"I know. Come on. We've got to find Frank and his new friend."

We piled into the car and I took the back seat with Alex, stretching out and lying my head against his back.

"Rylee, I thought you were joking." Erik shot me a glance over his shoulder.

"Nope." I cracked a yawn.

"I don't know where we're going."

Good point. I gave him directions as I dozed off, calling Berget's name in my mind.

She responded faster than ever.

"Rylee, do not come to Doran's, there are ogres here. Doran was in a trance and saw them coming with the end of the night, but only just barely. We almost didn't make it below ground before the sun kissed the Earth." Her long blond hair was disheveled and her clothes were rumpled.

"Too late, we've been and gone. There are two ogres that will side with us. A red and a green, Raw and Mer. They are going to bring what help they can."

Berget's eyes widened. "You think some of the ogres will side with us?"

"Raw seems to think so. Tell Doran I'm sorry, but I think he will have to be headquarters from now on. The farmhouse is gone, Giselle's home in the city is too small, and I don't know where else to set up."

"He won't mind." Her voice softened and I saw it in a brief flash. She cared for him. And he was in love with me. Shit sticks that was not going to be fun.

She smiled, reading me easily, seeing my discomfort. "It is truly all right, Rylee. He keeps me close and it is more than I could have hoped for. But I have other news for you."

"You do?"

She held my hand, seemingly crouched between the front and back seats, though I knew she wasn't really there. "There is a way to close the Veil to the deep levels if one is opened, like at the farmhouse. The blood of a guardian will do it."

In my mind I saw Eagle spread out in the bathtub, drained of all his blood, killed when he should have still been alive. "How much blood?"

She swallowed hard. "As much of it as you can. It will kill the guardian; it is one of the only things that will do it. Their body has to be opened with a weapon that has been cursed, and then they must bleed out."

Fucking hell, that was not the news I was hoping for. Though it explained a lot. The demons hadn't wanted us to follow them, so they closed the gate. My heart ached for Eagle and chilled when I thought about who was next. There were only so many guardians around. If they were captured by the demons and used to close gates as they needed . . .

"There is a catch, Rylee." Berget reached over and put her hand on my cheek. "But I am not sure my parents are telling me right. I think because the blood is forcibly taken from the guardian, the closure affects only the single doorway. There is more about closing off the Veil with blood than they are telling me. I will keep trying."

My brain and heart balked. I didn't want to go down that route. Something about it scared me, so I just nodded. "Be safe. Orion is hunting my allies and friends. Trolls, witches, and now ogres are working for him."

"Frank left for Dox's yesterday while the sun was high."

My brain ached trying to deal with the time difference between here and England.

"How did you know?"

She smiled. "He is rather loud and talks to himself, not realizing he can be easily heard. My memories of necromancers are not good, Rylee. I do not think it wise to bring Frank here again."

I let out a sigh. "Fuck, I really wish everyone could just get along."

With a nod she stood. "Yes, that would be easier, wouldn't it?" And then she was gone and I sat up.

Alex yawned, leaned over and put his nose to mine. "Hungry." I pushed him away.

"Yeah, I know. That isn't anything new." In fact, he seemed to be hungry more and more. Was there a tie between his appetite and his becoming less submissive? I rubbed my face. Something to think about another time, perhaps, but not now.

He flopped onto the seat, rolling his eyes up to mine, begging in the most pitiful way possible. I shook my head and yawned.

Rubbing my face, I let out a low groan. Power nap my ass. Sometimes talking to Berget did nothing but tire me out more.

"I think this is the place," Erik said, "but it looks pretty shitty and burnt out. Are you sure?"

Ahead of us was a charred and blackened shell of a building that had only a few timbers left standing, blasted from the fire Doran had set. The broken and abandoned pieces of the Landing Pad hurt my heart as I thought of Dox and his pride in his home and business. Of his unwavering friendship for me even when I was being difficult. I gritted my teeth against the emotions welling up in me. No time. There was never time for the grief that circled me like vultures waiting for me to finally let them at my heart.

"Yes. This is it." I rolled down the window, crisp air circling in with only a whisper of the burnt building tainting it. I leaned out and peered into the clear blue sky. High above us was a rather large bird floating on the drafts. So high, I was pretty sure it would be Eve. I Tracked her and sure enough, it was her.

Eve and Frank were here, but where was necromancer number two? Would she show up based on Frank's word?

Only one way to find out.

"Erik, wait in the car in case we need a quick get-away," I said, expecting him to listen.

"You got it." He tapped the wheel and I gave him a smile. Okay, so maybe he wasn't the brave, all-knowing mentor who could guide me through anything, but for now he fit in my life. Kinda. I couldn't take anyone bossing me around, and Erik didn't try.

The car rolled to a stop and I stepped out, Alex bounding behind me. He took one look into the sky and let out a long, deep howl. That was a lot easier than trying to call her down myself.

"Stick close, buddy. We're about to meet someone new." At least I hoped. I made my way toward what was left of the building, stared at the tattered yellow tape that fluttered in the wind around it. If I closed my eyes I could see the Landing Pad as it should have been, whole and full of laughter. Full of Dox and all his cooking, brownies, and ogre beer. A tear snuck out and trickled down my cheek. I let it go; he deserved more than one tear, but that was all I could afford at the moment.

"Rylee sad for Dox. I is sad," Alex said, sitting beside me. "No more brownies."

I dropped a hand to his head and roughed it up a bit. "Maybe you can talk Pamela into baking you brownies when she's back." Normally that would have cheered him. But not now, not this new Alex.

"Not the same," he said, then let out a heavy sigh.

Above us several beats of wings battering the air and then a soft thump.

"Rylee!"

I turned to see Eve, Frank, and our newcomer. The girl behind Frank had bright red curly hair that was wind tossed, making it even bigger. She peered around Frank's back, deep hazel eyes taking me in, her heart-shaped face uncertain. Shit, she was young, maybe as young as Pamela.

"Frank. Introduce me to your friend and tell me how the hell you think kidnapping a minor is good idea?" I wanted to save Milly and Pamela, but not by stooping to Orion's methods of kidnapping and coercing.

Frank slid off, stuttering and stammering, but the girl stepped forward. Not bold, confident.

"My name is Megan. And Frank didn't kidnap me."

I kept my face carefully blank. "No? And what will your parents say when they see you are gone?"

She bit her lower lip. "I'm in a foster home. They won't care much. And Frank said I could be trained, so I could be strong."

Broken wings, broken hearts, broken homes. They fucking flocked to me, no matter the place. Of course, this time I wouldn't be keeping this broken-winged one for my own family.

No?

Teeth tightening, I tried not to listen to that voice in my head. Already Megan impressed me, and I could see her and Pamela getting along well, their personalities a good match.

Instead of that, I changed subjects. "Eve, I need you to go back to the mineshaft, tell Blaz and Ophelia to come here and wait for us at Doran's. That is where we will meet. Can you do that?"

She swallowed and dropped her head to me. "The new dragon, I do not trust her not to try and eat me."

"Blaz won't let her."

Erik cleared his throat. "I could go with her. I'm used to flying and Ophelia will calm if she sees at least one of us is intact."

"And you would let me face the demons on my own?" I wasn't really surprised he wasn't trying to come with me. He hadn't exactly shown himself to be all that into the actual fights.

"Not much left for me to tell you. You've memorized the symbols and runes you need, and if I am honest with myself, this is overwhelming me. Vampires, ogres, witches and werewolves. I'd much rather deal with two angry dragons. Them I know how to deal with."

He walked over to me and pulled me into a quick embrace. "I've shared with you all I know. It isn't much, but it's all I have from your father."

I stepped back. "I think I will need you yet, old man. Don't think you can get out of your duties that easily."

Laughing, he walked toward Eve. "Yeah, I believe that. I just think that right now you don't need me at your side. In a while, perhaps. But not now."

Eve, happy that Erik would fly with her, took off without hesitation, leaving Megan and Frank with me and Alex. Alex circled Megan and she stared at him, her eyes wide with wonder.

"Wow, I thought Frank was shitting me when he said he knew a werewolf."

I glanced at Frank and he blushed and pushed his glasses up his nose but said nothing.

"Well, you're about to meet a hell of a lot more than that, kid. Can you control zombies yet?"

She nodded. "Yup, it's why my family booted me out. They didn't like the dead relatives showing up for family meals."

Again I looked at Frank. "And you too?"

"Yes."

"Good, because we're about to dive into the deep end. Alex, give Faris a call."

He sat back on his haunches and yelled at the top of his lungs. "Faarrrrrrrriiiiiiiis."

Megan slapped her hands over her ears, but when the slice of air opened and Faris stood far on the other side, deep in the protective shadows of his home, her jaw dropped along with her hands.

"Wow."

I nodded. "Here we go, kiddos. Off to meet your new mentor."

17

Faris didn't take us to Thomas's land, not right away. He took us back to his hidey hole, the one with the shuttered and blackened windows. I was just glad it wasn't his cement room. That I couldn't have handled.

And while Frank and Megan were somewhat squeamish around him—I was guessing their inborn dislike of vampires was making them uncomfortable—he was calm and cool. Like he really didn't care they were necromancers.

Which only intrigued me.

"Doran?" Faris asked the second we stepped through.

"He's fine, so is Berget. If you need us from now on, go to Doran. Whether he likes it or not, his house is going to be central command until all this shit is dealt with."

Frank gave a small smile and I winked at him. Yeah, I knew he'd be happy about that.

I waved my hands at Faris. "Come on, I don't want to sit around here all day, Pamela and Milly are waiting." Just saying their names, my Tracking kicked in and I felt the pulse of their lives. Pamela was awake and scared, but nothing was wrong with her; at least, she hadn't been hurt. But how would I know if Orion had broken her? Would she even know? Fuck, we had to hurry. We'd left them too long as it was.

Faris's lips twisted downward. "Thomas will kill you. He was one of the last necromancers held prisoner by the former Emperor and Empress." He tucked his hands behind his back, clasping and unclasping them several times. His nerves showed.

I let out a groan. That couldn't be good. "Let me guess, more than anyone else, he has a major hate on for vampires?"

Megan let out a squeak. "Vampires? Really, will I get to meet one?"

Holy shit she was green. Faris though, seemed more than a little amused. "I like this one, Rylee. She has spunk. Reminds me a bit of Pamela. Perhaps you would like to leave her here with me to train?"

"Yeah, that's not going to happen." I said nothing else, not really wanting to encourage him. Trusting Faris was like trusting a boomerang; it came and went but it was never right where you thought it would be.

"Really, honestly. There aren't vampires out there, are there?" Good grief, she sounded like a love struck teenager. Probably thought they sparkled in the sunlight instead of burning like a gasoline-soaked torch.

"My sister is a vampire. You might meet her," I said, keeping my eyes on Faris. His lips twitched. For now, Megan didn't have to know. Even though Frank shuffled his feet and his face went bright red with keeping a secret from his pretty young friend, he said nothing. Good boy.

Faris cleared his throat. "I believe it will be best if I open the doorway directly into the house Thomas lives in. That way the zombies he has roaming will not have as much of a chance to tackle you."

I licked my lips. "You can't kill him, Faris. We need him and so do Frank and Megan."

He put a hand to his chest and his eyes widened in mock innocence, the ass. "Why would you say that? You assume I would just attack someone?"

"Because I know you," I snapped. "I know if you have history with Thomas you want to see him face to face for some stupid fucking reason that will, in the end, ruin everything."

Faris's grin slipped. "He and I have unfinished business."

"I don't fucking well care. You can deal with him *after* he has helped us and *after* he has trained these two to their fullest potential. And not one second sooner. Got it?" By that point I was right in his face, physically crowding him. Of course, he didn't back down, that wasn't his style.

"You do nothing the easy way, do you?" Faris stared down at me.

"I do things the only way I know how." I took a step back. "Open the Veil, let's get this over with."

Frank and Megan crowded up behind me, and Alex sat quietly at my side. Faris flicked his hand and the Veil opened, giving us a perfect view of the inside of Thomas's house, a glaring Thomas and Liam staring past me at Faris. Grabbing a kid in each hand, I shoved them through ahead of me.

"There you go, Thomas. Two young necromancers who want to learn the ropes, you just have to teach them." Frank and Megan stumbled forward, and Frank flicked a glare back at me. At least he had a little spine. Alex bounced through next to me and I turned around, expecting to see the Veil had closed.

Nope, no such luck.

Faris strolled through, sweet as you please, a smile on his lips that was big enough his fangs showed clearly. "Hello, Thomas."

Thomas launched from his chair, his eyes darting one way and then the other. The zombies outside let out an instant, communal roar that shook the house.

"Faris, get the hell out of here!" I tried to grab him, tackle him, stop him from whatever it was he was planning. He avoided me with ease as the first window shattered and the ground shook.

"He has a zombie giant, you moron!" It took everything I had to keep my body between Faris and Thomas. This couldn't be happening.

"Frank," Liam yelled, "can you stop the zombies?"

"I'll try."

Megan was much more confident. "Hell to the yeah, I can kick those rotters to the curb."

I don't know what she and Frank did, but the zombies did seem to slow, or at least, they calmed down.

Faris on the other hand was still staring at Thomas, while I did my best to keep him from getting any closer. "Faris, we *need* Thomas. You can't kill him."

"I never said I was going to kill him, Rylee. I just want to talk to him."

Thomas let out a scream that was pure fear, the echo of it flowing through the house.

"I don't think he wants anything to do with you." I finally got my hands on Faris's arms. But it was weird; it was like I wasn't really there in a sense, like in that moment nothing existed for the vampire except Thomas. His eyes were focused only on the necromancer. After more than a few tense breaths, Faris slumped and he shook his head.

"All right, old man. I will go." He backed away, twisted the Veil and stepped through into a room I knew was his special dark place. Somewhere no one could find him, a cement room buried in the ground.

With Faris gone, the air around us shifted and mellowed. Thomas let out a long, low groan and slid to the floor, his back against the wall. "Why, why did you bring him here?"

"I didn't. I told him he couldn't come but as soon as he knew it was you . . . ." I didn't know what to say. How the hell did I make this right so Thomas wouldn't toss us out on our asses without helping Milly and Pamela?

Thomas rubbed a hand over his face. "I should have known he would find me. I have hidden from him for years."

At some point Liam had moved to my side, and his presence calmed me.

"Where is Erik?"

"Gone back to Ophelia and Blaz. He can't go with me through the Veil anyway." Hell, just the thought of going into demon territory on my own made my heart rate spike. Not that I wouldn't do it, I just wasn't real happy about doing it on my own.

"Thomas, how soon can you open the Veil?"

He blinked up at me several times, as if he'd forgotten I was there. I crouched beside him so I could look him right in the face. "Thomas. You need to open the Veil into the deep level so I can get my friends. Do you understand?"

As if he were coming back to himself he nodded, slowly at first, and then faster. "Yes, yes, I will do that."

Frank and Megan stood to one side, staring down at their new mentor. Megan gave a small cough. "Excuse me, this is our mentor? This old dude is going to teach us how to be powerhouse necromancers?" The disbelief in her voice was heavy and again I didn't really know what to say. I mean, Thomas looked like shit; I wouldn't want him to be my mentor either.

"Yes. He is. But right now he's going to do a job for me." I grabbed his forearm and hauled him to his feet. "Aren't you, Thomas?"

"You will need a timer so you know when I will open the Veil again and you can be there. Waiting. I will only hold it open a brief time, no longer than a minute, or we could end up fighting off demons and evil spirits of all sorts."

With great effort he seemed to be putting himself back together, though every few breaths he took his whole body shuddered lightly. I hoped that Frank and Megan hadn't noticed, though I was sure Liam had.

"Rylee." Liam said my name and the way he breathed it out tugged at my heart. He didn't have to say anything else. I knew what he meant. He was afraid for me to do this. Shit, I was afraid. But Giselle had always said bravery wasn't being unafraid, it was doing what had to be done even if you were terrified. Not really comforting in that moment, true as it may have been.

I touched my fingertips to his, just the tips. Anything more and I wasn't sure I would let go. "I'll be fine. As soon as I find Pamela and Milly I'll have lots of firepower at my back."

His jaw ticked and tightened and there was a faint glimmer in his eyes I couldn't look at. Nope, not doing this, not here.

Thomas pulled himself up to his full height, his vertebrae cracking and popping. He reached into his vest and produced out a thin, gold metal bracelet. Megan made a face and Frank carefully put himself a step in front of her.

"Rylee, wear this." Thomas handed the bracelet to me. "It is cool now, but as your time wanes it will begin to heat."

I was already shaking my head. "That won't work if it's magic; I'm an Immune."

"Then you will have no way to know if your time is up, if you should even bother to fight your way back to the pick up point." He didn't seem concerned in the least. I was betting the asshole zombie king knew I was an Immune. For some reason he didn't want to open the Veil. Or maybe he just didn't like me. That was a distinct possibility too. Wouldn't be the first time I'd pissed off someone to the point they were difficult just because they could be.

Teeth gritted, I tried to come up with a reason why he was being a douche, why he was trying to wriggle out of what he promised.

"There is a simple solution," Liam said, and I turned to face him, "let her take Alex. He can wear the bracelet and tell her when it gets hot."

Thomas rolled his head side to side. "I said only one could go through the Veil. Send Alex then."

"We can't send him!" I snapped. "And you damn well know that." Time to play the hard ass. "Frank, Megan, time to go. There is another necromancer we can go to." I pointed at the front door and they dutifully went.

"You cannot take them. My zombies will stop you." Thomas was all calm and cool.

Megan put her hands on her hips and squared off. "You think you're the only one who can take care of zombies?" She flicked her hand outward and, though I saw nothing, Thomas gasped and clutched at his heart.

"How . . . how did you do that?"

I leaned toward the closest window and peered out. Every single zombie had dropped to the ground. Except for the giant who was leaning . . . toward the house.

"Shit, everybody out the back." I grabbed Megan as I ran past her and then Alex bolted ahead of me, barreling out the back door. I didn't dare glance behind, just kept running even once we were outside. The giant was huge and when he hit it was going to be a big fucking mess. Each step I took I expected to get crushed, the immanent arrival of the giant's body on us with no way to avoid it. The thought only pushed me harder and I yanked Megan hard, forcing her to keep up.

Behind us there was an explosion of wood, metal, and glass as the giant's body hit Thomas's house. The ground at our heels erupted, the force of the impact dropping us to the unsteady earth, the rippling earthquake forcing us to stop running. I rolled onto my back to see the giant's head just a few feet away.

For a moment, there was nothing except the two of us breathing heavy and staring at the rotted head that had nearly taken us both out. The giant's eyes were liquid and oozed out of their sockets, and his blackened tongue was caught between broken and sheared teeth cutting it in half leaving it hanging by a shear thread of muscle.

Gross.

"Sorry, I didn't think that would happen," Megan whispered. Her face was as pale as fresh fallen snow. I doubted mine was any better.

"What did you do?" I pushed to my feet and then offered her a hand. She took it and the tremors in her body rippled up through mine. She didn't let go.

"I cut his ties to the zombies so they would go back to sleep. But I didn't know there was a giant." Her breathing came in rapid gusts and I knew she was about to pass out.

"Sit down. You didn't do anything wrong."

She plunked on the cold, damp grass but didn't let go of my hand.

Liam, Alex, and Frank came running from around the giant. Liam's eyes were frantic until he saw us and his body visibly relaxed. Alex jogged and danced, occasionally shooting out a paw to punch at the body of the rotting giant. "Stings like a butterfly," he chirped happily.

Liam pulled me into his arms, though I didn't let go of Megan. "Why didn't you dodge to the side?"

I shrugged. "I didn't think he'd fall that far."

Liam's jaw dropped and at my feet, Megan laughed. "Me neither."

Her face and cheeks had pinked and I pulled her to her feet a second time. "Okay, enough out of you. Looks like you'll fit in fine with the rest of us." I glanced at the massive body. The house was completely destroyed, as in gone. Looking like there had never been anything *except* a mostly rotted giant laying there.

Problem number one. "Did Thomas make it out?" I Tracked him and felt a thread taking me around the side of the giant. I followed it, and everyone else followed me. Megan clung to my hand and I let her. There was not any immediate fighting I could foresee and we didn't need her doing anything else without explicit instructions.

Thomas stood to one side of the giant, his hands in his hair, his mouth moving as he talked to himself. I interrupted him. "Thomas. Are you going to send me and Alex through the Veil now?"

His head snapped up as the giant's body bucked. Ah shit, not again. I backed away, letting go of Megan. "Get ready to run, people." .

The giant bucked twice, and then began to sink, dissolving into the ground. The earth seemed to reach up and drag the giant down, swells of dirt and grass tugging at the body until it melted back to where it had come from. The house that was under it was gone too now. So except for a few shards of wood and glass, there was nothing left of what had just happened.

"That wasn't one of us. What is that?" Megan whispered. The ground gave one last heave, a bubble of air that sounded distinctly like laughter curled up out of the earth and around us, the air crackled and danced.

Thomas backed away and said only one word.

"Elementals."

18

Megan piped up before I could. "Elementals? What are those? Like wind and fire and stuff?"

"I will not speak of the elementals our world holds. That is not the way we do things. Do not ask me again. None of you." He took a deep breath and again shook his head. "Rylee, I will send you and your Alex into the deep Veil. You have three hours. No more, no less."

Shit, I wanted to know about the elementals too. Something about what he said stirred a memory for me. A salvage I'd gone on years ago. I shook it off. Another time I'd ask Thomas.

Even though I was probably poking a bear, I couldn't help it; I had to know. "Why did you change your mind? Why are you helping me now?"

His eyes flicked to Liam and then he said very softly, "Perhaps even an old man wants to believe the darkness can be beaten back. Even if just for a moment."

Wow. That was not what I expected. Thomas barked out a laugh. "Then again, I also believe I would like you out of my life as soon as possible and this will be the only way. Chaos and danger, you Trackers are always the same. I'd forgotten that." He flicked his hand, tossing the bracelet to Alex, as if his earlier words were nothing.

Alex grabbed it mid air and the bracelet locked around his right front ankle. He gave it a shake, the gold catching the light. "Pretty."

"Three hours. That should be plenty." I stepped beside Alex and didn't look at anyone else. This was not goodbye, I would see them soon enough.

Frank and Megan wished me luck. I nodded at them, but said nothing. Liam didn't say anything either. This was just another moment in our lives together, yet always pulled apart.

"Megan and Frank, come here to my side. This is your first lesson." The two young necromancers went to him and he put a hand on each of their shoulders. "I will draw strength from you, and you will help me open the Veil. It is the only way. It will also show you how to open the Veil, both to the deep level and to any other place you should need to travel."

They let out dual gasps as his fingers tightened on their shoulders.

In front of me, the Veil opened, slowly, like it was being pushed through thick, black mud.

Yet it wasn't blackness that awaited on the other side, but a strange flickering twilight that gave me an instant headache.

"Bad light," Alex grumbled, blinking, his eyes watering. Mine were doing the same.

"Three hours, then be back at this point," Thomas said.

There was nothing for it but to go and go fast. I stepped through, Alex at my side.

The deep level of the Veil was odd. Really odd. Like everything had been drawn by a sketch artist, yet never fully finished. Grey and black, shades of white and off white. No color I could see. Hell, in a way, Alex and I would have fit in not too badly, if it hadn't been for my auburn hair and his golden eyes.

I took in where we were. An archway made of what looked like black steel, woven with bones, brittle and nearly grey with age. Each bone had symbols etched into them, so that not a piece went without a marking. Although I didn't recognize all the symbols, a few looked similar to those on the doorway in the castle. Which meant this doorway would either keep the demons out, or keep them in.

None of that mattered at the moment; we had to get Pamela and Milly.

I Tracked them and almost gasped. While I clearly felt them and knew what direction they were in, they were not close. Easily a thousand miles away. Easy.

Shit, shit, shit. Even if we had a car, there was no way we could do this in three hours! Panic nearly set in but I bit it back. We would find a way. We had to.

"Come on, Alex, we have to go." I started to run, as fast as I could, my heart pounding with fear for my friends. What I hadn't expected was the way the landscape shifted and turned under my feet. The ground blurred and I stumbled to a stop, Alex ramming into me and taking us both to the ground.

"Sorry, sorry. Didn't see you, ground is funny." He rolled up to his feet and brushed himself off. I looked around, behind us in particular. I couldn't see the archway. How was that possible?

"The deep levels of the Veil can do strange things, Rylee. You can travel hundreds of miles within minutes, if you so choose."

I spun, my jaw dropping. Giselle stood in front of me, a sword in one hand, and a thick, short spear in the other. She was younger than I'd ever seen her, her hair without a single grey in it, her face without a single line.

"Giselle, how the hell are you here?"

"When the worthy die, they are sent to guard the rest of the levels of the Veil from those cast into the deep level." A grin slipped up over her lips. "It is rather fun at times." Her smiled faltered. "But why are you here?"

"Orion took Milly and Pamela. And he plans to take Milly's child and possess it."

Giselle paled and lowered her weapons. "Mother of the gods."

"Come on, you can help us."

She shook her head. "No, these are the borderlands between the sixth and seventh Veil. I stand here, but cannot go deep into the seventh Veil."

Too good to be true, I should have known. "Then watch for us, because I'd bet my ass we're going to be running flat out in order to make it back here in time."

"I always watch for you, Rylee. Now go. Save them both as I know you will." She smiled and then lifted her spear in a salute. I turned away, my heart lighter for her belief in me. Time to run. Hundreds of miles, well shit, maybe we weren't so screwed.

Alex and I ran full out, the landscape blurry and strange around us, the smell of old basements closed for years then suddenly opened, the musty scent of eras gone by and perhaps of bad things in the past surrounded us. Not the worst smell I ever breathed, just off-putting. Here and there we glimpsed figures in the distance; no doubt they were demons but we didn't stop. And again I was glad Alex was covered in black fur and I had my black coat and dark jeans.

For now we were unnoticed, and though I didn't think it would last, I would take it while I could.

I clung to Pamela's threads, using her for the most part to guide me. She was scared, but calm and a shining piece of hope sung through her. She had faith it would turn out okay. Damn, I loved that kid. With each step we drew closer and closer, the feel of her in my head hopscotching rather than smoothly moving in my direction. Didn't matter, the end result was the same, even though it felt weird.

I reached out and put a hand on Alex, slowing us both. "We're close. How does the bracelet feel, is it warm at all?"

He shook his head. "Nope. Nice and coolio."

"You feel it warm up at all, you tell me, okay?"

With his eyes as serious as I'd ever seen them he nodded. "Gotcha."

I looked up and took a step back. A freaking high-rise building shot out of the ground, the dirt around the base looking like it had been planted and then grown as opposed to having been built.

At least a football length wide and several football lengths high, I'd never seen any building so fucking big in my life.

"Holy shit," Alex whispered. "Pamie and Milly in there?"

"Yeah, they're in there."

He let out a soft groan. "That's not goody good."

Above us the building seemed to answer him, groaning, the girders and whatever grinding against one another. I reached to my back and pulled my swords free. Just in case. I snorted softly. Who the hell was I kidding? I was going to need my blades, it was only a matter of time.

Approaching the building, I looked for an entrance. No doors, but lots of windows on the lower levels. Once we drew up against the behemoth I almost wished we hadn't.

It was a building, yes, but it was *alive*. The wall was skin, thick, dark, and pebbled, and whatever the building was made out of had been carved and hacked to resemble a building on our side of the Veil. I put a hand out, touched the wall.

Warm and slightly prickly under my hand, the skin had tiny little hairs all over it. Alex swallowed loud enough that I could hear him. "Can you smell what this is?"

"No, no, no. Alex no knows."

Shit, if he was reverting back to third person . . . I turned to see him peeing where he stood. Terrified.

I crouched beside him. "Alex, listen to me. I know you're scared; I am too. But Pamela and Milly need us, so we have to go in there. We have to get them out and take them home. You understand? We both need to be brave."

Whimpering, he nodded. "Pamie shouldn't stay inside the monster."

Monster, yeah, that was enough for me. I didn't really need to know what the demons had carved up in order to make their building. In fact, I didn't really want to know at all.

The first window I came to I peered in. Inside seemed again to be a mockery of an office building with a desk and chairs, a filing cabinet. Very strange. Some of it seemed to be carved directly out of the building, out of the creature. But there were spots where new material had been brought in, nailed and screwed into place. Where I saw the stains of old blood from those anchor points trickling down the walls. How long had this monster been kept like this? I shook my head. What a miserable fucking existence.

I lifted my hand to the window and, before I touched it, it slid open. A welcome to our home sign wouldn't have freaked me out as much. No matter. We needed in and we were going in.

Alex gave me a boost and then scrambled up the side. The building didn't shudder, but I almost felt its pain. I peered out to see Alex's claws dug in to make it up over the ledge. A strange sensation flooded over me and I let it take me and said the words rattling in my brain.

"Sorry. We just need to get our friends out. We mean you no harm."

The building/monster gave a slight shudder and went quiet and for a split second I almost thought I heard a whisper of words. So low I could easily convince myself I was hearing things. Except for the way Alex's ears perked up and he tipped his head.

I will help.

But that would be ridiculous. A demon wouldn't help me, a demon slayer. I pushed the words away and crept across the room to put a hand on the door. From what I could tell, we had to find a way downstairs. Milly and Pamela were way below us.

I did my best not to think about it. But before I opened the door, I waved my blade in the pattern Erik taught me and had Alex do the same with his claws. We were in full on demon territory. Seemed dumbassed stupid not to be as prepared as we could. But again there was no burning light, nothing to indicate the runes worked. Which gave me the willies.

Turning the doorknob slowly, it twisted with a soft creak that made me cringe even though it was pretty quiet. I opened the door enough to peer down the hallway, then put my head out further to peer down the other end. Nothing. Empty.

Somehow that didn't make me feel any better.

You wanted to feel good about being in a place where Orion existed in the flesh? Where demons lived and breathed and bred?

My body froze as the thought hit me. Motherfucking pus buckets. Sweat broke out along my brow and I had to force myself to move. I focused on the details around us and finding a way downstairs. The walls were almost iridescent silver, reflecting small bits of light, making it bright enough to see without any torches or electricity.

My breathing hitched and I fought to keep moving. The strangeness of our surroundings didn't help keep my mind from producing some seriously bad scenarios. Like walking around a corner and bumping into Orion.

Did I want to kill Orion? Hell yeah, in every possible way. I wanted to string him up and beat him to death with each of his own limbs as I hacked them off.

But I wasn't stupid. He was here, in the flesh, and I wasn't ready to fight him. No fucking way.

"Alex. You smell Pam or Milly?"

I looked back and he shook his head, his eyes all but shaking back and forth. His eyes were wild with terror, and it froze him to the spot. I needed him with me if we were going to get through this intact. "Come on, we'll find them. Then we'll get ice cream."

His ears perked up and he sidled up to my leg. "Tiger-striped ice cream?"

"Sure. And pizza."

His tongue flicked out as he licked his muzzle. "Hungry."

"Sooner we find Pam and Milly, sooner we can get out of here." The idea of feeding his belly was stronger than his fear. At least for that moment. He put his nose to the ground, breathing deep. I kept my eyes open for any sign of a demon. In some ways, I was more freaked out about their absence than by the fact we could get swarmed by them at any point. In my mind the devil you see is a hell of a lot better than the one you couldn't see, hiding in wait to ambush you. While I didn't want to fight any demons if we could avoid it, I hated that we hadn't run into a single one. That was too fucking weird.

We traversed the first floor, peering into rooms, checking for any way into the lower levels. Nothing.

"Warm," Alex breathed, then pointed to the bracelet. Fuck a duck. I stared at my feet, an idea forming. Cutting down through the floor would cause the monster building pain, but it might be the only way—

A high-pitched chittering snapped my head up and I stared back the way we'd come. Around the corner stepped a demon. No, not one demon—hundreds of them. They were small bugs, like a large roach, and they clung together to make the semblance of a man walking down the hallway. How did I know this?

The mini demons broke apart and flocked toward us, hissing and chittering, a steady stream of words barely intelligible, but I understood.

"*Blood and bones, fresh to eat, we love our meat, sweet, sweet, sweet.*"

Yup, not sticking around for that. "Run!"

Alex and I bolted from the horde of mini demons spewing their twisted poetry. Another corner and we ran smack into a large form and for a brief second I thought it was Orion, felt the chill of the possibility nearly take me to my knees.

But no, it was just a regular-ass demon. I screamed one of the words Erik taught me, "*Dabine!*" As I thrust my sword forward into his right eye, surprising him. Or maybe it was a her; I had no idea and didn't care. Alex snarled and took the demon out at the legs and then we were jumping over the body and dashing down the hall.

Behind us the chittering continued, the bugs singing away as they drew closer and closer, completely ignoring the fallen body. Apparently they only wanted us.

There were no doors to go through, no getting away from these things and they moved fast, like water rushing down a river.

"A door, a door would be fucking well nice," I breathed out as we ran, my eyes searching and then . . . shit, a door ahead shimmered into existence. I didn't question it, though a part of my brain said I probably should.

No time.

I grabbed the handle and swung the door open, Alex and I falling through before we slammed it behind us. This room was darker than the others. Darker and it smelled like *shit*. I stood and gagged, unable to keep my gorge from rising.

"Damn stinky," Alex grumped, heaving beside me. In the near dark, I barely saw him. Not that it mattered.

A shuffle in the room, a whisper of cloth, a sharp intake of breath neither mine nor Alex's. The bugs slammed into the door, and their chittering climbed into a higher pitch.

"Sweet meat, sweet meat, sweet meat. We love to eat sweet meat."

A rock and a hard place had never sounded so good as in that moment. Easier than the choices that faced us right then. "Alex. Stay close."

Somehow we had to go down. And if we couldn't find a stairway, I'd make one.

"Do you know who I am?" A voice, raspy with dis-use, called from the darkest shadows of the room.

"Nope and we aren't making any fucking introduc-tions. Come any closer and the only hello you'll get will be from the tip of my sword." I backed away, Alex with me.

"Little Tracker, little Rylee. Don't you want to see me, don't you want to know what your fate will be if you keep on this path of destruction? If you wish to finally face Orion, you need to know what he will do to you. What he does to all demon slayers."

That voice, it pulled at me, made me stop thinking about finding Milly or Pamela. For a moment, I for-got about the thousands of demon bugs waiting for us on the other side of the door, though they hadn't stopped their sing song of death.

"Who are you?" I whispered.

He shuffled closer. "Do you not know your own flesh and blood?"

A light bloomed and his face came into view.

Erik's face.

I stumbled back. "That can't be, I left you behind. With Ophelia and Blaz."

He let out a groan. "A doppelganger demon, one who took my face and showed you what you wanted to see. A family member, one who could teach you a little about demons, yes? Give you symbols and things that would help you stop them?"

I swallowed hard, my mind back tracking. Fuck me, how could I have not seen it? The pieces of the puzzle slid into place and I barely breathed. Erik, the one I'd left behind, and Orion had said the same thing.

The same quote about the blind not wanting to see. Or what about the fact our blades only burned bright when Erik was with us? Shit, it had been him making us think there was power in his stupid freaking words and symbols. He'd even convinced me not to Track demons so I wouldn't figure out what he was.

"Yes to all the above."

"Words that would keep them from you? That would end their existence? Words like *dabine*." The light around him grew stronger. "But did he say he had no real power, he was just a human, taking his brother's place?"

I nodded, numbed to the core. "But he helped me; you aren't telling me the truth."

The Erik in front of me gave me a tired smile. "Did he help you?"

Again, I was forced to see that while I'd wanted the other Erik to help me, he'd always hung back—doing the minimum, really just getting in my way, slowing me down. Putting me in danger on my own.

This Erik, the one in front of me, let out a tired sigh. "In families of slayers, every member has magic running through their veins. There are no words that work against demons. It is your blood, your blood and your heart and the innate power you carry. The fact you're Immune is proof enough. The fact that you carry a small ability to glamor, the fact that you're a Tracker, all of those are proof that you are a Slayer to the bone." He slumped to his knees, then fell back to his ass. It was then that I saw the chains, heavy black links that held him tight to the wall and allowing no more than a few feet in each direction.

"Ophelia vouched for him. Why would she do that?"

While I waited for him to answer I Tracked Slayers as a whole and got a solid ping right in front of me, but nothing else, not even on the other side of the Veil, not even from Alex who supposedly had demon slayer blood in him. But of course, that was a lie too.

More puzzle pieces came together. If Alex and Liam thought they could take down demons, they would leap into the fray, putting themselves into danger they couldn't truly face.

The demon Erik had been setting us up all along, hoping to kill off my allies. They would have believed themselves safe behind the demon Erik's silly words and symbols slashed into the air. Rage flooded my body as the real Erik spoke.

"Ophelia is broken, badly, her mind twisted when your father died. She would be very easy to convince, easy to control."

"Are you fucking kidding me?" I spluttered. "Easy to control?"

"That is what happens when the bond between rider and dragon is destroyed. The rider can survive, but the dragon, their minds are too deeply ingrained with the bond. Even if they seem sane they lose their ability to deeply read someone's mind; it burns that ability clear from them when their partner dies."

A sudden, sinking thought, like a half ton of cement slid through me. "If I don't have Blaz to ride into battle against Orion, what happens?"

Erik lifted his eyes to mine. "The world is done. If your dragon dies, and Ophelia dies, there are none able to carry you into the darkness. They are the only two who could do it."

Trust your heart, Rylee. Your heart will never lead you wrong.

Your heart will get you killed one day.

Love is never wrong, and your heart knows it.

My heart said he was telling the truth. I lifted my sword and he closed his eyes.

Only one thing left to do, and no time to second guess myself.

19

The blade on the chains caused a spark, but the blade prevailed, biting through the thick chain with relative ease.

"Come on, uncle. We're on a rescue mission. I just didn't know we'd be taking three out of this hell hole." He might not have been reliable in the past, according to my mother, but I didn't think he was that way anymore. The man in front of me was a solid rock of strength; I guess being captured by a demon changed you. Besides, I needed him at my side.

A breath whooshed out of him. "How do you know I'm your uncle and not a demon taking his place?"

I shook my head. "You wouldn't believe me."

"Try me."

"I Tracked Slayers as a unit. You're the only ping I got. That and . . . my heart tells me you're telling the truth. I trust that more than any words you say."

He whispered to himself as I turned away. "Just like Elena." That was my mother's name. "She always led with her heart. Always." There was a slight tremor in his voice.

"No time for crying and shit right now." I said, ignoring the shake in my own voice. "We've got to find a way downstairs. Pronto."

"There is only one way," he said, then pointed at the doorway behind us that bulged and sagged with the weight of those fucking bugs.

"You're shitting me."

"I shit you not." Erik, the real Erik, cranked the door open and swept his hand forward. The demon bugs fell back, curling in on themselves, the chittering easing off until nothing but silence.

Just that, a single sweep of his hand, and they were dying. It couldn't be that easy, could it? He saw my wide eyes, no doubt full of disbelief.

"Wait 'til you see what else we can do."

A thrill rushed through me, followed quickly by dismay. Time, there would have to be enough time for him to show me. He must have caught the look on my face.

"You have to believe, Rylee. You have to put your weapons down and believe in who you are. That is when the power will come, when you will truly be a Slayer in your own right." He strode forward and I saw the differences between him and the doppelganger. This Erik, though he'd been imprisoned for who the fucking hell knew how long, walked with purpose, with a determination I recognized in myself. He wore rags and no weapons and yet there was more danger in his one middle finger than in all of that demon who was impersonating him back home. There was no whining, puling puke afraid of his own shadow. I hoped Blaz ate the doppelganger.

I jogged to catch up to him. "Are doppelgangers easily intimidated?"

"They can be; depends on their acting skills. The tougher ones will hide behind a persona and can fake you out. But truly, once they are found, they are sniveling little shits who are only good for infiltration. They are not fighters, not really. They fear everything. You should have time to get to him before he harms the dragons." Of course, he was assuming we got out of here first.

"So Ophelia really didn't know it wasn't you, because her mind had been broken?"

"Not just that, she is not my dragon, my dragon was killed. Ophelia and I . . . we never got along well. So we never spoke mind to mind. She wouldn't know it wasn't me. And with her mind so broken, she likely didn't even try to find out."

His dragon was killed, maybe that was what had caused some of the changes in him, the differences between what my mother had known and what I saw now. Shit, I could only imagine losing Blaz. And in the scheme of things, I barely knew the big lizard.

I thought about the zombies and the doppelganger's reaction to them. "You ever face the undead?"

"Several times. Nasty fucking stinkers. Better than trolls though."

Alex grunted. "Yeah, nasty fucking stinkers."

Damn it all to hell and back, but I was liking *this* uncle more with each second. This was the uncle I needed. Not that ridiculous worm of an Erik I'd been presented with, the one I tried to trust even though my gut told me not to.

"Here." Erik stopped in front of a section of the wall that looked no different than the others. Except for a symbol etched into it.

"Demons love to mark their shit, claim it as their own, even their captives." He pulled the sleeve of his shirt up showing me his forearms. Up and down his arms were scars of the symbols the doppelganger had been teaching me. I shivered.

What would have happened if I'd faced Orion using his own words, his own symbols? I didn't want to know. And now I didn't have to.

Erik traced the symbol and the doorway opened, showing a huge wide stairwell with steps I would have to climb down, they were so far apart. Nothing for it but to get to it.

I started down the first step and Erik sat beside me. "For all that they are despicable shits, demons have a strange idea of fun." He clapped his hands twice and the stairs flattened out into a slide.

"How do you know this shit?"

"Study, lots and lots of study. That and I caught a demon once. I kept him alive long enough to dredge information out of him." Erik's eyes met mine and I understood clearly. He'd tortured a demon to get information. "He told me about the slides and how to activate them. Never thought I'd actually use that tidbit."

I spun to my back, the surface below us slick as if coated in a lubricant, yet it was smooth. Alex giggled as we slid, rolling side to side from his back to his belly and then sitting up.

Erik leaned back, crossed his arms over his chest and arched his back. In a flash, he'd shot by us. I mimicked what he'd done. "Alex, you too, we've got to go fast."

Alex took one look at me, did what I asked, and we were shooting down the curving, curling slide. I tried not to think how we were going to land when we hit the bottom, but there was nothing I could do about it now. All around us the walls glowed, giving off a shimmering light just enough to see by, though not clearly. Didn't matter, we weren't going to be there long. That's what I told myself.

Erik was ahead of us, his hair streaming out behind him. We took a long, looping corner and something snarled from the ceiling far above us. I stared up and, in that shimmering light, a deep black set of wings detached itself from the ceiling above and swooped toward us. Long, pluming feathers like some bird from a darkened Amazon spread out around it in shades of grey and black, and it had a beak at least four feet long with fangs protruding out of it. Peachy, just fucking peachy.

Erik called up to me. "Don't use your sword, Rylee. Use your hand. Pull your sword to fight while we slide and you'll lose momentum."

But how the hell did you fight without weapons? Shit, I had to roll to the side to avoid the first dive from the demon bird. Hands, hands. Fucking hell. I couldn't do it.

I jerked my whip free (see, I could sort of listen) and snapped it out. There was only a small problem with that idea.

The whip wrapped around the bird's feet, jerking them together, making it screech, but didn't slow it down. Nope, it started to pull me up, off the wicked slide. It snapped its beak at me, eyes glittering with hate I could only define as bottomless.

"Rylee, let go!" Erik yelled.

"No, I can do this!" The big-ass bird wasn't going to get the better of me. Power was there if I reached for it. I didn't need words.

Easy. Right.

I thought of the whip as a conduit, a way to transfer the power Erik said was in me. The power to stop a demon.

Sweat popped out on my forehead as I sought a part of me I didn't know existed. A part of my father, the past, the power left to me to stop Orion.

Heart, it had to do with my heart.

Just like that, the whip went stiff in my hand, gave a jerk and the bird exploded above me, black feathers drifting down for a split second and then I was sliding on my back again, breathing hard. Struggling to realize I'd done that.

All along I'd had a power in me that could stop demons. I'd just not known it.

I let out a whoop and reached behind my head, let my whip trail behind me. Alex yipped a couple of times.

"Good job, Ryleeeeeeeeeee!" He grinned back at me, tongue flipping around, spit flying every which way, even hitting me in the face. I didn't care. I'd killed a demon without my sword. Pretty damn cool.

Pretty fucking damn cool.

Pacing did him no good.

Yet there was nothing else but to move. Liam fought not to let out a long, steady growl. Rylee and Alex had been gone for over two hours. Two hours and every little piece of him felt each minute had been a year. Ten years.

"Do you not trust her to accomplish the task she faces?" Thomas asked.

Liam glanced at the necromancer sitting in a chair salvaged from the wreckage, his fingers steepled under his chin.

"I trust her. I don't trust demons."

Frank and Megan sat at Thomas's feet and they shared a glance, but it was Megan who stood and drew close to his side.

"Umm. Can I talk to you?"

What the hell could a teenage girl he didn't know want to talk to him about?

"Alone." She bobbed her head to one side, toward the tree line.

What the hell, it wasn't like he had anything else to do. He didn't answer her, just started to walk. Megan jogged to catch up, her bright red hair bouncing like crazy.

At the tree line he stopped. "What?"

Her eyes flicked back to Thomas, once, just once. "He's strong, but I don't think he intends to open the gate, or door, or whatever that was in the same place again."

If she had thrown a cup full of ice and water in his face he couldn't have felt the chill rush through his body any faster. "How do you know that?" Calm, keep calm. Ask questions, throttle Thomas only if he had to.

Megan licked her lips, then tucked her hair behind her ears. "When he touched our shoulders, we saw what he planned, how he opened the door thingy. But I knew Thomas didn't want to re-open the doorway when he said he did. And if he did, he would open it somewhere else."

"Why, why would he do that?"

Megan stepped closer. "He's working for someone else. Someone who wants her dead."

This was going down hill fast, faster than he thought possible. "Then why would he ask for new apprentices? Why not just kill us with the zombies out right?"

She shrugged. "Maybe greed. Why kill you if he could get something out of you in the first place?"

Liam leaned close and drew in a deep breath. There was no deception in her, no sour scent of lies, just a heavy perfume that seemed like something every teenage girl wore. Megan frowned up at him. "Why are you smelling me?"

"To see if you're lying."

Her jaw dropped open, and her eyes went wide with something akin to wonder, which Liam was not really happy with. She grabbed his arm with her tiny hand. "Frank wasn't kidding, you really are a werewolf. That's awesome!"

He had to get her back on track. "Listen to me, does Thomas know what you saw?"

She shook her head slowly. "No, I don't think so."

Liam started back toward Frank and Thomas. "I believe you, but unless you or Frank can open the Veil to where Rylee went, I need Thomas. And trust me, he will do what I want."

His eyes narrowed as he strode toward the old man. Yes, Thomas would fulfill his end of the bargain, or

Liam would make sure it was the last day he spent on this earth with his body still intact.

The bottom of the slide wasn't as bad as I'd thought. Nope, it was a big old pond filled with water, a thick coating of some sort of oil on top. Erik hit first, displacing the oil, then Alex, then me.

My body sluiced under the surface and I closed my eyes, held my breath and wondered how much shit I would have clinging to me when I stood. There was nothing to stand on, no bottom to the pond that I felt. Breaking the surface I wiped my face, the oily substance sliding off.

I swam for the edge where Erik and Alex were pulling themselves out. "Demons are disgusting. Do I even want to know what this is?"

"It isn't that bad. Leftover food grease if I remember correctly."

I grimaced. He reached down and pulled me out. Where we stood was a wide-open field of dead grass, acres and acres of dead grass and not much else. Like the demons decided to build their own terrarium inside the building.

"Alex, how's the bracelet?"

He shook his whole body, sending a spray of water and food grease into the air. "Warmer."

"Warmer than before?"

"Yuppy doody."

Erik glanced down. "Timer from a necromancer?"

"Yes." I nodded, Tracking Pamela. "And we're running out of said time. We have to hurry."

Pamela was close, real close. I almost called out to her. Of course, I should have known it wouldn't be as easy as fending off a single, large demon bird.

From the field of dead grass, the ground humped upward.

"Erik?"

"This one best we run from. Drovers are not easy to kill, though it can be done. It would take more time than we have."

Drovers. I tucked the name into the back of my head. "Run it is then." I turned and bolted along the edge of the pond toward where the slide hung. There was a door behind the slide, the only one available. It would have to do.

Erik beat me to it and flung it open, stepping through. "Dungeons?"

"I'm guessing. To the right."

He didn't hesitate. "That would be it."

We spoke as though we'd worked together for years, as if, hell, as if we understood one another in the way only two things can bring: genetics and time. Since time was an obvious out, genetics it was.

Behind us, the drover let out a high-pitched *ping* that shook the ground. I couldn't help but look back as Alex dove through the door after Erik.

Apparently the drover was like a giant earthworm, black like a night crawler, and there wasn't one, but three. Each one would easily dwarf Blaz, which was saying something. They humped across the ground, their open mouths pits of row upon row of teeth, tentacles reaching out and tasting the ground ahead of them. Yeah, I could see killing them would be less than easy.

"Another day, bitches!" I gave them a wave and stepped through the doorway, shutting it behind us. "Tell me we don't have to go out that way."

"Depends." Erik stood ahead of me, very still. "Don't move. Either of you."

Ah hell, what now?

There was nothing down the long hallways ahead of us. Or at least, nothing I could see.

Alex didn't move but I saw him shiver and lift his paw up ever so slightly. "Hotter, hotter."

Shit. "We don't have time, Erik. Whatever it is, we have to go. So either you move, or I do."

"Impetuous child." He snapped a hand out in front of his body and in front of us.

Oh boy, I suddenly felt ill.

Like watching ink drops appear in water, images fuzzed into view. Tall and short, fat and thin, there was no conformity other than the fact that they all were non-corporeal.

Ghosts.

"Demon ghosts are bad. They are the evil spirits that come through the Veil when called," Erik said, his voice taking on the tone of a lecture, monotone and droning. "Don't make eye contact, don't touch them. They won't touch you but they will try to spook you into running."

"I no likes ghosts." Alex pushed into my leg, his tremors traveling up through my body he shook so hard.

"Yeah, me neither, buddy. But we have to. Pamela and Milly need us. Close your eyes, and hang onto my belt." I dropped a hand to him. This couldn't be that hard. Hell, what could go wrong? I swallowed hard, my own body betraying me.

"Okee dokee," he whispered, as he squeezed his eyes shut, pinching them so tight his whole face scrunched up.

"Rylee."

"Erik." I stared at his back, the base of his neck. It was one of the few spots I didn't see ghosts staring back at me.

"Let's go." He stepped forward and I followed him, Alex clinging to the back of my belt, his claws brushing against the skin of my lower back.

Around us the spirits shifted and shimmered, their bodies pressing in tight. The back of Erik's neck was all I saw, the hint of a tattoo that I guessed traveled the length of his spine. Droplets of sweat running down his skin did not inspire me.

Then came whispers from every direction, teasing my ears with voices I thought I knew.

Dox.

Giselle.

Jack.

The Triplets.

"Don't listen to them. They prey on your loss." Erik's voice was tight.

"Are you hearing my parents?" I asked the question before I thought better of it.

He didn't stumble, didn't stop, but I saw the hesitation in him. "Yes. Their voices are calling to me."

This was a different kind of torture, and I'd have rather faced the drovers. Here, my guilt raged as the voices of my friends accused me, told me I'd used them. Left them to die to save myself.

Alex whimpered. "No, no, I save you."

"Alex, it's not real, don't listen, just hang onto me." My voice cracked on the tears hovering so close to the surface.

His grip tightened. "I save her. Save my sister."

I reached back and put a hand on the top of his head. "You did save her, it's okay."

He let out a long, low howl that shattered what was left of my control, his pain becoming mine. I let the tears come—who was going to see them? Just me, just Erik.

Of course, as hard as it was, I should have known the ghosts weren't done.

They changed tactics. The light in the walls grew dim and I found myself stumbling to a stop. "Erik!"

"Keep moving."

I took a step and then had to stop. A ghost floated between me and Erik.

"Little Slayer, look at me. See what you will be when we end you. See your future in my eyes."

Anger shot through me, annihilating the fear. "Fuck off and find yourself a too tight-fitted sheet."

The ghost swayed and ducked, trying to force me to make eye contact. And a little part of me almost let him. Just to prove they couldn't stop me. Or maybe even to see if they could show me the future. Bad, bad idea.

"Rylee, you're close, follow my voice."

"Not going to work." I slammed my eyes shut at the last second, as the ghost dropped and shoved its face right in mine.

Pissed off, scared, and knowing we were running out of time, I Tracked the demon ghosts. They lit up inside my head, a perfect outline of where they all were right in front of me.

"Don't mess with the Tracker, sheet heads!" I yelled, breaking into a jog and dodging around them with ease. A strong set of hands grabbed me and my eyes flew open.

Erik was smiling. "Yes, you are your mother's daughter."

20

We encountered nothing else until we reached the room where Pamela was being kept. I Tracked Milly, she was a door or two down by the feel of her threads. Sleeping, so at least that was good.

Pamela's door was heavily etched in symbols and as I lifted my hand to touch them, Erik stopped me.

"This one is alarmed." He pointed to a sunburst in the middle. "That one will unleash a venom that will drop anyone, knock them out for days the minute the door is touched."

I lifted my hand again. "Even an Immune?"

Erik frowned. "It is a risk."

"No other way, is there?"

"No. Here, these are the symbols to open the door." He pointed out three squares interlocked. "Trace them, open the door, get hit by venom. Pray to the gods you have the best fucking immunity out there."

He stepped back and took Alex with him. I didn't hesitate, traced the symbols, closed my eyes, held my breath. There was a puff of air, moisture tickled my face and then nothing.

Using the bottom edge of my t-shirt, I wiped my face. "It doesn't even smell."

Opening my eyes, I looked at Erik and Alex who watched me. Erik waved toward the door. "You are covered in that shit now. Don't touch your friends, or us."

Shit. I pushed the door open.

Pamela sat up, blinking. "Rylee?"

"Don't touch me, I'm covered in venom. But yes, who the hell did you think would come for you? Charlie?"

She jumped up, clapped her hands over her mouth and stifled a sob. "I told Milly you'd come. She said we were on our own. I think, I think she is trying to make friends with . . . Orion." She breathed out his name and I knew she'd met him, saw it in the way her voice hitched and her eyes dilated. Alex ran into the room and she dropped to her knees.

"Pamie, Pamie, Pamie."

"Alex, you came too!"

Erik clapped his hands. "There is no time. Alex, stick close to the girl. Things are about to get ugly."

I shot a look at him. "This wasn't ugly?"

"No one knew we were here, not until you touched that door."

Damn it all to hell and back. "Let's move, we still have Milly to get." I didn't want to think about the other problem we faced.

Thomas allowed us to bring two people out with us.

And I had three.

I would have to negotiate with him when we got back to the doorway; we were leaving no one behind.

Two doors down, and another doorway that was locked. Erik leaned in and traced the design. "No alarm on this one, no booby traps."

Why wouldn't they do anything for Milly's door? The answer didn't come to me until it swung open.

The room was sumptuous and filled with beautiful things, gold, silver, thick carpet, and food of all kinds laid out on a table. Orion wanted her well fed, well cared for. His breeding stock.

The mother of the body he wanted to possess so badly.

Milly sat in a stunning, low-backed green gown that matched her eyes perfectly. Her belly had swelled, even in the few days since I'd seen her last.

"Please tell me you didn't sign back up on Orion's team," I whispered.

She shot to her feet. "Rylee! You can't be here; Orion will kill you! Why did you come?"

My eyes met hers and the years between us rose. "You're my sister, as much as Berget, as much as Pamela. And I don't leave my family behind."

Her eyes welled, tears slipping down her cheeks, but she dashed them away. "Then we'd better haul ass, because if Orion doesn't know you're here now, he will."

I didn't want to tell her what we knew, that Orion wanted her for the child in her belly. That he wanted to possess her baby, not kill it.

No, this was not the place. We'd get her out and then tell her.

Erik led the way, but Milly was at his side, also helping to direct us. Pamela and Alex walked in between and I brought up the rear.

That Milly knew the lower hallways so well was . . . disturbing and my gut told me something was off. Shit.

"Wait."

They all stopped and looked back at me. "Erik. You lead. Milly, let him do his job."

"But I know where there are dead ends to avoid." She frowned at me, but it was confusion that covered her face, not anger.

"Let him lead."

She sucked her lower lip in between her teeth and slowly nodded. "I understand."

Erik lifted an eyebrow at me and I waved him forward. Slowly, my gut stopped clenching, and feeling like I was going to lose my lunch. Milly's back swayed ahead of me, supple and unbothered by the extra weight in her belly. Not at all how she'd been walking back at the farmhouse last time I'd seen her.

"Milly, give us some light, would you?"

"I can do it." Pamela said, lifting her hand.

"No. I want Milly to do it."

The doppelganger in the green dress stopped and planted her feet. "How did you know?"

"Does it matter?" I pulled a sword free as Erik spun. "Milly" was cornered; Erik lunged toward her, his hand out and she shrieked, her spine stiffening as she arced backwards, right in half, her head touching the back of her ankles.

Pamela let out a cry and flung her hand toward the demon. A burst of fire erupted, eating up the dress in a split second.

The demon scuttled toward us upside down and backward and still managed to dodge Alex and Pamela; I snagged my whip and snapped it forward. The leather coiled around the neck of the demon scuttling toward us.

Heart, it was about heart. I tightened my grip and felt the flow of energy—I could almost tell what it was—and then the whip tightened and the demon exploded without a sound, ash and dust floating down.

I turned and ran toward the room the doppelganger had been in. Tracking Milly, I felt her there, sleeping. Quiet.

The room was no longer furnished, but a bare cell, like Pamela's, and in the middle instead of a table full of food, was a large trunk.

"How did you know it wasn't her?" Pamela and Alex skidded into the room.

"Remember how much she was complaining about the extra weight, how her back hurt? She was walking fine. Like she wasn't even pregnant." My hands skimmed over the trunk, but there were no latches, no key hole, no way in or out I could find.

"Erik! How do we break this open?"

He was at my side, doing the same thing as me, his hands searching for an entry point. "I don't know. I've never seen anything like this before."

I Tracked Milly, could almost see how she'd be curled up in the box. Fuck, we didn't have time. I had to take the chance. I pulled a sword out. Erik stepped back and nodded.

"Do it."

I lifted the blade high, holding the handle tight with both hands and prayed I didn't hit her. With everything I had, I drove the blade down the inside edge of the box. I didn't feel anything like flesh and I let out a slow breath. Going slow wasn't an option, the box bit in hard to my blade, seeming to hold it tight and keep it from cutting. Teeth gritted, I jerked the blade to the left, hit the corner and then tipped the blade and went to the floor.

The box cracked, groaned, and fell open. Milly spilled out, her hair tangled and dirty, her face pale and bruised but she was alive. I bent to touch her, then remembered the venom.

"Erik, can you carry her?"

He didn't answer, just scooped her up in his arms. "We need to get out. Look at the wolf's bracelet."

I looked to see the bracelet fading. "Shit, we need a way upstairs or Orion is going to win by default."

The building around us shivered. I looked at Erik and he shrugged. "Don't know."

I directed my question to the wall, to the monster who made up the structure. "You can hear us? You know we want to stop Orion, but we have to get out of here."

The building again shivered and floor below us shifted, lifting us toward the ceiling.

"Oh shit."

That was not what I'd been hoping for.

"Erik!"

"Let me think."

I crouched as the ceiling touched my head. "Think faster. Pamela, Alex, lay on the floor. Pam, if it starts to squish us, you fire away, understand?"

She nodded, blue eyes hard, but not afraid.

Erik crouched, Milly unmoving in his arms. "The building is alive and can hear us, so I'm guessing that it doesn't like what Orion is doing to it."

The building gave a loud groan, pitched suspiciously like a "*Yes.*"

I ran with it. "Then you'll help us get out?"

Another groaning, "*Yes*."

There was no other option at that point. We had to trust the building that was alive, that was likely some sort of demon, and hope for the best.

Yeah, not really a gamble I wanted to take, but what other choice did we have?

I held my breath as the ceiling drew close and as Pamela lifted her hand, the ceiling shimmered and pulled back.

Only one problem. Seemed like we were about to get the express route. The panel below us began to pick up speed.

"Lie down, Rylee," Erik said, doing so himself and laying Milly flat. The walls around us flashed by and I forced myself to look up as each floor above us drew close and then disappeared a hairsbreadth before smashing into us. I didn't know why it had to be that way, but I didn't care. We were getting the hell out of here.

As fast as the ride up started, it was over, the building let out a final groan. "Go."

I sat up. Shit, we were in the room Alex and I crawled into what felt like hours ago. I glanced at his ankle. Only the faintest shimmer of gold showed. We were running against the clock, but I managed to keep my manners intact.

"Thank you."

I stood, Pamela and Alex scrambled toward the window and Erik followed.

I paused and put my hand on the building. "Why?"

The building, a living entity that demons carved out as their base, gave me an answer I didn't know how to react to.

"Not all demons bad. Remember."

Well shit. "I'll remember."

I climbed out the window. "Alex, you lead the way back to the gate. Smell our back trail."

He gave me a snappy salute. "Yes, boss!"

Behind us, the building groaned, the ground around the base shooting up in large chunks, and demons—lots and lots of demons—poured out of the windows.

"Time to go." Erik hitched Milly a little higher in his arms and took off, Alex running beside him.

Pamela stared at the demons, her eyes glittering with hate. "I want to kill them all."

How much had she seen, how much had they hurt her? I pointed after Erik. "Another time, Pam. We'll have another shot at them."

Running flat out, we barely stayed ahead of the horde. Alex ran in front, nose to the ground and then in the air, then back to the ground. I couldn't see any flash of gold, and that worried me.

We had to make it; Thomas had to hold the doorway for us.

Otherwise, we might as well give up.

Yeah, that wasn't going to happen.

Three hours. Thomas held up his finger. "I will open the Veil. If they are not there, waiting for us, there is no re-opening it."

Liam ground his teeth. "Thomas."

The necromancer looked at him. "Yes?"

"If she isn't there, you are holding the Veil open until I say. Understand?"

Thomas snorted. "Negotiations were made, you'd change them now?"

"These are lives on the line, not negotiations." Liam stepped closer, so Thomas and he were almost nose to nose. "They are lives that are needed more than any other in the world. You will hold that Veil open until I call cease."

He stepped back and nodded for Thomas to go ahead.

Megan gave him a look, her eyes full of worry; she mouthed something at him. Something that looked like 'kill him.' Yeah, that was not going to happen. Right at that moment there was nothing else he could do. Thomas would betray them, or he wouldn't. They would just have to wait and let the scene play out.

The necromancer put a hand on Frank's shoulder then one on Megan's, and the two teenagers slumped a little. Across from them, the Veil began to open, finally revealing the same archway Rylee and Alex stepped through only three hours past.

No one was there.

No Rylee. No Alex.

Just a vast empty plain. At least Megan had been wrong about that. Thomas had so far kept to his word. Now Liam had to get him to hold it a little longer.

Thomas let out a long sigh. "This is why I do not like opening the Veil into the deep level. No one comes out, not ever. I told you that."

Liam spun toward him. "You never said that."

"Didn't I? Well, it was implied."

"You hold that open." Liam stalked toward the open Veil, but whatever made him a guardian kept him from going any further. He stared onto the open plain. There was movement, far, far in the distance.

"There is someone coming."

Thomas snorted again, and his voice was strained. "Even if it is her, I am not sure how long I can hold this open, wolf."

"Thomas, hold it open. You have to." He strained his eyes, peering into the shimmering darkness.

The Veil slammed shut. "I cannot, Liam." Thomas slid to the ground between Megan and Frank.

"No!"

Thomas lifted his hand. "Let me rest. I am a fool, but I will open it again for you."

"He's lying," Megan whispered. "It's all an act."

Frank's eyes went wide. "Megan, why would you say that?"

Liam had a bad feeling this was not going to be easily cut and dried. "Megan, sit down." He pointed to the ground, a few feet away from Thomas.

Thomas lifted his head. "Someone has gotten to her, I think. She is marvelously strong, but . . ." He didn't finish. Megan lifted a hand and around them the ground shifted.

"I will kill you, old man. You're too stupid to see you're weak now. Too weak to stop me, too weak to open that gate. Orion will rule, and I will be his queen."

From below, the dead began to rise, pushing themselves out of the dirt. Liam didn't hesitate, though his heart faltered.

He leapt toward Megan, who had her back to him, and wrapped his fingers around her neck, lifting her from the ground. Quick and easy, he'd snap her neck; she wouldn't feel a thing.

"If you kill her, we won't be able to open the Veil," Thomas said, as though their lives weren't in danger, as if zombies weren't even now crawling toward them with open mouths and reaching hands.

"Knock her out. I can drain her powers. Permanently."

There was no other choice. She struggled in his hands, her face going red and then purple. He shifted his grip so the pulsing carotid artery was under his fingertips and then he squeezed.

Out like a light, she slumped, her body loosing urine all down her legs, urine he couldn't smell over the heavy perfume she wore. She must have known he could scent her lies and had covered them; the naivety had all been an act. Fortunately, the zombies she'd called stilled as she passed out, dropping where they were.

He all but tossed her limp body toward Thomas. "She is another of Orion's pets."

Thomas nodded. "It would seem that way."

Something about this bothered Liam, a piece that didn't make sense. "Why didn't he use her the way he used Talia?"

With a sigh, Thomas crouched beside Megan. "She is still young; likely, he was grooming her to be a backup. She is untrained, and without the proper training she could never have opened the deep level of the Veil for Orion."

A backup necromancer. Shit. There was nothing for her then, nothing to redeem her of this if she'd thrown her lot so fully in with Orion. Which was obviously the case. Liam's gaze met Thomas's. "Do it."

Thomas beckoned. "Frank, come, you must learn this too."

Frank stepped forward, his eyes glassy behind his too large specs. "I thought she was . . . I thought she liked me." He shook his head.

"We all get fooled by a pretty girl at least one in our lives," Thomas said, putting a hand on Megan's head, then taking Frank's hand and doing the same. "Likely, more than once, actually. This will help you in the long run, you will be stronger now than even she was."

Liam knew he couldn't rush them, knew that it was going to be close.

Come on, Rylee, let it be you. Come home to me.

21

We ran as fast as we could, but demons came from every side. Thousands upon thousands, more than I could comprehend. Most seemed pulled from the human psyche, nightmares lain dormant awakened, monstrous and terrifying. Others, though, were disturbingly normal.

Human like, and in that, all the more frightening. Because I never would have known them for what they were if they hadn't been chasing us. They would have fooled me.

Ahead of us, far ahead, I saw a speck of light. An opening into the world. Our time was up.

"Hurry, we have to hurry!"

But even as I said the words, the light disappeared, closing us off.

Alex whimpered and Pamela choked back a sob. I kept my focus straight ahead. "Keep going. Liam is with him; he will get that fucking Veil open."

And so we ran, an avalanche of demons closing in, tightening the deadly noose that would swallow us whole if we slowed for even a heart beat.

"Rylee, when we get to the arch, put the others inside and you and I will defend," Erik said, out of breath from running while carrying Milly.

We hit the archway a few minutes later. He dropped Milly to the ground and swung around. Pamela and Alex crouched beside her, and I spun to face the horde. But Alex didn't stay with Pamela, he pushed her down and then leapt up beside me.

"I protect you."

I wasn't going to argue with him. We were done.

Fuck me, we were so done.

I had no illusions; this was a last stand, a way to etch ourselves into the memories of the demons as the ones who took out hundreds of them. Erik's hands shot out, catching the first demon on the chin, his power vaporizing the monster before I even registered what it looked like.

"Rylee, you always bring the trouble, my girl." Giselle's voice made me smile. I knew she'd come; she wouldn't let us fight on our own.

"What happens if you die here?"

"Then I am gone. Gone to my reward, wherever that is." She loosened her weapons and steadied her stance. "There is no greater joy than to take a stand for those you love."

Erik grunted. "Fierce love is a power unto itself."

She smiled at him and gave him a wink, of all things. "That it is, Slayer."

And then they were on us. I used my sword, my whip, my hands. The power I'd not understood flowed under my skin, driving the demons back. From the heart, it was all from the heart.

Giselle fought like lightning, striking and withdrawing, her weapons dropping demons all around her.

And Alex, everywhere he bit, clawed, and struck, demons fell. It had nothing to do with symbols or etching designs into blades and weapons.

No, this was about the heart. Alex had more heart than anyone I knew, he fought for me because he loved me. And then it all clicked, and I finally understood.

Every person I loved, every child I'd brought home, every decision I'd made because it was the best I could do, that was what it took to take out a demon. This power was bottomless; there was no draining it, though I felt the toll on my muscles, on my stamina. The well in my heart would not run dry.

Liam.

Giselle.

Pamela.

Milly. All those I loved fed that power. Their love gave me this strength to face the darkest of hours without hate in me. Without anger. Without fear. That was why Alex could tackle demons. That was what the necromancer Talia meant when she said he had a pure intent. He fought from a place of love, he fought for those he loved.

The scent of roses swam up around me and I didn't look, I knew Milly was awake and she was pissed.

Her magic flowed and struck with a deadly aim, pushing the demons back. She wasn't killing them though.

"Milly, I know you want to hate them, but you need to let that go—you have to think of those you love. Of your baby. Then use your magic."

She stepped beside me, tears tracking down her cheeks. "Of you, too, Rylee."

Her power swept out in a bar of light and the demons cowered. To the other side of me, Pamela stood, her hands out, a smile on her lips.

"That's the key, isn't it?"

"I think so," I whispered, snapping my whip out, curling it around a demon's neck. There couldn't be hate, and even though there was, it wasn't the driving force. I did this for love, for those I loved. Not to gain vengeance or to make Orion pay. I did this to keep those I cared for safe.

Bar after bar of light burst out of Pamela and Milly, driving the demons back, way back. Far out of reach of my weapons or Erik's hands. The demons weren't dying from the magical assault, there was too much anger in Pam and Milly, too much rage at being held captive. Not that I was going to complain. They were giving us a respite, holding the demons at bay.

"Rylee. The door isn't going to open on its own. We're stuck here," Erik said. "And your girls, they will tire out sooner rather than later."

"Liam will come through." I stared at the archway.

"You are willing to bet your life on him?"

"Always."

Draining Megan took close to ten minutes, her pale face dipped into a shade of white Liam had never seen on skin before. She still breathed though; her body was alive even if she'd been stripped of every drop of power she had.

"It is done," Thomas said, his voice heavy with sorrow. "She had great potential, a shame she was tainted."

"Open the Veil."

"Wolf, let me get to my feet! I know you think they will be there, and I will open the Veil once, and once more only. If they are not there, I cannot open it again, not for days. And by then . . ." He lifted his brown eyes to Liam's. "By then it will be too late."

Clenching his hands into fists, Liam shook with fear, though by the look on Thomas's face, the necromancer thought it a more aggressive emotion that claimed his body.

He could barely say the words. "Open the Veil, she will be there."

Never in his life had he been so afraid. Even when Pamela and he had been separated from Rylee and Alex in the underground palace, when the water had come and swept her away. Even then he'd thought perhaps there was some way she would make it. But this time it was too close to the endgame; walking into Orion's own territory, no matter the reason, was a death sentence. And he'd let her go.

He should have fought harder, should have made her see that Pamela and Milly were not as important as she was.

The Veil sluggishly opened, the archway showing clearly. No one stood in it. A moment passed where he heard nothing and then . . . .

A deafening roar, the sounds of battle drove out of the opening, the scent of blood and magic lit up his senses.

"RYLEE!" He roared her name and then let out a howl he couldn't hold back, the cry of a wolf for his mate.

"Liam!"

Everything happened so fast. Pamela and Alex came through first, and then . . . Erik?

"What the hell, I thought you were with the dragons?"

Erik's eyes flicked over him and Liam caught a new scent. This wasn't the Erik they'd left behind. What the hell was going on?

"Where's Rylee?"

"Here." She stepped up to the edge. "Don't touch me, anyone. I'm covered in venom."

Behind her, he saw Milly.

Worse, behind Milly stood a figure who could be only one person.

Orion.

22

Like manna from heaven, the Veil opened behind us. Liam howled my name and I felt another prophecy slide into place.

And the great wolf will howl her name . . . .

Giselle stepped away, lifted her hand, and faded. "Love. That is what this is about. Remember that and look out for one another, my girls."

The others went through, but Milly hesitated. "Rylee. I can't leave. He has bound me again."

Behind her strode a figure, cutting his way through the mass of lesser demons. There was no time to be gentle; we had to go.

"No, you have to come. Milly, he wants your baby."

"I know. I will work for you from this side. I will slow him down. I won't let him take my baby. I can't leave, Rylee. He has me, there is no other way right now." Her eyes glittered with unshed tears. "I have faith in you, and if I'm wrong and Orion possesses my baby, I know you will do what you must to stop him. You were always the strong one."

I wanted to throw up with what she was saying, what she was asking of me. That I would kill her baby if necessary. Fuck me. "Just come with us. With me. Please."

She reached under the side of her skirt and pulled out a sheaf of papers. "Take them, they were all I could get, but they should help."

My fingers clenched around the thick paper and she stepped back, away from me. Away from the opening in the Veil.

"Milly." Her name choked in my throat. "Don't do this."

We were both crying, saying what I knew would be a final goodbye. I almost wished she hadn't redeemed herself, wished she hadn't come back into my life. It was easier to hate, far easier to hate than let someone go who you loved so dearly.

"Rylee, I love you the best, you have always fought for me, even when you shouldn't have. Even when I wronged you. Let this be the way I fight for you, for the world. I am bound to him. I cannot leave. There is no other way for me." Her green eyes sought mine and I knew she wasn't lying. I knew in my heart, but that didn't make it any easier.

"He'll force us to face one another."

She nodded and went to her knees. "Yes. I know. Go, Rylee. Sister of my heart, my one true friend. Go."

Everything she said was truth, everything. I backed toward the opening and fell through it into what felt like a brilliantly sunny day. The Veil snapped shut behind me.

Chaos was all around, talking over one another, Erik explaining what had happened, Pamela and Alex filling in the blanks. Megan lay beside me, and I gleaned from what I heard Frank say that she'd been a spy of sorts, infiltrating our ranks.

None of it really hit me though. Liam crouched beside me, put his face over mine. "Rylee, how bad is the venom?"

"Bad." I whispered, my throat closing off, the tears unstoppable as I lay on my back. "The worst."

"She loves you enough to die for you, Rylee," he said softly, his own eyes dripping moisture onto my face.

But that wasn't what I wanted to hear. "We have to go, Blaz is in trouble."

Liam nodded and moved so I could sit up. I wiped my face.

Before I could even ask him, Alex let out a howl. "Farrrrrrrriiiiiiiis."

Thomas visibly stiffened and turned his back. "Go quickly, I cannot stand the sight of him."

The Veil sliced open twenty feet away. Faris stood in the shadows of his room, waiting.

Liam put a hand on Erik's shoulder. "I cannot go. Send Blaz for me when you save his big leather ass. I'll be at Jack's."

Erik clapped a hand over Liam's. "I'll keep her safe."

The language of men, it was strange at the best of times.

I couldn't even kiss him goodbye. But for now, it would be enough. I would see him soon; there was no goodbye for us and as far as I was concerned, there never would be. I handed him the papers Milly had given me, wondered what they were, knew that at some point I'd finally be able to find out. Just not right now. "Here, hang onto these for me."

Faris took us to the farm without argument, without even a single snotty comment. "Doran and Berget are setting things up; over a hundred ogres have shown up to fight for you, Rylee."

"That's good. Thank you, for helping us."

He shared a quick look with Erik that I pretended not to notice. I knew I was not myself, I knew it. I just couldn't shake the last look in Milly's eyes as she bent to her knees, her hands cradled around her belly.

Mother of the gods, watch over her. Keep her safe.

Faris stepped through the Veil at the farm since night was heavy over the land. The scent of charred wood still filled the ice-laden air.

"Blaz?" I walked toward the barn.

Rylee, you are back? His head popped up behind the barn, like a giant Jack in the Box.

"Where is Erik?"

Ophelia's head appeared, rather close to Blaz's. Looked like they were getting along at least.

He is in the barn, shall I wake him? Her voice was almost tender.

"No. He's my uncle. I'll wake him."

I strode toward the barn, forgetting everything I'd learned about fighting demons. The hate and the pain was too strong. No one tried to stop me; my real uncle let me go. Pamela, Alex, and Faris stayed outside.

They all knew me.

I pushed the door open hard so it banged against the wooden slatted wall.

"Wakey, wakey, *uncle*," I snapped, uncoiling my whip. The doppelganger sat up and scrubbed his face.

"You made it?" His eyes were wide with shock.

"Yeah, probably didn't think I would, did you? Why didn't you want to go with me, *uncle*? Was it really because you didn't think you could help? Or was it because you knew the chances were too high that I'd find out what you really are?"

He pushed away from me.

"No, it isn't what you think. I had orders, yes. But Ophelia is such a dear and I've never had a friend. Ask the dragons. I did nothing. I just came and slept. I got rid of the poison I was to use on them."

"Demon!" I lunged at him, bare-handed, and he cringed; he didn't try and defend himself.

As I grabbed him, I heard the voice of the monster, the demon turned into a living building who'd helped us, in my head. *Not all demons bad.*

"Fucking hell." I pulled the pretender into my arms and the venom completely transferred. He took a breath and passed out.

Rylee, what have you done to Erik? The worry in Ophelia's voice was obvious. I let out a sigh and dragged his limp body with me. As I walked it shifted, the visage of Erik fading, replaced by one of a very small, very frail looking man. In some ways he reminded me of Thomas. All legs and arms. But he had a large head, and large eyes, and pale grey skin. Kinda human, mostly not.

"He's a demon. He was impersonating Erik to get close to us. To kill both of you." I flipped his limp body out into a pile of soot-covered snow.

Erik, the real Erik, poked him with a toe. "Why didn't you kill him?"

Ophelia's head snaked down. *How did he fool me? How do you know this one,* she shoved her nose at Erik, *isn't the one who is fooling you.*

"I still hate you, you big nasty bitch. What, did he tell you? He had a change of heart? That he could ride with another dragon now?" Erik swatted her nose and she pulled back, but said nothing.

In her eyes, I saw the confusion the real Erik told me about. The way her eyes were distant and faraway as she tried to process this turn of events. "Ophelia, you are not well. You haven't been since my father died. That made it easy for him to fool you because you wanted a new rider—"

NO! That can't be. This is not the way it was supposed to be. She trembled, her lovely eyes filling with tears.

I softened my voice. "It is. He fooled you, he fooled all of us."

With a wail, she threw herself backward, the ground shuddering under her weight.

I cannot stay. I cannot.

She let out a roar that made me slap my hands over my ears and with that she launched into the air. She fled from us, her silhouette fading from sight within seconds.

"Blaz, is she going to come back?"

I don't know. Rylee, he did nothing to us. There was no harm. Blaz's voice was quiet, for my ears only.

"Blaz, you said you wouldn't survive if I died, that we are bound. How come Ophelia didn't die when my father did? Or you, Erik, why didn't you die when your dragon died?"

Erik shook his head. "Every pairing is different. The one with my girl, she severed the bond as she died, to save me. Your father did the same for Ophelia. It is hard and painful, but it will leave the other half of the pair alive. Slayers keep their minds intact, but the dragons don't. Like I said, the bond runs too deep for them."

He speaks the truth, but don't even think it, Rylee. My place is with you, to the end I would not live my life well as a broken dragon. I do not know how Ophelia has done it this long. Blaz's eyes narrowed. At least I knew there was a way to save him if something did happen to me.

"Will you get Liam? He's waiting for you at Jack's. Bring him to Doran's."

You and your wolf. Of course I'll fetch him. Again. With a long snort Blaz leapt into the air, his path taking him in the opposite direction of Ophelia's flight. I wondered if she would come back, or if that was the last we would see of her. I wasn't sure we wanted a mentally unstable dragon, even if she was on our side.

"He will be gone three days at most," Erik said. "You need to decide what to do with him," he booted the passed out doppelganger, "before he gets back and your wolf gets a smell of him."

I knew what he was saying. There was no way Liam would allow the doppelganger to live knowing the danger he represented. And I couldn't blame Liam; the doppelganger had been so far within our guard we hadn't even known he was a danger. He could have killed Blaz and Ophelia and there would have been nothing we could have done to stop him. Hell, he'd been sabotaging my training and setting me up to be killed alongside Liam and my other allies.

I scrubbed a hand over my face. "I don't know. He didn't kill Blaz or Ophelia when he had the chance.

Do you think it's possible that not all demons are bad?"

Erik crossed his arms over his wide chest, his eyes narrowing in thought. "I . . . I think that not all of them are as bad as Orion. The creature who housed the demons was a demon that helped us. Perhaps there is a reason for this one yet to live."

A few hours passed before the doppelganger woke with a groan. He sat forward, swaying from side to side. Right away he changed his appearance to something far more human. He looked suspiciously like Bruce Lee.

"Why didn't you kill me while I slept? I know nothing, other than the orders I was given." His voice was lightly accented now, but not Russian like before.

I crouched in front of him and put a hand on his shoulder. He flinched as though it were a hot brand. "Not all demons are bad. That's what I've heard. Are you ready to renounce your previous master?"

"He'll kill me," he whispered.

I laughed, not kindly. "He's going to kill you when you fail to follow his orders, idiot."

"Right." His head dropped, black hair sliding forward to partially cover his face. "Our prophecies say he will win, that he will beat you, and he has the black book of prophecy now to guide him, as well as the violet book that has what you need from it." He lifted his eyes, they were completely black, with no iris, no white showing. Freaky.

"Well, all the other prophecies say I can beat him. The rest of the supernatural world has put their trust in me. If you won't renounce him, I'll kill you."

"I don't want to die. I like it here."

After that, it was simple. He picked himself a name. Albert, of all things, and Erik did some sort of binding on the doppelganger. I watched closely, that it was kind of like killing the demons, but only the reverse. Erik *pulled* the demon's essence close to himself instead of shoving it away. I watched, not because I wanted to bind any demon to me, but knowledge was power.

"He is mine, until I let him go or I die. If I die, he dies. It is that simple."

Albert shadowed Erik wherever he went, and soon enough we were calling him "Bert."

Faris took us to Doran's, though he was not happy about the demon coming with us.

The vampire pulled me to one side. "You walk a fine line, Rylee. Keeping a demon for a pet is not smart."

"He's not my pet, he's Erik's. And I will kill him if he steps out of line."

"I think you are going soft. Once you would have killed him and asked questions later, and now. . ." He lifted a hand and touched the middle of my forehead. "Something has changed within you. I don't know yet if it is for good, or for ill."

"And if I'd killed you when I had the chance Doran would not be the leader of the vampires and we all would have died at the hands of the old ones." I pushed his hand from my face. "So perhaps Bert has a part to play yet."

Ever so slightly, Faris inclined his head. "Touché. Now, I must be off. I have things to do for Doran."

He sliced through the Veil and was gone. I wasn't sure if I was happy to see him go or not. A powerful ally, but a mercurial one for sure.

The next two days passed swiftly. I met with Raw, who'd assumed leadership of this new band of ogres, then met with Raw, Doran, and Berget. Eve flew to bring the unicorns close to the borders of Doran's place. When I asked her about the harpies she shook her head. "I do not know, Rylee. They were non-committal."

Everyone had a plan, had a way to try and stop the demons. But I knew it would come down to what I had to do. The rest of them would be holding off demons, like Pamela and Milly had done for Erik and me.

Holding off the hordes long enough for me to do what I had to do.

Whatever the hell it was.

Three days and Blaz came flying into sight, three figures on his back. Shit, had he really brought . . .

Frank insisted. He said he wasn't leaving his family to fight demons without him. The boy has some spine.

Blaz landed and Liam slid from his back first. Shit, who the hell cared if we had a serious PDA?

I ran to him, threw myself into his arms and buried my face in his neck. His arms tightened around me and we stood like that, clinging to one another. Around us people swirled and talked, but for that moment it was just him and me.

No words were needed as I slid from his arms. We were together. That was all that mattered in that moment.

Blaz stood beside me picking at his teeth with his claws. *Chaos should have been your name. Everywhere you go, you bring change.*

"Complaint department is over there." I pointed at the ogre's tents, which were colored in the tones of their skin. Not a single black tent sat amongst them, a distinguishing mark. Blaz laughed and rolled onto his back, stretching out fully. As if Blaz's return was the signal, everything seemed to happen at once.

From behind Doran's abode came the clatter of hooves and within moments the black stallion of the Tamoskin Crush slid to a stop in front of me.

Tracker, the time draws near. We stand with you against the darkness. Nikko is what you may call me.

I gave him my thanks, nodded and headed inside. As night fell, I called a council meeting.

Doran, Berget, Raw, Liam, Erik, Pamela, Alex, Blaz, Eve, Nikko, even Charlie came. Faris was a no-show, off on some errand or another for Doran. Of Will and Deanna, I'd heard nothing. Which pissed me off to no end, but for all that it irritated me, there was nothing I could do about it. Not yet, anyway.

Before the meeting, I met privately with Thomas out near Blaz on the outskirts of Doran's property. He shook from head to toe, his lanky arms and legs all but knocking together. "Thomas. There are going to be a number of vampires at the council meeting, Faris included. Can you hold your shit together?"

He nodded slowly. "Yes. Frank and I spoke at length about what this trip would require of me. If the boy can do it, so can I. But I do not like it, nor will I ever trust the blood drinkers."

"You only have to trust me. Not them. That and do your best not to unleash a zombie horde on us, okay?"

Thomas gave me a tight smile and held out his hand. "You have my word I will do my best. If I must, I will walk away."

I took his hand and held it, my grip tightening. "Faris, he's more than just a vampire to you, isn't he?"

The necromancer's jaw twitched furiously and then he jerked his hand from mine. "Yes."

That was it; that was all I could get out of him. But it explained a lot if Faris had something to do with Thomas's captivity.

From there, the council was to meet.

We gathered outside where the fountain spewed water, teasing the lazy koi.

Of course, the council meeting never happened, or at least, not the way I'd thought it was going to. No, Blaz was right, my name should have been chaos.

Doran lifted his hand to bring the council to order when the Veil slashed open and Faris fell through, bloodied beyond belief. He was missing his left arm, taken at the shoulder; bite marks and wide, open wounds covered his body.

Confusion erupted and Liam moved first, opening a vein up in his wrist with a single slash and holding it over Faris's mouth before I could even suggest offering my own blood.

"Drink up, bloodsucker, it's the only time I'm giving freely."

Faris drank deep and his wounds healed, but his arm didn't grow back. The gaping hole sealed over with bright pink, new skin, but that was it.

He leaned on the tiles. "Orion is making a bid sooner than we thought." Faris's icy blue eyes found mine and for the first time, I saw fear in them.

"The doorway in the castle, the one that goes to the deep Veil, it has been . . ." His words dried up as he shook his head.

Faris didn't have to finish the words, I knew them already, but I asked anyway.

"He got it open, didn't he?"

Faris nodded, the council members around us hanging on his every word.

"Yes. And he's sending through his demons. Not in hordes, but carefully chosen packs. One of the packs did this to me like I was a child to be tossed between them. A toy to be broken."

There was the sound of sucked in air around the courtyard, the uneasy stamp of Nikko's foot on the tile. The idea of Faris being manhandled was . . . difficult to see, even in my mind.

"How bad could that be? Against all of us, the odds are in our favor, look at us," Raw said, his hand on his hips, legs spread in defiance. I caught a flash of red in his eyes as his anger and pride filled him.

Erik let out a low laugh. "The odds are not in our favor, ogre. This is bad. Yet bad doesn't begin to describe what we're up against if Orion is sending his packs through. They will make way for the demons who will set up Orion as king. The four horsemen. If the packs are coming through, the four horsemen will be next and we don't want that. Trust me."

I met his eyes, felt the blood pool from my face. He had to be shitting me, us. "Four horsemen?"

He nodded and everyone else melted away. The four horsemen of the apocalypse would soon be upon us, and Orion had set it in motion. He set them on us and now we had to face them.

This was not what we needed right now. But then again, when would there be a good time to have the four horsemen show up on our doorsteps?

Yeah, never.

Fan-fucking-tastic.

COMING AUGUST 2017 FROM TALOS PRESS

WOUNDED

A Rylee Adamson Novel
Book 8

"My name is Rylee, and I am a Tracker."

When children go missing, and the Humans have no leads, I'm the one they call. I am their last hope in bringing home the lost ones. I salvage what they cannot.

The clock is ticking, and I can feel the weight of the final battle with the demon hordes looming over my head. The puzzle pieces are becoming clearer, but the casualty list is growing. And with each name that is added to those we've lost, my confidence cracks a little more.

Yet there is hope.

A child saved.

A life lost.

A prophecy fulfilled.

$7.99 mass market paperback
978-1-945863-02-8

AN EXCERPT FROM *WOUNDED*

We were fucking surrounded. Erik was on foot, and wherever he went, the demons were driven out of the ogres' bodies. The ogres didn't survive the expulsion, but it still wasn't enough. We'd taken out at least two dozen of the hundred or so in the gang.

I trusted Nikko to keep me safe and finally Tracked Liam. Everything in me froze. He was hurt bad, his heart beating so slowly I wasn't sure we'd make it in time.

"BLAZ!" Fuck them all, they could roast, but not until Liam was out of the way.

The dragon had been waiting for me and dropped from the sky like an avenging big-ass angel. He swooped low, teeth and claws snapping ogres in half, following the thread I'd tied to Liam. When he launched back into the air, I could see the limp form of a black wolf in his claws. "Get him help!"

Pamela can help him?

I nodded, knowing Blaz could sense my intent as well as words unspoken. Liam was out of the way, but we were still in trouble. A flash of light drew my eye and I turned to find Erik had worked his way back to my side.

"Rylee, you truly have a knack for diving in, don't you?"

Erik parried with a green ogre who was small, at least as ogres went. Erik ducked inside of the ogre's guard and put his hand against the skin over his heart. The ogre fell, screaming as the demon ripped free of its body. Twenty-five down, seventy-five or so to go.

Piece of cake. Perhaps not so much.

Three arrows shot through the air, two driving through Nikko's side, and one through the red unicorn's neck. The red unicorn went down with a gurgling cry, his eyes rolling up and showing the whites as a group of ogres leapt forward, slashing and hacking him. Nikko let out a piercing scream that ripped through the night. I looked down and realized one of my legs was pierced through with the arrow, sealing my fate with Nikko's.

It has been an honor to know you, Tracker. Blood of the Lost, you will save us all.

His head whipped around and, with a sharp yank, he grabbed the arrow pinning us together, then gave a mighty buck, sending me flying through the air.

"That won't save us!" I yelled as I fell from the sky, only to be snatched up before I hit the ground by a familiar set of talons.

"Rylee, I see your lizard has left you alone again," Eve said as she tightened her grip on me. I twisted in her claws.

"Erik, we can't leave him!"

"We won't," she said, flipping me into the air and then diving underneath me so I landed on her back.

"Slick moves," I gasped out as I clung to her back.

"They have to be, to keep up with you."

I turned to see a blur of greyish silver wings dive and scoop Erik out of the melee, much to the roaring and consternation of the ogres. I couldn't see Nikko any more and my heart tore at the loss of such a pure spirit and a great ally. But like every other loss in my life, there was no time to dwell on it.

Life was about to get real ugly for the demon ogres, at least, that was what I was hoping. Fog rolled in around them and where it touched, ogres froze. Not all of them, but enough that I could see the fog was doing something to them. An undertone of screaming, faint echoes of voices trapped and now freed curled up through the air, tangling with the fog.

Those ogres possessed by evil spirits and not actual demons were no longer controlled by Orion. Doran had come through.

I opened my mouth to yell to tell them they'd been fooled and their friends could not be saved. But I didn't need to.

Those ogres released from the evil spirits fell on those who were truly possessed.

"I don't understand what's happening, why are they fighting now?" Eve called out. Erik answered her.

"Evil spirits can be expelled, they don't attach to the soul of the creature they possess like a demon does." Simple, yet still horrifying to think of a soul being latched onto by a demon.

Madness, total and complete, erupted as the ogres attacked one another. My heart sank as I watched the bodies pile and the number of the dead rise, and it was not on the side of those who'd been freed.

Erik and his ride, an odd-looking silvery grey harpy, caught up to us. "The weak ones are free, but they will be dead soon. We have to get the hell out of here."

He was right, this was a lost cause and we had to give way, much as it sucked shit.

"Eve, how far behind are the rest of the harpies?"

"They are on their way to London."

Her words stuck in my brain and I struggled to speak. "How could they have known?" Were they in on it? Shit, was I going to have to check every person who came within our close-knit circle?

"They have seers." She turned her head so I could see the chagrin in one eye. "I argued with them, told them they were needed here but they insisted they would meet us in London."

"Don't feel bad." I put a hand on her neck. "I would have done the same thing, argued 'til I was blue in the face."

The silver harpy swept in close, his baritone startling the shit out of me. "She made a good argument."

I cranked around in my seat to stare at the first male harpy I'd ever met. Now that I was looking at him, I could see the differences. He was far thicker in the legs, body and neck, and his face didn't have the feminine lines Eve did. His eyes were pale, a grey blue that would have disappeared if not for the black feathers around them like a mask.

"Zorro, how are you?" I blurted.

The male harpy chuckled, surprising me. "I see where Eve got her sass. My name is Marco."

The two harpies banked at the same time as we dropped from the sky, right into Doran's courtyard.

Pamela was crouched over Liam's body. Everything in me tensed, even though Tracking Liam I knew he was still alive. But barely.

I jumped from Eve's back before she had fully landed and ran to Liam's side. The werewolves had retreated and were pacing around, whining. Beauty stood to one side, buck naked, and leaning against Faris.

"Faris, get them all out of here. NOW," I said, doing my best to not let my voice break.

"They wouldn't go—how would you like me to deal with them?"

"Make them." I curled my hands into the thick fur around Liam's neck, trusting Faris would do as I asked. "Pamela, how bad is it?"

She lifted her eyes to mine for a split second before looking back at Liam, her hands cupping his muzzle. "Bad. It's very bad. I can heal all the wounds except the one on his chest."

The sound of footsteps running told me people were finally listening and going to safety. Which was good because I suspected it wouldn't be long before what was left of the ogres was over run and we'd be dealing with some pissed-off demons.

Sooner than you think. They are on their way to end us now.

"Blaz, can you stall them?"

On my way.

A whoosh of wings and the dragon let out a roar that shattered the air, pierced my ears, and made my heart pound. His battle cry stirred my own bloodlust. Seconds later, the sound of flames roaring across the open field reached us. A fire line would buy us a little time.

"Doran?"

"Nothing I can do, at least, not on my own. The blade was cursed. I'd have to have more of your blood and you have given too much as it is." He crouched beside me and held out a copper knife with a serrated edge, fresh blood on it. Liam's blood.

I leaned forward, Tracking Liam. Yeah, he was right there, but by Tracking him I could get a better idea of how bad it really was.

His heart beat at a strange cadence, and his soul was slipping. I could push some of my strength into him. We'd done it before, when we were in Europe, but it had mostly been me drawing from him. But what if I could give him some of my Immunity, enough to fight off this poison, or the fucking curse or whatever it was he was dealing with?

"Rylee, what are you doing?" Doran whispered as I drew on my own strength and gave it over to Liam. The energy flowed between us, the bond we'd made stronger than death, and his heart started to beat faster, became steadier.

There was a moment where I thought someone was trying to pull me off, to stop me, but nothing could come between us. Liam didn't shift under my hands, but his threads were stronger.

I pulled back, my vision doubling as hands caught me.

"You keep passing out like this and I'm going to think you like the head rush," Doran grumbled.

"He'll make it."

"What the hell did you do? You aren't a healer, Rylee." Doran didn't take his arms from around me and I didn't care. I could barely keep my eyes open.

"I'll explain later. Blaz, take Liam to London. Please."

Tracker, you gave him a lot of energy. Too much.

"Please, don't argue with me, I have a fucking headache." Which was the truth, my head was pounding, the sound of my own heartbeat felt like a bongo drum inside my skull.

You are coming with me.

"I'll go through the Veil."

Fine.

Damn, that sounded suspiciously like a woman would say 'fine'. Like 'fuck, I'm not excited about this, but I'm doing it anyway'.

Blaz winged over us, and scooped up Liam. *He'll survive the flight?*

"Yes. But he'll be out of it, probably the whole way," I said, feeling Doran's eyes on me. No one knew the bonding that had taken place between Liam and me. Though I suspected Doran was on to us.

Get through the Veil, Tracker. Blaz called back to me as he flew into the last of the night.

"Going, we're going!" I snapped. Of course, that was the plan. Problem was, we didn't quite make it.

At least, not all of us.

ABOUT THE AUTHOR

Shannon Mayer is the *USA Today* bestselling author of the Rylee Adamson novels, the Elemental series, and numerous paranormal romance, urban fantasy, mystery, and suspense novels. She lives in the south-western tip of Canada with her husband, son, and numerous other animals.